Roland Mann

BUYING
TIME

BUYING TIME

Published May 2010 by The Southern Cross

ISBN: 978-0-9834339-0-3

Cover © Emily Y. Kanalz
Cover design/layout by Emily Y. Kanalz

Second Edition

Dedication

For Mom and Dad for always encouraging me to do what I love, even if it rarely made sense.

Acknowledgements

My fear for this paragraph is that I'll leave someone off. If I do, the error is all my own and I ask for forgiveness now. I first want to thank God for saving me and for giving me any talent I might have as a writer. He gets all the glory for anything good found on these pages. I take all the blame for everything else. Thanks to my family: to my wife BJ for continuous love, support and encouragement; to my kids Brittany and Brett for trying their best to "let Daddy write" when they see me at my desk. Thanks to Emily Kanalz for such a fantastic looking cover! Thanks to my "First Readers" for the valuable feedback and comments received on an early draft of this book. Hopefully you will see your comments reflected in this revised version. Those readers are: Christy Butler, Carlene Blackburn, Jenni Gables, Ashley Koostra, Sharon Lavy, Angie Mann, Jerri Mann, Leean Mann, John Metych, Bill Sawyer, Genie Stracuzzi. Thanks to all my pals in the Byhalia Christian Writers group for their love and encouragement. And finally, thanks to you, the reader, for picking up a copy of this work. It is truly my desire that you are both entertained and blessed by it.

Buying Time

Prologue

Have you ever wished there was something in your life you could re-do? Slipped up and made a wrong decision and then wished you could get another chance at making it right? Turning a yes into a no, or vice versa.

Of course you do. Everyone does.

But once it's done, it's done. We live our lives and make mistakes and we're often told to be careful because we have to live with our mistakes.

Life isn't like a backyard basketball game—you don't get a do-over. Life isn't like a tape or cd...you can't hit the rewind or erase button and do it again.

Or can you?

Have you ever even really considered time? It is a topic many great minds have considered. Pericles told us that Time is the wisest counselor of all. That great Southern writer, Tennessee Williams, said that Time is the longest distance between two places. Thoreau said, "Time is but the stream I go a-fishing in."

But what do you really know about time? You know there are sixty minutes in an hour, twenty-four hours in a day and seven days in a week. We spend so much time thinking about time that time itself has become a commodity.

One can spend it, one can save it, one can waste it, and many can even do a good job of killing it. Astrid Alauda said that Time is the only thief we can't get justice against. Dion Boucicault said "Men talk of killing time, while time quietly kills them."

Sounds alarming, doesn't it?

Louis Hector Berlioz said that Time is a great teacher, but unfortunately it kills all its pupils.

To make matters worse, the older you get, the faster time flies. Of course, that can be explained away as all relative. What I mean is to a ten year old a single year is one-tenth of their life. But to a forty year old, one year is only one-fortieth. Hardly noticeable to the forty year old.

We never seem to have enough time to do those things we want to do. We frequently wonder where the time has flown when we're enjoying ourselves and having a good time.

Religious groups run ads on television that tell viewers

the most valuable thing you can give a child is your time.

One of the most famous lines that businessmen use is "time is money."

Yes, you can use your time wisely or you can waste time.

But, no matter what you do with it, "time" is incredibly valuable.

I should know.

I sell it.

Wednesday, July 19

Tom Morgan's day started out as usual—it stank.

"You're worth more dead than alive."

The words had echoed in Tom's mind earlier that day as he made the half-mile walk to Grady T's. Thanks to the Alabama humidity, he was thoroughly drenched with sweat by the time he arrived. It was the kind of day sun-worshippers loved.

A blast of artificially cold air struck him when he opened the door. His ears immediately turned to ice. Tom had to wait a moment for his eyes to adjust. All the windows in the building were tinted so dark it far surpassed the legal limit for an automobile. Of course, autos and restaurants are two different things, but it seemed to Tom that such dark tint was surely designed to hide something, whether it be in a car or in a restaurant.

His friend Mike waited for him at the bar, drink in hand. Grady T's, a restaurant/bar in downtown Florence, catered to the college crowd from the University. The sit-down restaurant occupied fully half of the building. An art-deco water fall/fountain stationed near the entrance at the center of the building and slightly across from the men's and women's rooms separated the bar from the restaurant. The bar patrons and the restaurant patrons could not see one another...unless they did so in the bathroom or at the front door.

Another door led from the bar to the patio. At the end of the building, the patio faced the street, but the street was elevated, forming a sort of natural walled-in feel for the patio, which was also covered to block the elements.

The patio was empty. It usually was during the hot days of summer.

For that matter, except for Mike, so was the bar. At 3 o'clock in the afternoon, most of the bar's regular patrons were still busy earning the hard earned cash that they might spend there later.

Without skipping a beat, Tom hiked himself up on the bar stool next to Mike. The two men nodded brief hellos, exchanging that look so that both knew that Mike knew Tom was late but wasn't going to say anything about it. It was enough though, that Tom felt guilty.

Mike's elbows were propped on the bar in front of him, his hands clasped together. He studied the silent baseball game on the television above the bar. Except for turning his head, Mike hadn't moved.

"Mike, I'm dying," Tom said. Mike turned his head slowly to Tom and his brows furrowed, as he tried to read his friend. It was just another way to lay on the guilt.

"Dying? What? How? What do you mean you're dying?" Mike put his hand on Tom's shoulder as he leaned closer for the explanation.

"Well, not dying like I've got to order my casket this week," answered Tom, wondering who would pick up the expense of his death. "But dying like I've reached that halfway point in my life and everything is downhill from here."

Mike took his hand from Tom's shoulder and returned it to the position from which it came--clasped with his other hand, inches from his face. Two glasses sat directly in front of him at the bar, one half full, the other empty. He slowly shook his head from side to side as he grabbed the glass still containing beer. It was, in a sense, his way of reprimanding Tom.

"Please don't start this again," he said. "You haven't even been to a doctor in years. There's nothing wrong with you. You don't even catch colds like normal people."

"It's true, though Mike," said Tom. "And really not just me, everybody is dying from the minute they're born." The bartender slid a foamy glass over to Tom. Tom had been there often enough that the bartender knew him. Tom and Mike knew him as "John the beer man." Tom contended that the beer-man had a genuine interest in the two friends. Mike argued he had a genuine interest in their tab. Tom guessed that Mike might be right, but wasn't ready to give up the long-running debate.

Tom looked up at John, nodded his thanks and did his best to wrangle John into the argument.

"Don't you agree beer-man?" he asked. "Don't you think everybody starts dying the day they're born?"

2

"You know me better than that, Tom," he answered, picking up a slip of paper pushed to him across the bar from a waitress. "All I really know is how to serve beer and mix drinks. It's what I was born to do. Anything else is beyond me. I leave all that other brainiac stuff to educated people like you."

"He agrees with me," said Tom without skipping a beat, "he just doesn't want to admit it to you, afraid he'll hurt your feelings."

"He's afraid he'll lose my credit card is more like it," Mike retorted.

"So what's on your schedule for today, Tom?" asked Mike, trying to steer the conversation in a different direction. Tom's car had been in the shop the last two weeks and Mike, having the leeway to make and keep his own schedule was playing chauffeur to Tom, at no expense to Tom.

The beer spilled from Tom's glass as he set it down in a hurry, eyes widening.

"I've got a really good one today, Mike," he said of his assignment, turning and grabbing Mike's sleeve. Mike released his own beer so as not to spill it from Tom's obvious excitement. "I'm going to interview some guy who spent something like seven years in jail for robbing a bank or something. Supposedly he was in cahoots with three or four other guys and he took the fall for them. They went scot free and the money was never found. Now, finished with his jail time, he's out and free to spend his share of the money."

"Get out..." was all Mike could manage, blindly grabbing his glass and taking a big drink.

"I'm serious as a heart attack," replied Tom, shaking his head. "He's turned in to some big philanthropist now, or something."

"I don't get it," said Mike, "why'd they let him keep the money?"

"Oh it's not that they *let* him. He didn't have it or they never found it or something like that." Tom guzzled the alcohol left in his own glass and hopped off his seat. It was paid for and he was always sure to take full advantage of that and not leave a drop.

"C'mon, let's go," he said.

Mike followed suit and tossed a bill he had folded in his shirt pocket onto the counter. The money covered the tip for the two of them. He knew that Tom wouldn't leave any money and so he always came prepared to tip the beer-man for both of them.

In minutes, Mike's Ford Expedition blazed along the highway as Mike pushed it far past the legal limit. Tom talked on and on about his most recent plan to delay his credit card bills once again. Tom had the terrible habit of touching Mike -- or for that matter, anyone he was talking to -- on the arm just before he said something. It wasn't a punch, but a light tap or touch to ensure that attention was being paid. With each tap Mike would glance over at Tom, who, despite the tap, was rarely looking at Mike.

It was one such tap that caused Mike to glance over at Tom and not see the old white Pontiac pull out in front of him. Mike desperately slammed on his brakes. His heavy Expedition spun sideways as he tried to avoid hitting the Pontiac. He slammed into the car anyway, pushing it into the lane of oncoming traffic and into the path of an eighteen-wheeler. The big truck's air horn was steadily blowing as it smashed into the innocent Pontiac, crushing it and then sending it back on Mike and Tom in the Expedition. And while this happened in a split second, the entire scene played out in slow motion in Tom's eyes.

* * *

Larry Pace had been on top of the world as early as lunch. He'd gone to work like any other day, but he'd gotten a letter in the mail that told him he'd sold his first novel.

He was flying sky high.

Larry taught accounting at the University of North Alabama, and it had been all he could do to keep from speeding on his way home. The speedometer crept repeatedly above the speed limit and Larry repeatedly backed away. He left work a little earlier than usual hoping to catch Gracie by surprise. He'd dialed six of the seven numbers to his home telephone several times before the day was over, hanging up before entering the last digit each time. He knew his wife Gracie would be excited about his novel as soon as she learned.

He pulled his small red pickup into his garage and noticed the absence of his wife's and his daughters' car.

4

Keying into the back door, it was only then that he remembered today was Wednesday and his wife would be busy at the church preparing supper. Disappointed, he sighed, pulled out the letter, read it one more time and placed it on the dining table at the place setting that was normally Gracie's.

The Pace family had only been out of the city limits for about five years, about the same time that they'd decided they were probably in Florence to stay. Larry had picked a place off the main road so his children would have a safer place to play. The yard of about three acres was big enough that he had plenty of room to plant a garden yet wasn't so big it could be called a farm. The garden was mostly Gracie's, but he enjoyed tinkering around in it also. Something about pulling weeds and grass from around the plants was therapeutic and it allowed him to spend some quiet time in thought and prayer.

He'd visited Ernest Hemingway's one-time home up in Piggott, Arkansas, and decided he wanted an office space like Hemingway's: a nice big solitary loft above the barn where no one could bother him while he worked. No distractions.

Actually, Larry's primary goal was to get a solitary place away from the house, it didn't have to be a Hemingway barn-loft. He'd made sure to run electricity but not a phone line to the room he called his office. He needed the electricity for his computer and his refrigerator ... and for his air conditioner. But he was determined to stay off the phone and off the internet.

It worked, too. That was partly why he was able to finish his novel.

While he got his long desired home office, Gracie got the house that she wanted. Mostly. Their daughters each had a bedroom upstairs and shared a bathroom. An empty bedroom up there served as the family "catch-all" room. The door stayed closed more times than not, but it was convenient to have. The master bedroom was tucked away on the bottom floor in the back of the house away from the noise of the traffic--which was negligible on their road anyway. A big bathroom was attached and was Gracie's domain, with a tiny not-in-the-way-spot for Larry's shaving cream, razor, deodorant and toothbrush.

5

The main room was a big room and was the room in which the family entertained company and themselves. The kitchen connected to the garage, but Gracie insisted on a heavy use of the back entryway--no muddy shoes would touch her floors. Below the girls' bathroom upstairs was a laundry room. Larry always teased her that the main reason she wanted that house was because of the laundry chute that ran from the girls' bathroom directly to the room below. Not only that, but it also had a door which was a "back" door to the laundry pantry from the master bathroom. No more collecting and carrying dirty laundry. Gracie was able to go directly to the laundry room and all the dirty clothes were there waiting on her. She had her daughters carry their own clothes up the stairs after they had been washed and dried.

Since it was Wednesday night, Larry changed into khaki's and a more casual shirt, one of the ones he bought when he was pretending to be a golfer. He only golfed because all the other accounting professors were doing it. He couldn't stand golf. He still had his clubs, but he wasn't sure where they were.

After changing, Larry hopped back in his pickup and began to pull away. He knew he still had an hour before supper began, and he thought he'd show up and offer his help—something that he rarely had time to do and another way he thought he'd play at telling Gracie the news about his novel. He was unsure whether to tell her or wait and let her find the letter on the table.

As he pulled out of his driveway and onto the road, a police car pulled into his driveway. Larry touched his brakes and pulled over to the side of the road as he noticed the officer waving him over.

He threw his truck in park and left his engine running as he opened the door. He met the police officer behind his truck.

"Mr. Pace?" said the officer.

"Yes, that's me," Larry answered, "What can I do for you?" The police officer looked away into the woods and subtly shook his head. The shake was barely discernable and Larry wasn't even sure he'd seen it.

"Mr. Pace," the officer continued slowly as he removed his hat. "I'm Sergeant Rainer. Mr. Pace...I'm afraid I have

6

some very bad news for you." The officer quite visibly did not want to pass the information along, but knew he had to; it was one of the bad parts of his job. "There's been an accident--"

"An accident?" asked Larry, now alarmed. "Oh no! Which one of my daughters?" he asked as horrible images of his daughters' pain flashed into his head.

"Which one?" began the officer. "No, it's your wife, Gracie--"

"My wife? Is she okay?"

"No sir," Rainer paused. "Look, why don't you shut off your truck and come along with me." Rainer twisted his hat in his hands and stared at the ground. Larry was stunned.

"What do you mean? She's not okay? Where is she?"

"Mr. Pace," said Rainer. He stopped twisting his hat and stared Larry straight in the eyes. "Your wife has been killed in an automobile accident."

Saturday, July 22

"Larry, I'm sorry for you and your daughters." The voice belonged to a man but Larry barely noticed. He sat next to the coffin in which his wife's body rested, a daughter on either side of him. The last forty-eight hours had been a complete blur to him. Sergeant Rainer had carried him down to the morgue to identify the body. Larry had never even been in a morgue before that day. Rainer carried him home again and Larry had the unfortunate task of telling his daughters, both of whom were the spitting image of their mother.

A sleepless night and then a day of burial and funeral service arrangements had brought a solo visit from the preacher, a man who had been very instrumental in their emotional well-being the last two days.

"Why Gracie?" Larry had asked the preacher at the visitation Friday evening.

"Larry, I don't know the answer to your question," said Brother Joe, "I can only tell you what you already know. God has a plan for us all and maybe it was time for Gracie to go home." Larry knew Brother Joe would say that, knew they would all say that.

"She worked hard for God while she was here," Brother Joe continued. "Maybe it was just time for the reward of hard work. She'll be there waiting on you." And while they meant well, they all said essentially the same thing.

The room had been arranged with flowers, more flowers than Larry had ever seen. He knew they were from friends and family members all sending well wishes and condolences. There were so many arrangements in places that it crowded the chairs and made it hard to sit. Some people were sitting anyway. Many others were standing. All spoke in hushed whispers, sometimes stealing glances toward Larry and his daughters. At times Larry felt they were invading some of his most private time, and at other times, he was glad they were there, even if he was not talkative.

One man in particular grabbed Larry's attention. He

stood alone and studied Larry and his daughters throughout the entire evening. He had no idea who the man was, but it must have been someone who Gracie's life had touched.

It was pleasing for him to see that Gracie had touched so many lives. He knew that God had chosen a good woman for him, but he never realized others knew that as well.

As the evening wound down and most of the well-wishers had departed, Larry finally stood to say goodbye to Gracie. His daughters moved away to give him some time alone. Larry didn't hear the man walk up behind him.

"We never know when it's our time, do we?" said the man.

Larry turned to find the man who had earlier been studying him so intently.

"You know," he continued, "they say everyone has a time and a place already picked out."

"I'm sorry," said Larry, "but I can't place you. Do I know you?"

"No," he said, "I wouldn't think so. My name is Ben, people call me Big Ben. Odd, isn't it. I'm not really that big, huh?"

"Listen," Ben continued, "I'm not going to take up too much of your time. I know that you have a lot on your mind right now."

Ben reached into the inside pocket of his jacket and produced a business card.

"When you've recovered from all this," he said, "Give me a call. I have a proposition for you—might allow you to buy back some of that precious time with your wife."

"Buy back?" asked Larry. "What on Heaven's earth do you mean by that?"

Becky spotted her Dad's sudden ashen face and grabbed her sister by the elbow. They couldn't hear what the man had said, but both knew they were needed.

"Don't worry about the details," said Ben. He'd spotted the girls making a bee-line for their dad. "Just call me when all this is over and we'll talk."

"Are you ready, Dad?" said Becky, as both daughters approached like some sort of SS goon squad.

Ben said goodbye to Larry, bowed slightly to the daughters and made his way to the exit.

"What was that all about?" asked Cindy.

9

"I dunno," said Larry.

"What'd he say?" asked Becky.

"It's not important," said Larry. "C'mon, let's go."

Larry's daughters had taken Gracie's death surprisingly well, much better than he had expected. Possibly, even better than he was. Gracie was not only his wife, she was his best friend. He knew when he married her that any kids they had would eventually move on, and in the end it would be just him and Gracie.

Now, when the girls finally did leave the house, Larry would be alone.

Monday, July 24

On the second floor of Shoals Hospital, nurses shuffled back and forth around Mike's unconscious body. Somehow, miraculously, Tom had come out of the accident unhurt.

Unhurt physically, anyway. He was in more serious mental anguish than he had ever been before. The lady in the car they'd hit had been killed and Mike was fighting death, hanging on by the proverbial thread.

He sat in the waiting room where he had been for three days straight. *It's a Wonderful Life* played in his head as he contemplated suicide.

"You're worth more dead than alive."

The movie ranked as one of his all-time favorite movies. Inevitably, he cried like a sissy when one of the stations showed it during the Christmas season. Always available at Wal-Mart, he'd purchased at least half a dozen copies one right after the other as his VCR ate them up. He was pretty sure it was available on DVD, but he still didn't own a DVD player. Still, he watched it on television when the stations ran it, preserving the current copy he owned for at least one more showing.

His favorite scene was the one in which George Bailey is told "No securities, no stocks, no bonds. Nothin' but a miserable little $500 equity in a life insurance policy. You're worth more dead than alive." Of course, Tom knew the ultimate idea of the movie was that George had been such an influence on the people around him that his life wasn't just about money.

But this is America, and Americans today are all about money. Tom told himself the movie was old and the ideas presented in it were outdated. We've all become Mr. Potters, at least that is what Tom believed.

The difference between Tom and George Bailey was that

George would have been worth something dead.

Tom Morgan would not.

If he died—if it was him in the hospital instead of Mike—he was dead. Pure and simple. Nothing more than a rotting corpse. There would be no angel working to get his wings come and show him the error of his ways.

Actually, Tom knew that somebody would have to fork out a couple grand for a casket. Tom wasn't sure who that would be—probably the city. Or they'd find some way to put it on his bill in the afterlife, his "death bill," he was now calling it. So, in death, not only was he not worth anything, but he would be dead…and further in debt.

Tom had lost all sense of time as a doctor emerged silently from behind one of the big swinging doors. Tom had become so accustomed to the comings and goings that he didn't really pay attention anymore.

"Excuse me," said the voice from above. Startled, Tom look up into the face of the doctor. A man with gray hair and a speckled beard peered down at him with a slight side smile.

"How's Mike?" Tom could not manage anything more.

"Mike will survive," the doctor said as he sat in the chair beside Tom. "He'll need lots of rest and some serious TLC, but you could use the rest, too. Why don't you go home? You've been up here for several days—I know because I've seen you in this exact same spot wearing the exact same clothes. And I'm a doctor, I'm supposed to notice that kind of thing. Now go home, sleep until you wake up, and then come back and check on Mike. Maybe by then he'll be awake."

Tom nodded, knowing he needed to listen to the doctor's advice, but he didn't budge. Without realizing it, he was suddenly walking out the door, the doctor's hand firmly wrapped around his arm.

"I've taken the liberty of calling a cab for you," the doctor said as Tom's glassy eyes finally made contact with him. The doctor smiled. "No charge," he said, and turned Tom over to a hospital volunteer, a young girl, dressed from head to toe in hospital scrubs colored pink. Except for the color, she might have been a nurse. The girl smiled at Tom and took the other arm after the doctor gave her instructions regarding the cab.

"My name's Becky," she said, "You look like you need to hibernate a while. I'm sure whoever you're here to see would agree with us that you need your own rest. Won't do them any good if you're exhausted, now will you? Plus, the doctors here are great ones, but there are some things that are in God's hands, even when we don't know why. We have to put our trust in Him to work it all out."

Tom stopped. The mention of God made him wonder if there was something to what she said. Living in the South did give one a perspective on God and religion not usually enjoyed elsewhere. Even still, Tom generally shrugged it off as fantasy, a good story. But just a story. But if not a God, then what?

Becky urged him forward and he took another look at her before he moved again. He finally decided that she was too young to understand what kind of pain one can experience in life like he had. Give her a few years, then she could tell him about how good God was.

* * *

Larry and his youngest daughter Cindy entered through the sliding hospital doors moments before his eldest daughter Becky exited. A volunteer there, she waved to her father and sister as they entered.

The two stood in the lobby until Becky returned from helping a dazed man into a cab. She looked her father deep in the eyes, seeing the pain she knew he was trying to hide.

"Dad," she said, "Are you sure you want to do this?"

"I tried to talk him out of even coming up here," said Cindy, "but he wouldn't even listen to me."

"I appreciate what y'all are doing," he told his daughters, "but I have this feeling we should do this, plus I know it is what your mother would have done."

"But Dad," Cindy protested, "We don't even know the guy. What if his family is there and they don't want us there?"

"That's a chance we'll have to take," he said. "The police said there was alcohol in his blood and he may be charged for accidentally killing your Mom, negligent homicide or whatever that's called. But I know your Mom and she still

13

would have wanted us to do this.

"Now c'mon, let's go and pray for this man before Satan convinces me to go back home." Larry stopped, opened his Bible, and began to read. "For the Lord shall be thy confidence, and shall keep thy foot from being taken."

His daughters stared.

"God placed this verse in my heart this morning," he told them. "I can't explain it more than I just felt like I had to turn to Proverbs and read chapter three."

Larry smiled. "C'mon," he said, "let's go!"

Moments later the trio arrived near Mike's door. Larry uttered what must have been the twelfth or thirteenth silent prayer asking for strength. He knew if he had to depend on his own strength, he might very well wish the man would burn in hell. But he didn't rely on himself and called on the Lord's strength as he had done for years.

A nurse spotted them at the door and immediately recognized Becky.

"Hi Becky," she started, then realized what she thought was going on.

"Hey there" was Becky's short response. "Is this the guy that ran into Mom?" she asked before the nurse could steer them away. The nurse turned her head away. She didn't know Becky very well. Becky had already seen it in others at work. Some people have a tendency to become shy or distant when someone they know has experienced a loss. Becky tried to tell them all that she knew her Mom was in a better place.

"Look," Becky said, "we're not here to condemn the guy or to try to make him feel bad."

"We're here to pray for him," said Larry, interrupting his daughter. "The accident he caused took my wife from me. She is in a better place now, but I know she would want us to pray for him. Matter of fact, I think she may be praying for him through our prayers." Becky smiled when Larry gave voice to her very thoughts. She had learned it all from her mom and dad, so it was only natural they would think the same way.

The nurse half-heartedly rolled her eyes. Saving souls from eternal damnation was clearly not something that interested her. Saving lives and helping the helpless was. Had she mentioned this to Larry he would have tried to tell her how different yet how similar the two ideas were. Larry knew that Gracie would be interested in working to save the soul of the very one who took her life. He also knew she would be happier now that she was in the Kingdom of God.

Catching the eye-roll and never afraid to go on the offensive, Larry asked the nurse, "How about you? If you were to die today do you know that you would go to heaven?" The nurse looked to Becky for help. The only help she received came in the form of a smile.

"Look... I..." the nurse stammered.

"It's not a trick question," said Larry. "Either you do or you don't." Larry's forwardness bothered some, but his daughters were accustomed to it and had grown to expect it. Larry knew that by setting the example where they could plainly see, his daughters would search for Godly traits in the men they considered for marriage. But he sure didn't want to think about them marrying just yet.

"I just..." she said, "I don't think I need you to save me today" when she finally caught her breath.

"Oh, 'I' can't save you," said Larry, "but I can certainly show you the way and introduce you to the one who could do it. Only Jesus can save you."

Larry thought he could see the mind of the nurse working, but her patience had reached an end. He'd shared his faith with enough people that he knew many of the signs. He knew God has his own perfect plan and it may simply have been Larry's role to plant the seed. Someone else would have to come along and water it.

"Well, look," he continued, "you think about that a little while. Eternal damnation is not a pleasant thought. Meanwhile, would you mind showing us in?" The nurse eagerly opened the door and stood aside for the trio to enter.

Larry entered first and immediately took a chair near the head of the bed. Cindy sat next to him and Becky stood near the foot of the bed. The nurse slowly stepped back into the hall, attempting to be unseen by the praying family.

And pray they did. Larry began by praising God's wonderful mercy and awesome power, and thanking Him for sending Jesus to die for their sins. Larry then asked God to remove the hardness from his heart toward the man in the bed and to work His mighty power on him and speed him to recover, if that were His plan. He asked God to bless the life of the man and hoped that he would learn from his mistakes and find Jesus upon his recovery. Larry asked that he play a part in helping the man find Jesus if that were in God's will. Larry prayed for the better part of a half hour, seeming to have all the time in the world. When he stopped, both his daughters echoed "amen" in unison. It was clearly not the first time they'd prayed together as a family.

Tuesday July 25

The phone rang in Tom's apartment. It was about the fifth time it had rung, but the first four times Tom was in too deep a sleep to move.

He threw the covers off his face and peeked through squinted eyes at the clock. It read 5:17 p.m. Tom had no idea what day it was. He'd lost all track of time the minute Mike's Expedition hit the Pontiac. He wasn't even sure now what day it was when the accident happened. He wasn't sure he wanted to pick up the phone.

"Hello."

"Tom?"

"Yeah."

"Did I wake you?"

"No—yeah. It's okay. Marty?"

"Yeah, it's me. It's five o'clock on a Tuesday afternoon. What are you doing in bed?"

"I love you, too, Marty. I'm not a staffer, so I can sleep whenever I want to. And I want to right now. What do you want?" Tom rolled over and tried to see what kind of light was coming around the curtain on his window. Was it a hot five o'clock or an overcast and muggy five o'clock?

"What do I always want when I call you? Work! How's that story you're working on?"

"Story? Oh no," said Tom as he sat up in bed. "Marty, I haven't done anything on it. I never even made it there. I was in a car accident."

"Car accident? How? Did you get hit? You don't even own a car, do you?" Marty knew about Tom's car, but because of its perpetual state of disrepair, Marty always joked Tom didn't own one.

"No, I was a passenger," Tom said. "You remember my friend Mike? Owns the computer consulting thing?" Tom continued only after the voice on the other end grunted the affirmative. "It was his car. I guess it was totaled. I don't really remember, but now he's laid up in the hospital."

Tom swung his legs off the side of the bed. His entire body ached from the hibernation length sleep. He knew he needed it after the accident and several days of little to no sleep, but sleeping so long always made him feel as if he'd wasted some of his life, slept so long and could never get part of it back. What a waste of time.

Suddenly, the scene from *It's A Wonderful Life* crept into his head. He wondered if Mike had any insurance. He was, after all, self-employed.

Mike and Tom's friendship went back some ten odd years, when they met in school. Tom was just about to graduate from the University's journalism school and Mike was close to a business degree. They met one night at the sorority house as they arrived to pick up the same girl for a date. Seems she forgot she'd made a date with Tom and at the same time made one with Mike. Both men were so thoroughly angered at the girl that they went out together, leaving one very hot, very frustrated sorority chick at the house.

They got so drunk that night that neither of them remember how they got home. But they'd been fast friends since, and that night was frequently a topic of conversation for the two. It reminded them regularly that even two very different lives could have some things common between them.

Mike ran his own business, a computer consulting firm. The Muscle Shoals area of Alabama wasn't exactly a hotbed of activity for computer based businesses, and Mike had been told more times than he could count that he should move elsewhere to make the really big bucks. Mike told Tom he didn't want to go, though. Sure he'd like to make the "big bucks," but he liked his home in the little town of Killen, about fifteen minutes from Florence where his business was located. Since they finished four-laning the bridge into Florence, his morning commute had been cut in half. He wasn't ready to give up his home just to make the big bucks.

"So?" came the voice on the other end of the phone.

"So what?" replied Tom. He'd been so lost thinking about Mike, he forgot the question.

"So are you gonna go finish up that story? I'd planned on running it this week."

Tom stood, slowly stretched, slightly grunted into the phone as he did so. "Yeah, I can do it." Then, after a short pause, "Can I borrow your car?"

* * *

Larry entered the house with the mail in his hands. He had been lost in his own thoughts when he passed the kitchen table and tossed the mail into his chair. His daughters were busy preparing the evening meal as they'd been doing since Grace's death. He knew they were doing it to take care of him, and part of him felt guilty. He was the father, the head of the house. It should have been him taking charge of things, seeing to his daughters.

He shook his head to clear those thoughts and noticed the envelope sandwiched in between two solicitations for credit cards. His heart skipped a beat. It had all the markings he had anticipated only a matter of days ago. He reached for the envelope with one hand, and with the other scattered the other mail off the chair and accidentally onto the floor.

It was. The publishers return address was clearly marked. He sat down with the envelope in his hand and remembered the call he started to make less than a week ago.

A week ago, Larry Pace's life was everything he thought it would be. While at work, he had received a letter that told him he'd sold a novel. The University had given him the money to put food on his table for twenty-one years but it was this novel that might bring about retirement.

Once upon a time he had harbored the idea that he would move on and work at a major University, maybe even an SEC school, but after his two daughters entered school he decided with his wife that UNA wasn't such a bad place to be.

On top of that, the university's primary focus was on teaching not research. He enjoyed teaching, molding—some said warping—young minds. The problem, among his peers at least, was one of perception. Accounting professors aren't usually known for writing Science Fiction novels, but Larry

Pace had done it. Not only had he written one, but he sold it. The letter he that day confirmed it.

The letter also said that in thirty days or less he would receive a royalty advance of thirty thousand dollars, not quite his yearly salary, but it was his first novel and a good way to start.

He'd been to writers conferences and most "professional" writers told him to be happy if he received about ten percent of that.

Larry wasn't ready to hand in his letter of resignation just yet, nor was he really ready to talk about it amongst those in his department. Why give them yet another reason to harass him.

He had picked up the phone and dialed the first six numbers of his telephone number. He couldn't bring himself to dial the seventh number and hung the phone back down.

He hadn't called Gracie yet, nor did he plan to even though he was incredibly tempted to do so. Rather, he had planned to pick her up as was usual, and carry her out to eat in celebration of the fact of his pending publication. She'd been his biggest supporter and it was only fitting that the two share the moment together.

He also hadn't shared it with his best friend, Dr. Steven Dale, a faculty member from the art department. Steven was out of town on a mission trip and not expected back for almost a week.

Larry was a member of the local Baptist church and quite committed to his faith. Thus, when his church family learned he was working on a "science-fiction" novel, they privately questioned him, taking the assumption that anything science fiction wasn't quite the model of Christianity.

Like any writer, though, Larry welcomed the opportunity for critical readers, and he invited several of the more vocal members of his church to read and comment on his novel. Larry asked the Pastor if he would read it and offer suggestions, particularly pertaining to scripture and theology.

Larry's church family was quite amazed and surprised. It was true, they reluctantly admitted, that Larry's novel was different from anything they'd expected and quite suitable for a Christian audience. It refrained from the vivid descriptions of sex that so often permeated modern "literature." That is not to suggest that Larry's characters were sexless, but the sex they practiced was done so in a manner according to the institutions of marriage set up by Christ.

And while some of the aliens might worship a fictitious god other than Christ, very specific parallels could be drawn to Christ. The heroes were of devout faith, a faith which caused them to be victorious in the end.

Larry's novel also refrained from the continual use of profanity. Larry knew from personal experience that it was both possible and "realistic," (a term he frequently heard from other writers who suggested he insert profanity in order to make his story more "realistic") for a person to live for years and years and not speak vulgarity. "Realistic" was a term amateurs used, those who had not lived life but assumed they knew what it was supposed to be like.

Some members of Larry's church not only thought it was suitable but also an example of good Christian entertainment. Many of them expressed an interest for more Christian fiction like Larry's and wondered why there was not more on the market. Many suggested that he would be to Christian Science Fiction what Harry Potter was to secular writing. They even suggested he write a second novel. Larry just laughed and told them "one book at a time." To which they usually responded for him to get to work!

Unnoticed by Larry, both his daughters had seen him brush the mail into the floor and had paused to watch him lost in thought. Their sudden non-movement caused him to notice them.

Becky broke the silence. "Everything okay, Dad?"

Larry looked her in the eyes and then turned to do the same with Cindy. Tears were welling in his eyes. Both of his daughters noticed and moved to sit in the chairs beside him.

"It just completely slipped my mind," he said, slowly and carefully examining the unopened envelope.

"What did, Daddy?" said Cindy, "You're not making any sense."

"Girls," he said, placing the envelope flat on the table, both hands holding it down so as to not let it slip away, "the day your Mom died, I received some incredibly fantastic news." The sisters looked at each other and shrugged.

"And?" said Becky.

"I sold my first novel," he said. Their eyes widened and they squealed delighted congratulations. He uncovered the envelope and slid it slightly toward the center of the table.

"Open it," he said.

Becky, whose one hand was covered with a pot-holder and the other with a long mixing spoon, reacted first. She dropped the spoon and glove on the table, reached for the envelope and tore it open. She began to remove the contents.

"It's a check," she said. She stopped. Her eyes opened as wide as silver dollars and her mouth dropped open. She slowly lifted her head, briefly made eye contact with her sister and then stared at her father.

"Is this real?" she asked.

"What?" interrupted Cindy. "What is it?"

"As unbelievable as it seems," said Larry, "it is very real indeed."

Becky, mouth still gaping, eyes still wide, passed the check over to her anxious sister. Cindy quickly grabbed it and examined the amount.

"Thirty thousand dollars? Good Lord!" she said.

"That is exactly what it is, Cindy," interjected Larry, "the Lord has decided to bless me—bless us with this for some reason. A reason I don't know, but one that I discovered the day of your Mom's death."

"You make it sound like a bribe," snarled Cindy.

"Not at all," said Larry, placing his hand atop of hers. "The Lord gives and the Lord takes away according to his own plan. What have I always tried to tell you girls? Everything here is His, we're just His stewards. As much as I love you both," he continued, "you belong to Him. He has just allowed me to watch over you for a while."

"Will you pay off the house?" asked Becky. She was always the practical one when it came to finances. She worked and saved her money and Larry was quite proud of the way she oversaw her own finances. She was exceptionally devoted to her tithe, and had started when she was in elementary school tithing on her allowance.

"No," Larry said, slowly. He took the check from Cindy,

examining its details for the first time. "This is something extra, something completely unaccounted for." Never missing an open opportunity to provide an example for his daughters, Larry then asked, "What do you think we should do with it?" He carefully chose to say "we" rather than "I," something he'd started doing many years ago at Grace's suggestion. She had said it helped give the girls ownership and feel like it was really something they had done rather than simply been a witness to. Larry found that it worked and he tried to use that approach whenever possible.

"I think we should give it all to the building fund at church," said Cindy.

"Boy, wouldn't they like that," added Becky. "But what about giving it to an organization we don't normally get to give to. We give to the church regularly, but what if we could give this to an orphanage or something."

"Hey!" said Cindy, "We could give it to the poor or needy people at our church."

"Wait," said Becky, "What would you think about starting a scholarship in Mom's name? Maybe something particularly for kids in our youth group who display a willingness to walk with God?"

Larry smiled.

Becky's eyes brightened. "Hey!" she said, "what if we made it to the Christian college up the road? It could still be for members of our church, but specifically for those seeking to enter into the ministry. They always need money, and it would be going to help make disciples."

Larry's smile broadened. He liked the idea. He liked that while not exactly what he had in mind, it was close enough--it was God's work. And this way, he could honestly say the idea came from his daughters. Even better, he liked the fact that both his daughters took to the idea of giving away thirty-thousand dollars.

Thirty-thousand dollars. It had yet to sink in what a huge amount that was. And neither of the girls have their own school paid for. Thirty-thousand dollars all to help kids pay their way in education for the ministry.

It was then that Larry cried. His sudden outburst startled his daughters, but he simply bowed his head and began to pray. It wasn't a prayer meant for them and they knew it. They couldn't understand it through his tears and mumbled speech anyway. Larry had set this kind of prayer example for his daughters their entire life. To them both, it WAS the way of life.

They each slowly got up out of their chairs and resumed their previous activities as quietly as possible. Cindy prepared a glass of cold, sweetened tea and set it near her father's bowed head. It would be a much-thanked refreshment when he finally lifted his head.

* * *

Not long after crossing the Tennessee state line, Tom pulled the borrowed Toyota 4runner off highway 43 and onto a long-ago-blacktopped road. His directions indicated that the house was not far from the highway itself, but could not be seen from the road because of the enormous trees on the estate. As he inched the vehicle forward, he spotted white columns through the trees and a small opening indicating a drive somehow wound its way through.

Turning left, the tires crunched as they moved on the gravel drive. Tom let out a low whistle as the house slowly came into view.

The house was a Greek Revival style with six large columns spanning the two floors in front, three to each side of the large front double-doors. It seemed freshly painted a bright white, even the detailed molding seemed unnaturally clean. A small balcony, enough for a couple of people, hung immediately over the front doors, the railings a shiny black wrought-iron looking job.

Tom felt like the temperature must have dropped a degree or two as he stopped the truck and got out. A beagle of some sort of mix came around the left side of the house, barking and wagging his tail. Tom wasn't sure whether the dog wanted to be friends or to fight, so he produced the best "dog-friendly" voice he could muster.

"Hey there puppy dog," he said, and squatted, inviting the dog to approach with some dog-kisses. The dog ceased barking and trotted over, tail steadily wagging and tongue hanging out. Tom grabbed both his ears and rubbed appropriately, creating a friend for life in the dog.

With his new canine friend tagging along, Tom slowly walked to the front doors hoping someone would come to them before he actually had to knock. Normally he wouldn't be nervous for a simple interview for a newspaper story, but he'd never interviewed an ex-convict before. Not that Northwest Alabama didn't have its share of ex-convicts, just that he'd never had to interview one before. His interviews were usually odd people with odd hobbies.

He rapped loudly on the door. He'd learned long ago that if you knock loud the first time, you wouldn't have to knock a second time.

Looking down he noticed one of his shoes untied. As he bent to tie it, he read the neatly placed welcome mat. Decorated with watches, clocks, sundials, and other items which must have been time-keeping devices of their appropriate ages, the mat read: "Welcome again" in big red letters. Tom exhaled sharply in a half laugh-snort. He wasn't sure he got the joke, or if it even was a joke, so he stood again and watched the doorknob. He was oblivious to the approaching figure around the side of the house.

"Hello there," said a voice nearly in Tom's ear. Tom jumped slightly, startling the dog that took one look up at Tom and the newly arrived stranger on the porch and then trotted off. "Didn't mean to startle you," continued the man. "I was in my shed out back and saw you pull up."

"Mr. Selling? Benjamin Selling?"

"Please come in," he said, as he pushed the door open and stepped aside so Tom could enter. The rush of cool air from the air-conditioned home caught Tom full in the face. Tom entered and it was his turn to step aside so the man could close the door behind him.

"It is Ben Selling, isn't it?" asked Tom as his eyes adjusted to the dim lights of the front foyer. He heard the easy click of the door behind him. The front entryway was bigger than the living area in Tom's apartment. It stretched upward to what Tom could only guess was the attic. A grand staircase spiraled up on both his left and right, converging at the top. Pictures, portraits, awards, certificates, anything that could be put in a frame adorned the walls.

"Actually, it's Chapman, but my friends call me Big Ben. You're welcome to use that," said the man.

"Nice place," said Tom.

"Thanks," replied Big Ben. "You really haven't seen much of it yet."

25

"Maybe," he said, "But I can tell from here how nice it is. Heck, this place is bigger than all the places I've ever lived...combined."

Big Ben led Tom to the doors immediately to their left. He grabbed the crease where the two doors met, not exactly a doorknob, and slid them both in opposite directions into the walls, effectively hiding their existence.

The room beyond was dark.

Tom sensed the absence of floor immediately to his front, and as his eyes adjusted to dimmer light once again, he noticed the entire room was sunken by a few feet. Big Ben adjusted a knob somewhere from beside the door and the room flooded with light. Tom let out a low whistle as he caught sight of the room. Decorated from top to bottom, wall to wall, the room was filled with clocks of all sorts.

"You must really be into clocks," said Tom.

"Yeah. But not clocks so much as time itself," replied Big Ben. I discovered it while I was ... locked up." He said the last part with a bit of a chuckle himself.

"I guess having the time to reflect helps reflect on time itself, huh?" asked Tom, trying to keep the conversation moving in a pleasant manner in order to help break the ice.

"As a society, we don't realize how valuable time is until it's gone," said Big Ben, "don't you think?"

"Oh, I don't know," replied Tom, "all I ever seem to do is waste it."

"Exactly!" came an excited burst from Big Ben. "And it is incredibly valuable. We never tend to think of time in precisely that way, though." Big Ben moved to the center of the room to an old rock structure which Tom assumed was a sundial. Having never really seen a sundial except in pictures, the object looked like something that could only really be a sundial in light of all the clock company. Immediately in front of the sundial sat a chair. Tom wasn't sure if it was a recliner or not, but it looked to be as comfortable as any chair he'd ever owned. "Come here," continued Big Ben.

Tom stepped slowly, taking in the wide assortment of time pieces. Two steps down placed him in the center of the room next to both Big Ben and the sundial.

"Do you know what this is?" asked Big Ben.

"Not really, but I'd guess it was a sundial."

"You'd guess right. Put your hands on it," said Big Ben as he moved his hands to show Tom what to do. Tom followed his example and placed his hands on the old rock. It was surprisingly smooth, but he wasn't sure whether that meant it had held up well under time or it had been weathered.

"This is a Celtic sundial from about two thousand years ago. If you place both hands on it and shut your eyes, you can almost imagine yourself there." Almost in a reaction to Big Ben's suggestion, Tom closed his eyes.

Suddenly he felt a rushing sensation and the backs of his eyelids acted as giant screens flashing before him the wreck that claimed the life of a woman and may yet claim the life of his friend. He yanked his hands off the cold stone and felt dizzy.

Big Ben was close to him, their faces only inches apart.

"What was it?" Big Ben asked, "What happened?" Tom remembered he was the one who was supposed to be asking the questions.

"Nothing," he answered, realizing only then that he was out of breath.

"Not nothing. Something. Maybe some time you wished you could take back...relive maybe?"

Big Ben's frankness surprised Tom and it showed on his face.

"Don't be surprised," Big Ben said, backing away. "Time is an awesome thing. One can spend it, one can waste it." He began to circle Tom and the sundial on the first step up. "You said so yourself. Many even do a pretty good job of killing it. But no matter what you do with it, 'time' is incredibly valuable."

Big Ben had come half way around the room so that he was behind Tom, whose focus was still on the sundial. In so quick a movement Tom did not notice until Big Ben was in his very ear, Big Ben leapt down and had one arm around Tom, his mouth so close to his ear that Tom thought for a moment he would kiss it.

"Do you know how I know this, Tom?" Tom, stunned and still a little dizzy, only grunted.

"Because I sell it!"

"What?" This exclamation shook Tom from his dizzy stupor so that he stepped out from under Big Ben's arm and turned to face him. "What do you mean? You sell these clocks? Are the valuable?"

Big Ben laughed and took three steps up toward the door, the same door they entered the room through.

"Clocks? No, I collect these clocks," he indicated with a wave of his arm, "but I sell time."

The silence lingered as Big Ben allowed the idea to sink in. Tom glanced again around the room. Every one of the clocks were different, yet each one had the exact same time, down to the second on those that indicated such. They seemed to come from all corners of the globe and from all time periods. It was the biggest, most unusual assortment of clocks he'd ever seen, not that he'd seen that many.

He looked back at Big Ben, still standing in the door, and sighed before taking his own labored steps toward him.

"You don't believe me," said Big Ben, as he stepped aside to allow Tom to pass. Tom slowly brushed by him and Big Ben slid the doors shut behind him.

"Not at all," said Tom. He was, after all, here to interview the guy for the paper, not to call him a liar. "As a matter of fact," he said, turning and removing his reporter's notepad from his pocket, "I find it quite interesting, though I'm not sure how it directly relates to the reason I'm here."

"Oh!" said Big Ben, "you're not to include that in your story. This is for you and me only. If you include it in the paper, no one from the paper will ever be allowed on the property again."

"Is that a threat?" asked Tom, slightly surprised.

"No threat. A promise." Big Ben walked away and into another door, motioning for Tom to follow.

"It was something I thought would interest you and you had not yet asked me about why you were here, nor had you removed your notepad, which you have now done. It was between me and you. Personal. Not for publication."

Generally Tom felt like a pretty smart guy, but he always hated it when someone he was interviewing got him on some silly technicality like removing his notepad. This Big Ben was indeed a smart guy, Tom was anxious to see if he could learn whether this guy stole money or not, and why he became the fall guy for others.

28

Big Ben led Tom into a parlor with big bay windows overlooking the backgrounds of the house, including the shed off to one side. Big Ben sat and indicated with his hand for Tom to also sit. Tom proceeded to ask him about the reported stolen money, the other accused thieves and the whys and hows of the robbery and his time in jail. All the while, though, he kept going back to what this Big Ben had said about time.

When the interview was over, Big Ben once again escorted Tom to the front door. Tom folded his pad and returned it to his pocket.

"Thanks for your time," he said.

"It was my pleasure," replied Big Ben. "Is the interview over? Are we off record now?" With a hesitating sigh, Tom nodded.

"I want you to think about what I've said about time. It's not cheap, but if you ever want the chance to relive a part of your life...you come see me."

With that, the two shook hands. Big Ben closed the door before Tom was down the steps, rejoined by his new canine friend.

Who wouldn't want to relive some part of their life, he wondered. Sounded too much like science-fiction, though, and he laughed at the idea as he drove off.

Wednesday, July 26

The hospital room was cold and quiet as Larry finished his prayer. Since the first day he and the girls had visited the driver of the Ford expedition, he couldn't bring himself yet to assign a name to the man even though he knew he had one. He was afraid it would make it more personal and that he would quickly forget what the man had done. He knew that God would forgive the man and that God would forgive him for harboring the thoughts...but it was his wife who was killed and he just couldn't bring himself to forgive the man completely... not just yet. He wanted a few more days to be mad.

But he knew that wasn't the way God wanted him to think, and he asked for forgiveness... the same way he'd done every day before that one.

He sighed as he whispered amen and lifted his head only to see Dr. Steven Dale, his colleague from the university. Surprised, Larry stood quickly and offered his hand. Dr. Dale, who taught art, took his hand and shook it. The two had met Larry's first year, which happened to be Dr. Dale's second.

"Larry," said Dr. Dale.

"Steven," said Larry, his voice revealing his surprise, "what are you doing here? I thought you weren't due back for a few more days."

"I heard about the whole thing from Christy last Thursday. I couldn't get back until yesterday. I talked to one of your daughters on the phone last night and they told me you'd be here. Larry, I'm so sorry that I was not here."

"Steven," Larry said, beginning to walk away from the door, leaving the sleeping boy alone in the room behind, "I don't want to even hear that again. You couldn't help it; you had work to do. And from what I hear, you had the chance to do God's work, too!"

"You heard right. We took fifteen workers with us, and six natives came to know Christ."

"But there you go again," Steven stopped abruptly, "changing the subject. I'll tell you all about my trip and the victories later, you talk to me now. You talk, I listen."

The two friends stepped through the open doors of an elevator and pushed the lobby button.

"Steven," said Larry, after the doors closed behind them, "it's hard."

"I know it is, Larry. Remember, though, with God --"

"All things are possible, I know. But that doesn't make it any easier."

"Larry, God gives us trials to make us stronger, not to torture us or to simply be cruel to us. I can't begin to tell you why He would want you to go through this trial, not at all. Matter of fact, I desire some logical explanation. But there is some reason. Be sure to open your heart and learn what it is He wants you to learn. So, Larry, what are you doing here? Why are you coming up here?" Steven asked the one question Larry was hoping he wouldn't ask, but knew he would eventually.

"I'm praying for that guy," Larry replied.

"What guy?" asked Steven.

"The one who hit and killed Gracie."

"Larry, you know I wouldn't normally ask you this kind of thing, but what exactly are you praying for?" The two men had reached the front lobby and made their way past the sliding door and past a few nurses standing in the smoking section, quietly puffing away on their cigarettes.

"I know what you're thinking," said Larry, "but I'm okay. The first day I was very, very bitter. Then I got to thinking what would Gracie do if the roles were reversed. I knew immediately that she would be praying for the recovery of that man so that she could speak with him and try to introduce him to Christ after his recovery. She would be praying for him and not me, because she had confidence that I know the Lord, but not so for the man."

"Steven," Larry continued, "Gracie was the strongest Christian woman I know, maybe the strongest Christian I know." And then, after what seemed like a long pause, "I miss her, Steven."

"Larry," Steven said, "Grace was a great woman, and

31

you know what the Bible says about a good wife, right? Proverbs 18: 22 says 'He who finds a wife finds what is good and receives favor from the Lord.' Don't you ever forget that God will keep his word. You will receive favor."

"But I've already received so much," Larry replied. "I couldn't ask for two better kids, especially when I hear some of the stories other parents tell. I've got a good job where I'm able to talk about Christ without fear of repercussion. Well, at least without fear of being fired as long as I use common sense.

"And I sold my novel. I --"

"You what?" asked Steven in surprise.

"Yes, I sure did."

"Get out! Tell me about it." Larry did not immediately reply, and instead the two walked quietly to Steven's truck, which Larry had spotted almost immediately. Steven had a fondness for old beat-up trucks, saying if it was good enough for millionaire Sam Walton, it was good enough for him. Besides, he figured maybe if he tried to act like a millionaire it might just happen. It was one of the many running jokes between the two men.

"Not much to tell, really," said Larry. "You remember when I sent it in. I got a letter a short while back that said it had been accepted, and then shortly after that, I got a check." He leaned against the bed of Steven's truck, folded his arms and looked out across the parking lot.

Steven leaned against the truck just beside him, removing the keys from his pocket and tossing them inside the window and onto the seat. "You mind if I ask..." he started.

"Thirty thousand," answered Larry without hesitating a beat.

"Thirty?"

Larry smiled and turned his head to face his long time friend. "Thirty thousand," he said, emphasizing the thousand. "Yeah, it surprised me, too."

"Wow! God is good!"

"God is sovereign," Larry countered. Steven chuckled at the long time joke between the two, but was still too flabbergasted to really respond.

"Man," Steven finally said, "what're you gonna do with it?"

"Here's where it gets even more fantastic," Larry began. "I told the girls about it and asked them what they wanted to do with the money, not really suggesting one way or another. The idea of paying off the house came up, but believe it or not, it was their idea to give it all away."

"Give it-- What do you mean?"

"Not just haphazardly, but maybe set up a scholarship of some sort for kids in our church to go to Trinity Christian University down the road."

"Larry," Steven said, finally turning and opening the driver's door, "you are truly an inspiration to me and I daily draw strength from your own strength. I know that I've told you before, but God blessed my life bringing you here."

"God is good," Larry said.

"God is sovereign," Steven answered with a smile, fully recovered from the shock of the news.

* * *

Later that day, Larry sat at the kitch table eating lunch. He had only taken one bite of his sandwich when the call came. The man had come to. He rushed through the front doors of the hospital not noticing Becky's waving arm across the lobby. He made straight for the elevator and the doors opened just as he approached.

At the sound of the elevator bell his feet were moving again. He'd been there enough times and could probably make the way with his eyes closed. A few people were gathered around the door to the man's room, suggesting there were more inside. As Larry approached, a nurse ushered everyone out of the room and into the hallway, claiming a need for more rest for the man. A few doctors walked off in the opposite direction with an elderly couple Larry assumed must be the man's parents. He turned to the man standing beside him, a young man who hadn't been in the room when Larry approached, but who appeared as if he desperately wanted to enter.

"What'd they say about him?" Larry asked.

"Said he still needs rest," the man answered.

"Will he be okay? I mean, will everything..."

"Will everything still work? They didn't say, but I think they feel he'll do well in physical therapy."

"Better than Gracie," Larry responded, mostly under his breath.

The man looked closely at Larry, studying him. "Are you family," he asked, "I don't guess I know you or have seen you before."

"No, not family," Larry answered, "but a very concerned party." After a moment's hesitation, Larry looked back at the man, studying him in return. "What about you?"

"No, I'm not family either," answered the man, "but I'm a good friend."

Larry stuck his right hand out to the man. "Larry Pace," he said.

"Larry..." began the man as he slowly accepted the handshake, "'Pace?' Are you kin to..."

"To the woman he killed?" Larry asked before answering his own question, an edge in his voice. "Yes, I was... am her husband."

The man sat down suddenly in the chair behind him, his face turning ashen white.

"You okay?" Larry asked. The man did not immediately respond, but slowly shook his head back and forth.

"I'm so sorry," he said, finally. Then suddenly looking up at Larry, "it was probably my fault. I distracted him. I have a terrible habit of doing that to anybody who knows me."

Larry sat in the chair beside the man. "I'm sorry," he said, "I didn't get your name."

"Tom," said the man, "Tom Morgan. I was in the car with Mike when it hit...when we...when it ... when your wife was killed."

* * *

Big Ben poured a glass of wine for his new guest, setting aside a still fresh glass from his last visitor. This new guest stood studying the sundial in the middle of his clock room, speechless by all the ticking going on around him.

"This is just amazing," he said.

"Yes," said Big Ben, handing the guest a glass and hoisting the other up slightly in the air, "it is." The two raised the glasses to their lips and quickly downed the liquid.

"So," said Big Ben, sitting in the single chair in the room,

"If you could relive part of your life, what would it be?"

"Oh, I don't think I'd want to live my life again," said the guest.

"You mean, you've lived a perfect life?" Big Ben replied, feigning surprise. He leaned back in the chair, crossing his legs. He pulled a cigar out of the inside pocket of his sports jacket and stuck it in his mouth, unlit. "That's simply amazing."

"No," said the guest, "I'm not saying that. But life is linear, I don't want to start all over again. I'm pretty okay where I'm at."

"Linear? Oh, you believe that?" asked Big Ben. "What about all that history is doomed to repeat itself stuff?"

"Well, I don't know much about that part, but yeah, I do believe life is linear. You're born, you live, you die. Point A to point Z."

"Well, what about just reliving a part of your life? Y'know, either that week long love affair with the secretary, or maybe even the week before your mother died."

The guest reacted with surprise. "I've ... I've never told you my mother was dead. How'd you know?"

"I told you on the phone," answered Big Ben, removing the cigar from his mouth as if it were actually lit. "I sell time, it's my job to know about my customers ... or potential customers. Call it ... market research."

Big Ben smiled and stuck the cigar back in his mouth, twirling it between his teeth. He wanted to light it, desperately wanted to feel the taste of the smoke moving down his throat and into his lungs. But ... he resisted the desire. He knew it was addicting.

He had other desires, stronger desires now.

"That's a little eeric," said the guest, finally sitting back on a step near the top. He had to look down at Big Ben and slightly around the sundial in the middle of the floor on the bottom level.

"Look," said Big Ben, once again removing the cigar, "it's not really important how I know, but that I know. We could waste the time talking about it, but I'm in the business of selling time, not wasting it.

"Now tell me, isn't there any time at all in your life you wish you had a 'do-over'?"

The guest was quiet as he peered off in the distance,

seemingly at one of the clocks, yet at nothing at all.

"Yeah," he finally said, and then seemed in no hurry to go on. Big Ben knew the signs. He'd been selling time long enough to know when that thing they call memory was working hard on a person. Regret, remorse, rejoicing, romance, retribution. The 5 R's, he'd called it. All these things flashed through a person's mind as they remembered.

"Yeah, I do," he said before finally returning his focused gaze back to Big Ben, "but you already know that, too, don't you?"

This time Big Ben let his own silence hang heavy on the room. He already knew his answer and already knew he wouldn't offer more explanation, but it was the only answer he was going to give.

"I do," said Big Ben, not bothering to remove the cigar.

* * *

Larry drummed his fingers on the table as he held the phone to his ear awaiting an answer on the other end. After the tenth ring, a groggy voice answered something that sounded like a hello.

"Brother Joe," asked Larry, not quite recognizing the voice.

"Yes," said the still sleepy voice, "who is this?"

"Larry Pace." Then after a brief pause, "Did I wake you?"

"No, I mean, yes, but that's okay. What time is it?"

"It's almost two o'clock," said Larry, not really sure why the preacher was asleep in the middle of the afternoon. "I'm sorry," he said, "I never thought I'd wake you at this time of day."

Larry, like many members of his church, had this supernatural image of the preacher. He was God's man and did God's work. He was perfect and never sinned. He never needed sleep or food or any of that other stuff that "normal" people needed. Larry discovered he was wrong about the food at last year's "dinner on the grounds" the church held one Sunday afternoon. Larry was a personal witness to Brother Joe's devouring several plates of food, each stacked with a generous helping of assorted prepared foods.

"Well," said Brother Joe, "normally you wouldn't at this

time of day, but old man Jones died last night and I was with the family until about four in the morning."

Larry remembered that Brother Joe had been the first to arrive at Gracie's wake and the last to leave. He remembered Brother Joe was also there the night Gracie died, but he couldn't have repeated times or verbal exchanges if it had mattered. He remembered only that he cried with his two precious daughters for what seemed like hours upon days and Brother Joe was waiting in the wings in case he was needed, a spiritual EMT.

"I'm sorry," Larry said once again, "I wasn't trying to suggest--"

"Larry," said Brother Joe, stopping Larry in mid-sentence, "don't worry about it. I was in the office this morning and decided to catch a catnap during lunch. Now it's time to get up again anyway."

Larry laughed to himself at yet another reminder that all men are equal, even preachers. He couldn't count the number of times he'd closed his eyes intending to get about a fifteen or twenty minute nap, only to wake up an hour later.

"What's on your mind?" said Brother Joe through a stifled yawn.

"Listen," Larry began, excitement bubbling over the phone like molten lava, "I need you to go visit someone for me."

"Okay," said Brother Joe, waiting for the "but" part of the story. And there usually was a "but" when someone called asking him to visit someone particular.

"This guy was in the car that killed Gracie," Larry said after hearing what he thought was a less than enthusiastic response, probably because Larry himself was so eager about this one. "And," he continued, "he's feeling like it is his fault. Just a while ago at the hospital --"

"The hospital? You okay?"

"Yes, I'm okay. It--"

"The girls, then? Which one?"

"No, no, Brother Joe, they're fine. They called me to tell me he was coming to."

"The girls called you?"

"No, the hospital called me."

"What happened?"

"They called to tell me the guy who hit Gracie was coming to."

"I see," said Brother Joe, though he sounded not quite sure, "so what did he say?"

"I didn't talk to him."

"But I thought you said he was feeling guilty?"

"Not him, the other one."

"What other one?"

"The other man."

"Larry," said Brother Joe through a sigh so big Larry felt the hair around his ears move, "you have me utterly and totally confused. How about starting over."

So Larry took a deep breath and explained it all.

"Wow," was Brother Joe's reply when Larry finally stopped. Larry felt as if he'd told the entire thing in a single breath. The silence that followed seemed to stretch for minutes to Larry. He thought Brother Joe would follow immediately with a diatribe that would ramble on par with the one Larry had just finished.

When he couldn't take it any longer, he said, "So, can you go visit the guy?"

"You bet I can," came the immediate answer, causing a flood of great joy to sweep over Larry. "Where does he live? I'll go now."

"Now would be great."

* * *

It was unusual that Cindy ever called Becky while she worked. Becky worked only one day per week, and that day was usually Wednesday. She left school just a little early and was able to put in nearly five hours before time for church.

"Becky," started Cindy, "I'm real sorry I called you at work." Becky wondered what it was this time. Because of the rarity of the calls, they usually brought either really good news ... or really bad.

"That's okay, Cindy," she answered in her best big-sister voice, "I've always got time for you." She knew that would put Cindy a little more at ease with whatever she had to say.

"Becky," she repeated her sister's name in order to buy

her time to think...and her sister knew that. "I'm really worried about Dad," she finally said with a big sigh.

"Dad? What about him?"

"I think he's becoming obsessed with the guy who killed Mom." They'd talked with their Dad before about referring to the man who'd been in the car that struck Gracie's as the man who killed their Mom. While he didn't take out a gun or knife and purposefully kill Gracie, it was still an act of taking a life, and in their eyes, that was killing. Larry was very careful to try and get the girls to not say it with any sort of malice and to state it as fact, the same way they'd say Cain killed Abel.

"Obsessed? You mean like you think he's planning revenge or something?" asked Becky. "How's he obsessed, Cindy?"

"He's still praying for that guy every morning, and I just overheard him talking on the phone to someone about it. I think it is really getting to him."

"How's this, then," started the older of the two girls, "you and I will make a deal and we'll bring it up after church when we get home. I'll take the phone off the hook and you get him into the living room. We'll gang up on him and make him talk about it. Sound like a deal?"

"Deal," came the younger sister's reply. And after only a short pause, "Thanks, Becky."

"Love you, sis!"

* * *

It had turned into a beautiful day, thought Brother Joe Hallmark. The sun was shining, the birds were singing, the kids were playing, and the fish were probably biting.

A wonderful time to be alive.

And a wonderful time to be a Christian and realize that everything he enjoyed was created and belonged to God. And he hoped that he could convince the young man he was going to see of that very thing.

Larry was not one of those people who frequently asked him to go see anyone. Larry was strong enough with his own faith that he usually just did the going and seeing himself. But Brother Joe had recognized the anxiety in Larry's voice and knew that the knowledge of this man's relationship or connection with Gracie's death was still wearing on Larry. Brother Joe was glad he had called.

He parked his car out in front of the apartment complex, a habit he'd gained when he first started witnessing to people. He figured if he had further to walk to get to the door than pulling up in a parking slot immediately in front of the door that God might give him an opportunity to share with someone other than the one he'd come to visit. It was something that happened on occasion and thus Brother Joe decided one out of ten was worth the extra walk.

In a matter of minutes, he was standing at the front door to the apartment. He said a silent prayer asking God for wisdom and direction and raised his hand to knock. Before his hand could connect with the door, it swung open wide, causing Brother Joe to react with a start.

"Whoa!" he said, his clinched fist perched inches from where the door should be. His sound startled the man on the other side.

"Huh?!" he said as he jumped back. "Oh Jesus, you scared me." His shirt was untucked and mostly unbuttoned, something he was trying to change as he stood in the open doorway.

The door wide open, Brother Joe got a good look inside. He'd taken courses in Seminary that helped him to "read" the home of someone to get clues to not just their living conditions, but to their spiritual well-being.

Tom's apartment was very dark. Brother Joe noticed lights on, but bulbs missing from the multi-bulb fixture. The carpet appeared as if it hadn't been vacuumed in more than three months, possibly longer.

Clothes, books, papers, video tapes, music cds, magazines, dirty clothes—and even some likely clean ones—were strewn all over both rooms. A footpath led from the front door to the refrigerator and then to the couch in the tiny living area and also to what must have been the bedroom. Brother Joe thought to step from this obvious path would result in stepping on something unseen underneath, possibly something alive.

"Fear of God is a great first step," said Brother Joe, smiling and lowering his hand to extend it for a handshake. "I'm Joe Hallmark, preacher of First Baptist Church."

"Tom Morgan," he said.

"Yes, I know," responded Brother Joe.

"Why is it everybody knows things about me?" Tom asked. The question was not directed at Brother Joe, but in a general sense.

"Believe it or not, Tom, I know a lot about you that you yourself may not even know." That was a line Brother Joe frequently used to get "in the door," as he would always say. If he could get past the barrier of the door, something that was so easy for so many to close, he felt he could say things that would reach into their heart. It wasn't Brother Joe doing the reaching, but God. But it seemed to work often. It was one of the gifts God had given him.

"You and everybody else," he said. Tom stepped out of the door, slightly edging his way past Brother Joe, who moved back to allow the man room to pass.

"You've had other visitors?" asked Brother Joe.

"No, not really," said Tom as he pulled the door closed behind him. Brother Joe had seen this act before, most of the times by people who knew he was coming. They would see him pull up outside (which was another reason he parked on the front street and walked) and grab their keys and meet him at the door, acting as if they had somewhere important to go in a hurry. Brother Joe often wanted to say they were headed to Hell in a hurry, but he never did. On the one or two occasions where he actually hung around and waited, he noticed that they merely got in their car, drove around the block, returning slowly to make sure he was gone.

"Have I caught you at a bad time?" asked Brother Joe.

"Time? I'm so confused about time right now. When is a good time?" he asked, inserting a key into the lock and turning it.

"There is no time better than the present," continued Brother Joe, unsure where this direction of conversation was taking them. "If Jesus comes tonight, you won't be able to ask him to come back tomorrow." Brother Joe liked that line, though he couldn't claim it. He'd read it out of an old country preacher's memoirs, and the line was directly linked to the days of the high-volume door-to-door salesmen.

"What?" said Tom, having locked the door and returned the keys to his pocket. "Oh, that's right, a preacher. Look-
-"

41

"Not just any preacher," interjected Brother Joe, "but one sent by God, and requested to come see you specifically by a man." This, of course, threw Tom for a loop.

"Huh?"

"Larry Pace, I believe you met briefly today, asked that I come see you." Tom searched his memory, then it clicked.

"Pace? Oh! Larry Pace," he said, "yes, I did meet him today. Though had I known who he was, I might have tried to avoid him. There, that's kinda like a confession, will that help me for the day?"

"Tom, I understand you're in a hurry," said Brother Joe, once again extending his hand. "May I come see you again? Maybe when you have a little more time?" Tom smiled, accepted the preacher's hand and shook it vigorously.

More time was exactly what he was going to look into. It sounded just nutso enough that ... well, it was worth another trip to check it out. If it didn't work, so what? What was lost? Only a little time. Really, how valuable was Tom Morgan's time anyway?

"Preacher, you certainly may. How 'bout you come back tomorrow? If I don't have more time then, I'll be sure to make some especially for you."

* * *

Larry turned the key and opened his office door and entered in a hurry. It wasn't that he needed to do anything fast, but he was anxious and couldn't get the possible conversation that Brother Joe was probably having even now out of his head. If they could help lead Tom to Christ, then... well, then what. Maybe it would help ease the pain of Gracie's death...but it would never bring Gracie back.

The sun shined brightly through his window as his mind raced back to the day he'd opened the letter. It still seemed like such a dream...not just selling his novel, but losing Gracie.

He leaned back in his chair and examined his office. It was the same office he'd occupied for the full twenty-one years he'd been at UNA. It wasn't a corner office, but he was happy with it nonetheless.

A single window filled the far wall. The window, which went to the ceiling from about knee-high, was surrounded by floor to ceiling bookshelves on either side. The entire length of one wall, approximately ten feet, also contained floor to ceiling bookshelves. The bookshelves ended to make a slight square space for a closet.

The other wall was plain, but Larry had his desk against it, and it was filled with pictures and other assorted paraphernalia that had gathered for twenty-one years. The books on the shelves were in perfect order according to Larry's preference, and looked as if they had been dusted just that morning. His desk was clean and free of clutter, only his open briefcase broke a picture perfect image.

A picture of Gracie sat next to his phone. He wished he could talk to her just one last time. He knew God had a plan and he was not about to suggest to God what his timetable should be...but he wanted to talk to Gracie just one last time to tell her he loved her. Just to make sure she--

Wait.

He remembered some guy at the funeral telling him something about getting another shot or something. He'd given him a card.

Larry felt around in all his pockets as he tried to remember what he'd done with the card. He didn't really expect to find it on his person, but went through the motions while he thought about it.

He remembered getting the card, but he couldn't remember what he had done with it. He looked through his desk drawers, not really expecting to find it in any of them either. Most likely, he'd left the card at home.

A quick light rap on the door and a familiar and friendly voice interrupted his brief moment of solitude.

"Hey buddy! You back and ready to pound the pavement? Warp the young and fragile minds of the incoming freshmen?" From his office on the third floor, Steven had seen Larry drive up and walked down to see him.

Larry turned to shake the hand of his good friend. He hadn't thought of it until just now, but this was his first time back to his office since Gracie was killed.

"Well, not really. I mean sure, but that's not really why I'm here." Steven plopped down in the guest chair in Larry's office, put there for students and one-on-one conferences, but often occupied by Steven.

"Larry, old boy," said Steven, slumping down in the

43

chair, obviously making himself very comfortable, "you're not making much sense."

The phone on his desk rang and Larry sat in his chair before answering. After his initial hello, he became excited when he learned the identity of the caller. However, he slumped back not attempting to hide disappointment in either his voice or his posture. He said thanks and hung up. Steven said nothing, but looked at Larry with anticipation.

"That was Brother Joe," said Larry.

"Yeah, what'd he want?"

"Oh, I met a young man who was the passenger in the car that hit Gracie. He was feeling all guilty and so I asked Brother Joe to pay him a visit. He did, but he just returned and said the guy kinda rushed him off." Larry sighed and swung his chair to stare out his one window.

"I know you know it, but I'm gonna remind you anyway," said Steven to Larry's back. "God has His own time and His own schedule. We can't mess with it, but rejoice that we can be a part of anything He has planned."

"I know." Larry's answer was short and distant. He watched the squirrels playing in the trees in front of his window, but he didn't really see them. "Gracie would have said the same thing."

Larry continued to stare out the window. Steven stood and stretched. Through a partially stifled yawn, he said, "God is good, Larry. Don't you forget that." Steven waited a moment for the anticipated routine reply. It never came. He quietly let himself out of the office, saying a prayer for Larry as he returned to his own office.

* * *

The house hadn't changed any since Tom was last there. He wasn't sure why, but he had expected something to be different. There was a vehicle parked where he'd parked the last trip. It was a nice one, too. Expensive. Some foreign made sports car. Candy-apple red. Waxed shiny and clean.

Tom pulled up next to the car, careful not to come too close. He turned the engine off in the SUV he had borrowed. He was unsure whether to get out or not. What if Big Ben was busy and was only kidding about that time thing? He'd had dreams about this kind of thing since he was a kid, and couldn't stop thinking about it since his visit. His current life was so worthless, it would be nice to return to a time when things were better; maybe he could actually change something or do something worthwhile.

Before he could make a decision, the front door opened. Out walked a beautiful blonde in a very trim-fitting knee length dress. The dress was also candy-apple red. She was quite a sight and Tom let out a soft whistle heard only by him. The blonde stepped out onto the porch and Big Ben followed a step, just far enough to pull the door somewhat closed behind him.

Big Ben spotted Tom and motioned with his hand for Tom to come up. He did not seem surprised at all; rather he acted as if he was expecting Tom... as if Tom had an appointment.

Tom sighed and decided he didn't have anything to lose, so he might as well see what it was all about. He removed the keys from the ignition, opened the door and stepped out. He closed the door and placed both hands in his pockets as he slowly walked toward Big Ben and the red dress.

"-it's really that simple," said Big Ben to the red dress. She turned and flashed a friendly smile to Tom as he approached. He smiled and nodded a hello back. He suspected why she was there and by her return look, he figured she guessed why he was there.

Big Ben stepped back and opened the door once more, indicating for Tom to step inside.

"Call me when it's done," he said to the girl as Tom stepped by him and into the house, "I want to know your first reactions." With that he closed the door and finally spoke directly to Tom.

"Hello Tom," he said, "decide to take me up and buy some time?"

"I thought I'd look into time-sharing," Tom said, trying to be funny but not really knowing what he should expect. "I'm pretty poor as a freelance writer, just ask my creditors."

"Ah," said Big Ben, shrugging off that suggestion, "the time I sell is affordable by all. So what are you interested in?"

Tom pulled his hands out of his pockets and held his palms up for examination. "See," he said, "no notebook or pencil today. I'm here for me."

"Great," said Big Ben, "follow me." He led Tom back into

the room with all the clocks and shut the doors behind them. Big Ben motioned for Tom to sit in the single chair in the room and then he sat on the steps nearby.

"Let me tell you about it," said Big Ben, "I said you could afford it, and you can. But it is not cheap. And there is a single problem." Tom half-expected this, something where on every other third Thursday on the full moon was the only time it would ever work. And that was only when Jupiter was visible to the naked eye which wouldn't happen again for ninety-nine years...or some such nonsense.

"I've never put money into a Swiss bank account before," said Tom. Big Ben stopped his thought with his mouth open and simply stared at Tom.

"Tom," he started, "you must be deadly serious about this or I have no interest doing business with you. I have many, many customers who are completely content and I simply do not have the time to waste if you are not serious."

"I'm sorry," said Tom, as he examined the tops of his shoes. He noticed and was suddenly aware that one of his shoestrings was white and the other was bright red; something that he had done around one a.m. one morning in the offices of the newspaper, thinking it funny at the time. "Look," he said," I'm interested in this, but I just don't know if I can afford it."

"If you will kindly shut up long enough for me to finish, you will understand.

"It is very simple. You pay time and a half for whatever amount of time you want."

Tom furrowed his eyebrows. The explanation sounded simple, but it still didn't quite fall into place for him.

"What do you mean? I have to work for you?"

"Not at all. Say you want a week of time," began Big Ben, "you simply agree to pay me a week and a half. No money, no swapped work, no Swiss bank accounts."

"How do I get it to you?" asked Tom.

"You don't have to worry about it. I can handle the technical aspects. It'll simply come off the end of your life."

"Huh?" said Tom. Now he was lost.

"If you want to purchase a week of time. You pay me a week and a half. That week and a half you pay comes off the end of your life."

"You mean, like I'll die a week and a half earlier than I

would have?" asked Tom, thinking his answer bordered on ridiculous.

Big Ben simply nodded.

"You know when I'm gonna die," asked Tom, somewhat surprised.

"It's not something I've committed to memory," answered Big Ben, "but it is something I could easily learn. You'll never miss it, the week and a half you pay, I mean. You'll simply die a week and a half earlier than intended."

Intended by whom, Tom wondered. "What was the drawback?" he said aloud, "You mentioned some problem."

"It's a warning I feel obligated to tell all my customers," said Big Ben, "and especially those with a history or tendency to substance abuse." Tom was shocked. He'd never thought of himself as an alcoholic or druggie or any kind of substance abuser.

"I'm not sure I'm in that category," he said defensively.

"Regardless," said Big Ben, "it's something I go over with everyone anyway. See, it's like a drug."

"Oh," said Tom, almost sounding relieved, "you mean it's something I take?" Immediately, he suspected some sort of advanced hallucinogenic.

"No, not that at all," said Big Ben. "What I mean is that it is very addictive. After you've gone back once, you'll want to do it again. And once you've done it again, you'll want to do it again...and again and again. Remember, that for every trip you take, the payment comes off the end of your life. A couple of weeks are not that big a deal. For the addicts, though, they can considerably shorten their expected lifespan.

"I speak from experience here, too, I've used it before." Big Ben's voice trailed off here and that made Tom curious. But there were enough questions bouncing around in Tom's head. He decided to leave that one for a later time.

"Couldn't you stop them?" asked Tom. "From going back, I mean?"

"Tom, I'm in the business of selling time," answered Big Ben. "There is nothing illegal or immoral about what I do. Okay, maybe immoral, but nothing illegal.

"I do not sell time to anyone under the age of 18, so anyone who buys time from me is a responsible adult. Well, an adult, anyway.

"As you have no doubt seen, I don't pressure anyone into buying time. I simply present you with the option to do so."

"How's it done?" asked Tom, genuinely.

"Tom," said Big Ben, "we could waste a lot of time on the hows and whys, and it probably wouldn't be any more clear to you. Frankly, however, I don't have the time to waste."

"What do you get out of it?" asked Tom.

Big Ben smiled. "What," he said, "you don't think I do this because I'm a kind man?" He laughed, mostly to himself. "I'm on commission," came the rather unexpected and short answer. Tom sighed. He felt like he was in some really bad B movie, but he had decided to go with the flow before he got here regardless of what happened.

"Okay," said Tom, "sign me up, I guess." He stuck his wrist up in Big Ben's direction. "You need some blood?"

This time Big Ben laughed, then pulled out a piece of paper. "Nope," he said, "just your signature here."

"You mean there's no deal with the devil or I don't have to give my soul up or anything like that? I just give up some time at the end of my life?" Big Ben nodded yes to Tom's questions.

"This ain't what I'd expect to see in the movies," said Tom as he moved to sign the contract.

"You're not in the movies, Tom," said Big Ben, "This is real. And I assure you, though you may not think it much more than a sheet of paper, this contract is very real."

Tom took the offered pen from Big Ben's hand, and began to read the contract over. It was titled "Do-Over Agreement," and it already indicated his name, the length of time, and the date of when he wanted to get a do-over. All it needed was a signature.

Tom sighed to get rid of his chill bumps. True or not true, he didn't know. But it didn't matter to him, it was worth the risk. Or the pretending. It wasn't costing him any money, so if it wasn't real that meant it was just pretend. His life wasn't much anyway, and if he lost some time off the end of his life, so what? Nobody would know...plus nobody would miss him anyway.

Tom signed the contract and offered the pen back to Big Ben. Still it actually felt as if he'd signed a deal with the devil.

"Why Big Ben?" asked Tom. Big Ben examined the signature on the contract, nodded his head approvingly, folded it in half and stuck it in his pocket. He looked thoughtfully at Tom.

"There's a clock with that name. Famous one."

"Yeah, I know about it. Has a song, too, I believe," said Tom. Big Ben nodded in agreement. The silence ticked by. Tom thought Big Ben was waiting for him to say something else. When he offered nothing else, Tom turned to leave. He stopped short at the front door, looking as if he'd left something behind.

"How do I ... you know ... go?" he asked. "Is there some sort of time machine? A fancy watch or something?"

"No, Tom," said Big Ben, "it doesn't work that way. It is far easier than that. When you're ready, you have but to go to sleep. When you wake up, you'll be there."

"Be where?"

"Where you want to be," said Big Ben.

"How do I get back?" asked Tom.

"Same way," replied Big Ben. "Listen, Tom, don't worry. There's momentary confusion, but your brain and memory arrive intact so you'll know exactly what is going on. Keep up with the days while you're gone, and you'll know exactly when you're coming back.

"And when you wake up, it will be like a dream. No time will have passed here. Not a minute. But your soul will have aged a week and a half. Now, have a nice time."

Big Ben smiled and slowly shut the door. He was finished with the conversation even though Tom still had a few curious questions.

Tom wasn't necessarily a believer as he walked to his borrowed vehicle, but he smiled at the thought of his soul aging and not his body. Well, Big Ben hadn't actually said his body wouldn't age, but if he fell asleep and time traveled with only his mind or soul, or whatever, how could his body age?

And what about his soul? What was that exactly? He shrugged off those thoughts. While he may not exactly have sold his soul to the devil, he felt just rotten enough that he figured God or Jesus or whoever the great spirit in the sky was, that He certainly was not interested in him now, not after a deal like the one he'd just made. Tom had crossed the line of no return.

* * *

Larry's daughters beat him home from church that night, not unusual except Becky had parked the car in the middle of the driveway. Larry laughed to himself. It was a ploy the girls learned from their mom. It wasn't unusual for Larry to return home to find Gracie's car in the middle of the driveway. She knew that Larry couldn't do two things: first, he couldn't get his truck around the car and into the garage; second, he couldn't stand to see the car all "cattywhompered" as he called it. It was simply something Gracie did to stall Larry, to buy her a few more minutes for whatever it was she wanted to finish before Larry came in the house.

He stopped short of the car, turned the truck off and removed the keys. He wasn't in any hurry, he figured one of the two girls had spotted him or would soon spot him. Moving quickly would only make them nervous. He entered the car and moved it forward and into the garage. He piddled as he returned to his truck by picking up oddball trash that had blown into his yard, eventually tossing it into the back of his truck. He climbed into the cab and pulled his truck into the other spot in the garage. He piddled more as he took the collected trash from the back of his truck and placed it in the trashcan. Since Thursday was trash day, he decided to take the can to the street, even though he hadn't collected the garbage up from inside the house.

As he slowly walked back up his driveway to the back door, he saw one of his daughters dash from the window. They were indeed watching him. He smiled inwardly, but managed to suppress the outward smile so the girls wouldn't know he'd seen them. But he'd delayed long enough, it was time to walk into the ambush.

* * *

Tom entered his apartment in the usual manner: He followed the path of visible floor to his refrigerator, placed his keys on top of the microwave while opening the refrigerator. He reached in, grabbed a beer from where they always were: Long ago he'd bought one of those cheap little plastic drink feeders for his refrigerator. Every time he grabbed a beer, it cycled down and put another one-- already cold—in its place. When he refilled it, the warm drinks went in on the top. He often wondered why more people didn't buy them; after all, it took up less space in his refrigerator and it was cheap. Cheap was the part that attracted Tom.

Drink in hand, he navigated the mess on the floor, his obstacle course, as he referred to it, and found the way to his small corner of the couch. Staring at the television, he blindly reached his left hand to the cushion beside him and grabbed the waiting remote. Without attention to his actions, he hit the power button and the television slowly came to life. He knew the tape was in the VCR and queued up to the spot. That spot. He hit play on the remote.

"No securities, no stocks, no bonds. Nothin' but a miserable little $500 equity in a life insurance policy. You're worth more dead than alive," came the voice from the television. Tom wasn't even watching. His eyes stared unfocused to that little spot just below the television. He hit the rewind button, he had the timing to an exact science, and the VCR clicked as it rewound the picture on the screen.

"No securities, no stocks, no bonds. Nothin' but a miserable little $500 equity in a life insurance policy. You're worth more dead than alive."

He hit the rewind button again and then hit the power, shutting down the TV with the tape once again queued to the appropriate spot.

Tom hit the rewind button as soon as the words were finished. The VCR whirred noisily as the tape rewound. As long as Tom held his finger on the button, the characters on the screen moved in that funny going-backward way. It was that kind of way that made you laugh so hard you cried as a kid, but as an adult, you found it only slightly amusing. Tom let his finger up when he spotted the beginning of the scene.

He watched for a third time.

At twenty-eight, Tom's life hadn't exactly gone the way he'd imagined it. Maybe it was all just a dream anyway. He remembered that somebody once said life is nothing but a dream, but he couldn't remember who said it. Not that the "who" would matter. They were probably paid a bunch of money to say it anyway. At one point in his life, Tom figured that by the time he reached thirty he'd be rubbing elbows with the John Grishams and Stephen Kings of the world, worrying about the plot of his next novel, kicking back in the Bahamas or some other exotic location.

Instead, he was just a freelance writer with the local paper, and not a well-liked one at that. A company in New York owned it and most of the local residents resented that. So Tom spent his time worrying if his car would get him to work and back without breaking down. Or without running out of gas. The breaking down part wasn't what worried him so much as the embarrassment that the car might break down. Which it often did. It was, in fact, in that state of disrepair even now.

Growing up a white southern male, certain expectations about the ability to repair a car were part of the baggage. Along with expectations of being a redneck and a racist. But Tom had skipped "shop" in school, electing instead to hang out with his friends in the study hall.

Not that they ever really "studied" in study hall. A game of chess was always interesting so long as Sheila was there to study. And if all else failed, reading the latest sci-fi novel also surpassed shop as exciting. He'd made it through *The Hobbit, The Chronicles of Narnia*, a whole bunch of stuff from H.G. Wells, and Asimov's *Foundation* series during study hall. All in one year. High school seemed like such a long time ago, yet somehow only like yesterday. One kid and one ex-wife had changed that.

He sighed and tossed the remote back onto the cushion beside him. He often thought that was the spot most people reserved for dogs or cats, loved animals and companions.

In Tom's home, it was the throne of his remote.

He leaned his head back on the couch and closed his eyes. It was all too much for him to comprehend. How could all that stuff Big Ben said be real? If it wasn't real, how could he fake all that stuff? How could he know what he knew? How? How? How?

As he considered the hows and whys, Tom thought of the time he'd return to. As he wondered truly what it would

52

be like to return there, he slowly drifted off to sleep.

* * *

Dr. Steven Dale took the last sheet from the printer, looked it over one good time and placed it on top of the other sheets fresh from the printer. Creating a syllabus for his classes was one of his least favorite things to do as a teacher, but it was one of the necessary things. He jokingly referred to it as one of his necessary evils of teaching. That and grading papers were his least favorite aspects of teaching.

But now he'd finished his syllabi for the fall term, which did not begin for another month. He'd finished it so early because he was not teaching any classes during the summer. Instead, he'd gone with the school Christian group on a mission trip to Africa. Steven was one of three adults who went along with fifteen college students. As mission trips sometimes go, it was the students who were touched by the ministry of their group. Often, Christians from the United States realize just how fortunate they are only when they see people from another country in their natural state and not on television. Not just to see them, but to actually get down and live with them as they live for a week. This opens the eyes of many missionaries.

And it was no different this time. Six of the students committed their lives to Christ, either as a profession of faith, or simply as a devotion of their life's work. Regardless, to Steven Dale, any time new souls were won to Christ, it was a victory worth celebrating.

Steven took the paper and put post-it notes on each indicating he wanted thirty-one copies of each syllabus. The school never placed more than thirty students in his classes, so thirty-one gave him one for all the students and one for his classroom copy. Post-it notes attached, he walked to the Art department office and placed them in the copy stack. A student worker would make the copy the next day and place it in his mailbox. Everyone was gone for the day, so nothing would happen now.

Another benefit of staying a little late was that the halls were empty. Come four O'clock, it was often hard to find instructors hanging around their offices unless they had a late class. Steven didn't mind this because it let him feel a little more... free.

Steven was one of those Christians who liked to talk to God regularly, and he frequently did so as he walked or simply as he went through his daily routine. However, he'd heard on more than one occasion folks from the university had accused him of talking to himself. He'd been called into the Dean's office several years ago and grilled for several hours. He didn't find out until later, but the Dean had a psychologist beside him during the entirety of the interview. Oh, Steven knew the lady was there and that she was taking notes, but he figured it was for "file" purposes and not for psychology purposes.

He had ended up arguing theology with the Dean who was of a completely different faith. It was one of these faiths that conveniently left the morals inside the church doors. Steven reluctantly admitted that it might not be so much the particular denomination as it was this one church. Steven had been to that church before and it seemed more a who's who of the university than a house of worship. Initially he had been excited to see so many faces he recognized from the campus, after all, universities are not traditionally known for their Godly beliefs. But when he realized they were there simply to be seen and not to worship, he decided to never go again.

The Dean had reluctantly concluded that while Steven may be fervently religious, that did not make him crazy. Nuts maybe, but not crazy. A fine line, granted. But not crazy.

Since that day, Steven had had an uneasy relationship with the dean and did his best to stay out of any possible conflicts. Not only was this best for him, but Steven felt it was following the teachings of Christ as well.

He sat down in his chair with a short burst of a sigh. Had anyone been in the room with him, they would have heard "Larry, Larry, Larry." The minutiae of the day done, his good friend Larry came immediately to the forefront of his mind again. He'd been percolating in the back of his mind all evening, and now it was time to think about Larry and lift him up to God.

Steven rocked the cushioned chair back and swiveled around to look out the window. On the second floor, he had a pretty good view of ... a tree. Initially wishing the tree removed so he could have a better view, he'd come to appreciate the tree after a few years. He realized that it forced his mind not to wander on the things around campus that could so easily distract him. Not that his mind couldn't still wander when staring at the tree, but there were no moving objects, students going back and forth, on which to focus his attention. The tree simply stood and swayed in the wind (when there was wind).

He tried to put himself in Larry's shoes, but knew he couldn't do it. No matter how much someone ever tells you they know how you feel, Steven knew it wasn't true unless they had also experienced the same sort of thing. And Steven had never lost his wife.

Larry's strength was a constant reinforcement of his own inspiration and strength, though. When Steven had the problems with the dean, he frequently spent time in Larry's office behind a closed door, pouring out his heart and his problems. Larry had always listened and then usually offered up some inspiring words and some scripture, giving Steven additional strength and encouragement to carry on. Not only that, he occasionally felt a burst of energy at times when the only two people who knew what was going on was his wife and Larry.

Once, when Steven had an important meeting, he asked Larry if he had prayed for him during the meeting. Larry's response was that he frequently prayed for his friend. Sensing his avoidance, Steven asked specifically if he prayed while the meeting was going on, because he felt a renewed strength. Larry simply smiled and gave the usual, "God is great!" response the two had become so accustomed to.

Steven knew his wife Christy prayed for him. He'd asked her and she gave him direct answers. He'd turned to Christy the last few days asking for help in praying for his friend as he went through his loss. Steven felt it had actually drawn he and his wife closer over the last few days as they both realized they could go home to be with God at any time, that they were on God's clock and not their own.

He sighed once again and drew a deep breath. His mind now cleared, he dove in and began to pray for his friend. He prayed first for a peaceful, calm assurance of God's love and grace, an assurance he knew everyone needed after a loss of a dear loved one. He asked the same thing for Larry's daughters, and that the family would draw together and gain strength from one another. He asked God to ease the pain and remind them that their dear wife and mother was in a better place. Lastly, Steven prayed about Larry's obsession with the man who was in the car. He prayed that Larry was being forthright with him and that it was not an obsession but was truly a Christian care and concern. Briefly Steven wondered how he would feel in the same situation. Would he be obsessed and possibly angry, or would he have true care and concern for the eternal salvation of the one responsible for the death of a loved one?

He returned to his prayer and asked God to guide and direct Larry when it came to the man. He asked that if it be God's will, and if the man wasn't already part of the family, to bring him into the Christian family, and allow Larry to be part of it. Mostly, he asked for God to heal Larry's pain, and return him to his life of worship.

Steven found he wasn't ready to end the prayer, but anything more would be repetition. Plus, he frequently was never ready to end prayers. He could pray with the best of them at church, and from the heart. But he said Amen, clicked off the power to his computer and went home to his wife, saying another silent prayer as he went. This time it was one of thanksgiving...for his own Godly wife.

* * *

Larry opened the door slowly and half expected to be nabbed immediately. He resisted the urge to smile, seeing the girls mimic so many things their mom had done over the years. Having to pass through the kitchen, he found it all shut down: dishes done, lights off, breakfast bowls out for the next morning. Just like Gracie used to do. No distractions, nothing to give him the desire to stop and help clean up and set the house to order before night.

He set his Bible down on the table so it would be handy for his morning reading and proceeded to the living room where all the lights were on.

As he entered the room, both his daughters were seated in their usual seats, busy "reading" something or other. Except he had seen them scurrying about as he pulled in, and that he could now see little beads of sweat on the face of each daughter, it was a perfect ambush.

"Hi Dad," said Becky as she looked up from her reading. "What took you so long?"

"Nothing particular," he said, "just a little this and that." After his short pause, he began to walk slowly down the hallway toward his bedroom. "Gonna call it a night," he said, "I'll see you girls at breakfast."

Larry knew he would never go to bed without first kissing his girls good night, or without at least offering and asking for a good night kiss. If his memory was correct, both daughters had refused only a few times, and it was always when they were mad because he wouldn't allow something. They later came crying and apologized and then showered him with kisses, but those times were very rare. He wasn't mad now, but it was funny to see how his daughters reacted.

"Wait! Dad!" called Cindy after him. "Come sit down with us for a few minutes. It's still early."

Larry took the few steps back so that he could see both his daughters. They were both anxiously looking his direction to see if their ambush was going to fail or not.

"I don't know," he answered, "I'm pretty tired."

"Ah, c'mon Dad," said Becky. "We haven't seen you all day long. You could sit down with us just a few minutes before you go to bed. You're not that old yet that you have to go to bed so early."

The trio laughed at the age joke. Becky had heard that said in some movie a few years back, and periodically called her dad "Old man," something that first shocked Larry but now he found it quite funny.

"Well, I guess I can find the time to sit for a few minutes," he said as he returned to the living room and took his seat on the couch.

"How was your day today, Dad?" Asked Cindy.

"Fine, I guess. How was yours?"

"Mine was fine, too," came her response. "What'd you do today?"

"Same ol same ol, really," he said, nearly having to bite his tongue to keep from laughing.

"Dad," said Becky forcefully, "did you go see that man again today?" There. It was out. Larry hadn't expected it to be about this; he figured it was about chores, his health, the money.

"And exactly what man are you talking about?" he asked. "If you think I'm trying to arrange a husband for you, you can think again. You'll have to do that on your own."

"You know the one we're talking about," added Cindy. "The man who was driving the car that killed mom."

"I found out he was not in the car alone," said Larry.

"What? What do you mean?" came the quick return from his daughters.

"Simply that while the guy in the hospital was driving, there was a passenger with him who came away relatively unscratched. I met him today."

The girls fell silent and Larry didn't offer anything else up. He knew they needed time to digest it all the same kind of way he did. Finally, Becky broke the silence.

"Dad, we're worried about you," she said.

"I worry about you, too, Becky."

"No. I mean we're really worried about you. Like you might be becoming obsessed with the man and everything. Now that there's a second one, maybe him too." Becky took a deep sigh before continuing, "Dad, we just think you're spending too much time worrying about this."

"And Dad," Cindy added, "you're the one who taught us what the Bible teaches us about worrying. Luke 12 says not to worry about your life, what you will eat; or about your body, what you will wear. God feeds the birds, aren't we more valuable than birds?"

"I'm not worrying about him," Larry said, "I'm praying for him. It's what your mother would have done."

"Dad," said Becky, "I have to disagree. Mom would have sought God's will, not yours. You're worried about what Mom would have done. Have you prayed about what God would have you do? We are supposed to use Jesus as our measuring stick, not Mom."

Larry could actually see what the girls were saying. He wasn't sure it was what they meant to say, but he could see it anyway. In a sense, he was proud of his daughters for being able to both discern and to know scripture to support their argument.

On the other hand, being rebuked was never easy. And it was especially hard when it came from his daughters.

"You're right," he finally said after a long pause, "I have been doing what I think Mom would have wanted and using that as a measuring stick. How about if I promise you to seek God's will daily on this? Will that make the two of you feel better?"

"Yes," was the harmonious response.

"Okay," he said, time to test again, "I'll start in the morning."

"We can start now," said Cindy. She shot a glance over to Becky. Had she overstepped here? Becky looked expectantly at Larry. Larry smiled. They passed.

"Yes," he said, "let's start now." Larry bowed his head and began to pray.

Thursday, July 27

om awoke to hear the sounds of the dogs barking outside. The light from the window caused him to squint so that he couldn't see much more than the light itself. He threw back the covers and prepared to jump off the top bunk of his bed only to find his feet already on the floor.

"Mom?" he yelled, nearly slipping on a magazine as he stood. He didn't remember leaving a comic book there, he always put them away, protected.

"Mom?" he said again, this time a little more loudly. If she was busy with dishes or laundry, she'd have a hard time hearing him. He cleared his eyes and made his way across the room...which seemed oddly unfamiliar.

He stopped at the doorway and stared at...the wall? Where were the stairs? He rubbed his eyes once more and looked around again.

It began to come back to him then. It was a dream. He was actually in his apartment. Alone.

Not a dream.

He'd traveled.

He'd gone back in time.

He'd visited the past. It worked.

But now he was back in the present. The here and now. The here where he had to write his articles and pay his bills. The here where he was still worth more dead than alive.

He turned back, kicking the Sports Illustrated magazine under his bed and he collapsed in despair.

* * *

arry opened the door to his office to hear the phone ringing. He dropped his bag at the door, propped it open and ran behind his desk to pick up the phone.

"Dr. Pace," he answered, slightly out of breath.

"Dr?" came the voice on the other end.

"Yes," said Larry, "That's me. Who are you trying to reach?"

"Larry Pace."

"That's me. Who's this?"

"My name is John Newcastle. I'm calling about your novel. I'm with the marketing department trying to schedule some things for you. Your editor didn't mention you were a doctor."

"Ah!" Larry laughed not quite to himself. "I'm not a medical doctor. I'm a professor at the college. And I may have neglected to mention that. I hope that won't change anything," Larry said, a little concern in his voice.

At about that same time, a knock came on Larry's door. Without even an opportunity to answer, the door creaked open slowly and in popped Steven's head. When he saw Larry on the phone, he held his hand up as if to suggest he'd come back later. Larry, however, wrinkled his brow and shook his head as he motioned Steven in.

Steven sat in his usual spot as he listened to Larry's repeated short answers of "uh-huh," "yeah," and "okay." Larry flashed him a quick smile and a thumbs up before he finished with "sure, just send me a list of the dates."

As he hung up the phone his excitement was visible to Steven.

"What was all that?" asked Steven, knowing it had to do with Larry's book, but playing in to his friend's excitement.

"That was some guy from the marketing department of my publisher." Larry's words came quick. Steven wondered when Larry had last taken a breath. "Seems they want to send me on a short promotional tour. It's not a big thing at all, only about a dozen spots. But they've picked out some important stores and a conference or two. I'm not speaking or anything, just signing books. Pretty cool, huh?"

Steven chuckled at Larry's continued excitement. "Take a breath, my friend, or you'll pass out from lack of oxygen."

Larry gave Steven a puzzled look and then broke out in laughter himself. "I guess you're right. I'm sounding like a fast-talking Yankee, ain't I?"

"Ain't?" asked Steven, mocking surprise. "Ain't? Didn't you just sell a book? Aren't you supposed to know that ain't ain't a word?"

The two friends laughed for a minute, sharing in intimacy that only a deep friendship can bring.

"It's good to hear you laugh again, Larry," said Steven, finally.

"Yeah," answered Larry, slowly. "It's good to laugh again.

"But hey!" he interjected quickly, "Let me tell you what the girls did last night. They ambushed me!"

"Ambushed?" asked Steven, sitting up slightly in his chair. "What do you mean?"

"Do you remember how I told you once that Gracie used to ambush me sometimes? She'd leave the trashcan out in the middle of the driveway trying to make it look like the wind blew it there, or something else like that. Didn't matter what, but I would have to move it before I could pull on into the garage.

"She always knew that once I got out of my truck that I'd get distracted and piddle around with this or that before going inside. It took me a few times to figure out that it was her. The only way I figured it out was that every time I had to get out of the truck like that, she waylaid me with something that had been heavy on her mind.

"Well, the girls must have been really paying attention to their mom all that time and I didn't even know it. The same thing happened yesterday. At first I thought it really was the wind, then I spotted them running back and forth in the house. It became so predictable it was funny."

"Hey," said Larry, interrupting Steven's laughter. "I've got a question for you."

"You ever heard anyone say something like buying back time at a funeral?"

"Buying time?" asked Steven, still chuckling over the story of the previous night. "No, I don't guess so. You talking like some sort of corporate thing or something?"

"No," answered Larry. "I don't think that was it."

"So what was on their minds," Steven asked.

"Who's minds?"

"Your daughters," said Steven. "You said they ambushed you last night. Earth to Larry."

Larry's eyes focused on something in the distance as his mind recalled his conversation with his daughters. "Well," he started slowly, "seems they're worried about me."

"Worried?" asked Steven. "That's not so unusual, though, is it? It's natural for a child to worry about a parent. And what with Gracie and all." Steven wasn't sure he was following. Further, he wasn't sure he'd be able to because Larry was still lost in his mental daze.

"Larry?"

"Hmm? Oh. Sorry," said Larry.

"I said I didn't think it was so unusual for kids to worry about a parent, you think?"

"Nah, it's not really unusual. They were actually able to point something out that really struck me," said Larry, fully returning to earth.

"What was that?"

"Well, all this time I'd been telling them that I was praying for the man because I know that's what Gracie would do. Y'know, I was thinking about her and all that. The girls reminded me that I should be doing it because it's what God would want me to do."

"Ouch," said Steven.

"Yeah," came Larry, "But you know even though it stings a little coming from my daughters, I was very proud of them to be thinking along those lines. They didn't get all wrapped up in missing Mom... I mean, Gracie. They were sincerely thinking about Christ.

"And you know," Larry said, slowly pausing, "that made me proud."

"And you very well should be. You and Gracie have raised some good fine Christian girls. Heck, I'm proud for you."

"Thanks. You've got some good ones yourself," Larry said, returning the compliment to his friend.

"Ah, mostly Christy. I'm just kinda along to make mistakes for Christy to fix." He laughed.

* * *

Brother Joe Hallmark parked around the corner from Tom's apartment complex in order to get in his usual walk. He'd greeted an older couple that smiled and told him God loved him before he'd had the chance to say those very words. Smiling and nodding that gave him a good feeling about the upcoming meeting with Tom.

Standing at the door he'd been to once before, he said his silent prayer once again asking for God's wisdom, direction and words. Loudly, he knocked.

After a few minutes, the door slowly opened, revealing a sleepy Tom, hair tussled, t-shirt wrinkled, eyes squinting in the sudden flood of light.

"Morning, Tom," said Brother Joe, extending his hand. Tom smacked him tongue against his teeth a few times as if trying to get a bad taste out of his mouth. He slowly produced his own hand for Brother Joe.

"Did you forget that you asked me to come back today?" said Brother Joe as he slowly shook Tom's hand.

"I did?" was the inquisitive reply.

"Hmmm," started Brother Joe, "I can see you don't remember. Maybe you'll remember once you're more awake. Can I come in?"

"Uh...sure," said Tom as he slowly opened the door. As Brother Joe stepped across the threshold and into the darkness, Tom reached behind him searching the wall for the light switch. A faint click and light invaded the small apartment.

Brother Joe was only about half surprised to find such a messy apartment. Tom was, after all, a bachelor with no serious commitment. He had no real reason to keep his apartment clean. It didn't look any better or worse than when he'd had the opportunity to peek in earlier.

Tom shut the door behind him and stood silent for a second. Brother Joe, stopped right in front of him, turned to look at Tom. There was really nowhere to move or sit. Tom, slowly realizing the predicament, rushed in front of Brother Joe and began shifting magazines, books and other assorted papers off a small section of the couch for Brother Joe to sit on.

"Here, preacher," said Tom as he tossed items here and there, "you can sit here. Sorry about such a mess."

"Thanks," said Brother Joe as he took the offered seat. Tom watched Brother Joe sit, an armful of books and papers still in his hands. Still seemingly half asleep, he stepped over Brother Joe's legs and walked around behind the couch, dropping his stack onto a hidden pile out of Brother Joe's line of sight.

"You, uh, want something to drink?" asked Tom, "a beer or something?"

Brother Joe laughed. Often people would try to test him just to see what he'd say. He didn't think Tom was testing. He thought Tom was still asleep.

"No thanks, Tom, I don't drink alcohol."

"Don't drink?" replied Tom, puzzled. "Oh yeah. Preacher. Sorry, I forgot." Brother Joe heard the refrigerator open and bottles clink around inside. Probably trying to hide the beer bottles, or at least shift them to the back of the refrigerator. "I've got a can of Mountain Dew, you want that?"

"It's not open, is it?" Brother Joe was just joking, but usually his jokes were only funny to him.

"Huh? Open? No, it's not open."

"I was just kidding," said Brother Joe through a stifled chuckle. "I don't want anything to drink. But don't let that stop you, go right ahead and get something. I know that I need my coffee to get started in the morning."

"Yeah, okay."

Brother Joe heard more clanking, hair of the dog, he guessed. That's when the smell hit him. It wasn't alcohol he didn't think. It could have been drugs. He certainly didn't know all the drug smells. It didn't exactly smell like dirty clothes, either. It was just ... odd.

When Tom reappeared he carried a half finished Dr. Pepper. He made his way over to the other side of the couch and simply plopped down on whatever was there: papers, magazines, a computer floppy disk.

"So what was it you wanted to talk to me about, preacher?" said Tom, putting the Dr. Pepper to his lips.

"Well," began Brother Joe, "I think I mentioned to you that Larry Pace asked I come see you."

"Uh, yeah, you mentioned that. Why'd he want you to see me?"

"Well, Larry's a unique man. You know, he just lost his wife and when he met you, well, he was just concerned."

"Concerned?" said Tom in surprise. "Concerned about what? My eternal soul?"

"You laugh," replied Brother Joe, "but yes. Don't you find that amazing? He's lost his wife and should be mourning, but he's calling me asking me to see you."

Tom rolled his eyes but didn't think Brother Joe could

see him. He shrugged his shoulders before Brother Joe began again.

"Would you mind telling me about what happened?" Tom looked at him with an inquisitive look.

"You mean at the hospital?"

"No," said Brother Joe, "the accident."

"Oh." Tom paused, looking off in the distance.

"I'm not reporting to the insurance company or police or anything." Then, after his own short pause, "I report to a higher authority." It was another of his jokes that obviously was funny only to him.

"I don't see why not. Be kinda like a confession or whatever for me, wouldn't it?" asked Tom.

"Well, I'm a Baptist preacher, we don't really do confession or anything like that. I mean, we're all about confessing because we have to confess our sins. But if you want to look at it like that, sure. It's always good to get it out to someone."

"Yeah, I guess." Tom paused again as he remembered the events that led to the accident. "Mike was actually driving me to a job. I write for the paper and my car was on the fritz. I needed a ride to my interview. Mike does that for me often."

"What was the interview," Brother Joe asked, trying to keep Tom talking.

"Some guy--hey! That piece might have run by now; I haven't even looked. It was some guy who served time in prison for robbing a bank. But they never found the money. This guy supposedly takes the fall for a couple other guys but no money was ever located. And he's not even ticked.

"But anyway," Tom continued, "we were headed there and I was just talking to him. When I talk about something I get excited about I have a tendency to touch the person I'm talking to repeatedly during my excitement. It's a bad habit; I know it is. I kept touching Mike while he was driving and one time I touched him and he didn't see her pull out in front of him."

A deeper silence followed as Brother Joe thought about what Tom had said. Tom was still miles away, anyway.

"So," Brother Joe finally said, "you blame yourself for the accident?"

"Yeah." Then "Well, no not really." And "But yeah, sorta.

I just wish I could take it all back." Tom thought back to the night he'd just spent. He'd gone back in time somehow and experienced it—lived it all over again. Wouldn't it be great to be able to go back and change that so that he didn't actually touch Mike and Mike could see the car and stop and not kill that lady?

"Tom," said Brother Joe, interrupting Tom's thoughts, "would it surprise you any if I said it was all part of God's plan?" Tom's response was a short burst of air through pursed lips. It was the sound of disbelief. Brother Joe had heard it many times before. Once it fazed him, bothered him, but no more.

"It wouldn't matter," he continued, "if you could go back in time. You couldn't change anything. God has chosen for this to happen exactly as it did. He has His reasons. I can't explain them. I can't tell you why. I just know it's so."

Tom looked up from his daze and stared Brother Joe right in the eye. What he'd said was eerie, almost like he'd read his thoughts.

"How do you *know*?" he asked.

"Because God says it, that's how."

"What? Did He come to you in a vision?" Tom's voice was filled with sarcasm. It was obvious he had a problem with anything relating to God and His word.

"No, Tom," replied Brother Joe, no hint of aggravation in his voice at all. Instead, it was the model of patience and compassion. "It's all in His word, the Bible. I didn't bring one with me today, but if you have a copy, I'd be happy to show it to you."

Tom looked away again. Brother Joe could see he was deep in thought. His words, God's words were penetrating Tom's heart. God was convicting him.

"Nah," he finally said, "I believe you. You know that stuff so I trust you. I just don't think that it's for me."

"What, you don't think Heaven's for you?" asked Brother Joe.

"Well heaven, sure," said Tom. "But all the religious stuff that goes with it, I guess."

"It's for anyone who will believe. Regardless of race, creed, age, job, doesn't matter. Anyone."

"But don't you just wonder what it would be like if you *could* go back and change things?" asked Tom. "Don't you

67

wonder?"

"I guess everyone does," answered Brother Joe, "we're human. It's only natural for us to want to undo wrongs in our life. Set things right. But you know, Tom, that the Holy Spirit is at work in you. He's convicting you, telling you what's wrong and what's right."

"My own Clarence," Tom chuckled.

"Clarence?"

"It's a personal joke. An old movie reference."

"Old movie?" Asked Brother Joe.

"Yeah. *It's A Wonderful Life.*"

"Oh! Yeah. The angel! I love that movie," said Brother Joe, excitedly.

"You do?"

"Sure. George contemplates suicide but God reveals to him all the truly wonderful things he really has, in *spite* of the difficulties of life."

Tom wasn't so much surprised that Brother Joe knew the movie, but was surprised to meet someone else who apparently loved the movie like he did. But Brother Joe continued, "I guess you could say the Holy Spirit is kinda like that. He's more of a conscience really. More like Jiminy Cricket."

Tom laughed, "Always let your conscience be your guide."

Brother Joe chuckled a little but said, "Yes. That's the Holy Spirit. He's the conscience for all Christians and He's the one who tells non-Christians they're doing wrong and really works on their hearts to get them to trust Jesus." Brother Joe, chuckling no more, got deadly earnest.

"You think maybe that's what's going on with you?"

"Preacher, you gonna try to save my soul now? Tom smiled. "I can tell you before you answer, my soul cannot be saved."

"Anyone can be saved, Tom. Anyone."

"Well, I appreciate your concern, but not today." Tom stood, a signal that the conversation was over. Brother Joe stood after him, but was not yet finished.

"What if Jesus returns tonight?"

"Well," said Tom, opening the door and holding it open for Brother Joe. "As you yourself said, God has a plan for everything but we don't know it. If He comes, He comes.

Thanks for coming preacher."

"May I come again?" asked Brother Joe. Tom grimaced slightly, trying not to make it obvious that he didn't really want the visit, yet unable to do so.

"Yeah," he finally said, "sure, you can. Don't come tomorrow or anything. But you can come and we'll have another deep conversation about time."

"What?" Brother Joe stopped in his tracks.

"I said we can have another deep conversation about time," Tom repeated.

Brother Joe laughed. He didn't tell Tom, but he thought he first heard "conversion." Converting was certainly what was on his heart. But he knew that Tom had repeated a truth: everything is on God's timetable, not ours.

"Sounds good, Tom," he said, walking away, "We can even talk more about *It's A Wonderful Life*. I'll see you later."

* * *

Larry felt better after he told Steven of the girls' ambush. He nearly always felt better after he'd talked to Steven. He hadn't told Steven, though, what he planned to do today. He knew that Steven would try to talk him out of it. But he was determined to see the man who had driven the car that hit Gracie. Not just to see him, but to talk to him. He'd seen him many times before, but never did he have the chance to actually talk with him. And he'd done what he promised to the girls--he had sought God's will and he believed he should share with him about God's love. If God's love was so great that the husband of the woman he'd accidentally killed would come to tell him about it in love...well, that seemed pretty convincing to Larry.

So Larry waited until he knew Steven had stepped out of his office and then called and left him a voice mail. Told him he was going to the hospital to share with the driver. He knew Steven would know what driver he meant.

The drive to the hospital was longer than it should have been. Larry was actually a little nervous. He talked out loud to God the entire way. He asked for guidance and patience and, most of all, absence of any sort of anger.

He parked, entered the hospital, still praying under his

breath. When he reached the man's room, he stopped. The other guy, the passenger Tom, was sitting with his back to the door up next to the head of the bed. He was talking to the sleeping driver. Larry inched closer, trying not to make a sound.

"...was incredible," said Tom to Mike. "I really thought I was there. I mean, it *felt* like it was fifteen years ago." Tom spoke as if Mike were awake and listening and carrying on a conversation with him. But Larry noticed that Mike was sleeping soundly, not hearing a word that was said.

"And all I had to do was go to sleep. I mean I always thought time travel would be like the H.G. Wells book, y'know? *The Time Machine?* Can you imagine--" the door creaked as Larry pushed it open trying to quietly enter the room more.

He knew what he thought he heard, but he was trying to get closer just to make sure. It made him immediately think of the man at Gracie's funeral—he still couldn't find his card anywhere.

Tom, stopped in mid-sentence, turned to see Larry smiling and entering the room. He stood.

"Nah," said Larry, motioning with his hand, "keep your seat. Is he sleeping" He was still thinking about what he thought he'd heard: time travel?

"Yeah," answered Tom, looking down at Mike. "I haven't been here very long, but he's been asleep the whole time."

"You mind if I come in here and join you?" asked Larry. "I really didn't expect to find you here." Had Tom just been telling Mike about a dream?

"Huh?" asked Tom, "Why not?"

"What I mean is," said Larry, taking a seat at the end of the bed, "I came to see him, not thinking I'd find you."

"Umm." Was the response from Tom. He turned the chair so that it faced Larry, the bed--and Mike, to his side. He continued, however, to keep his face looking at Mike.

"So what do you do...Tom, isn't it?" Asked Larry simply to break the tension in the room.

"I write for the paper," said Tom. "Oh! Hey! Why'd you send that preacher over to see me?"

"You've just gone through a pretty traumatic event and I thought you could use an ear, someone to talk to," answered Larry. "Did he come see you?"

"Yeah," said Tom, "came this morning."

"Nice guy, isn't he?" asked Larry.

"Yeah," said Tom, looking off in the distance, "persistent." Larry laughed.

"I hope he was able to help you some. That's great you write for the paper, though" said Larry. "What an incredible talent God must have given you. I can't imagine always having to write on such a deadline."

"You get used to it."

"What happens if you miss your deadline?" asked Larry.

"Depends," answered Tom, going through the situations in his mind. "A lot of the time they can just get something else and push the story back a few days. Well, that after they've chewed me out royally."

"I wrote a novel but my deadlines were pretty easy and I pretty much set them myself."

"Cool, a novel?" asked Tom, genuinely interested.

"Yeah, just a little science fiction novel," answered Larry, "not that big a deal, really."

"Cool. What's the name of it?"

"Well, it's not out yet and the editor and marketing crew are still tossing several options around. They want to come up with a title that'll draw the most interest. Not sure how much say I'll have in it, but I'm okay with that."

"What kind is it? I mean is it horror or crime or..."

"Science fiction. Bunch of aliens fighting each other. Say, you ever wish you could just buy yourself some more time on those deadlines? I mean, if you wanted to do that, what would you have to do?"

A chill went up Tom's spine. He realized that Larry had probably heard him talking to Mike. He'd thought he was just talking to his sleeping best friend. He didn't think or realize that someone else could be interested in anything he had to say.

But then again, even though Big Ben had said the information wasn't for publication, he never said he couldn't tell anyone about it—not specifically. He might actually want him to tell others. Ben had said he was on commission, and any other sales would bring him more commission.

"Well, just call the editor and tell them you need more time," he said, "I do it all the time." He laughed. He wasn't about to fully unload on this guy.

And Larry hadn't gotten the answers he wanted. He wanted Tom to just volunteer to repeat his story. But he didn't want to come out and ask him what he'd said. Number one, it just flat wasn't polite to listen to someone else's conversation. Number two, if he hadn't heard what he thought he'd heard, Tom would think he was crazy. How could he ever talk to him about Jesus if he thought he was certifiable? He found himself drifting off in a daze and so he allowed himself to go halfway there because he knew Tom was watching.

"I wish real life was that easy," he said, "don't you?"

Tom chuckled, "yeah, like when we shoot hoops and you can't agree on the foul and you get a do-over." He didn't have to ask. He knew what Larry was thinking. He knew Larry would like to have a chance to do-over the loss of his wife. It was obvious simply by the look on Larry's face.

"Yeah," Larry responded, barely audible. "Like that." Do-over. Larry drifted completely away. It would be nice to see Gracie just one more time. It wasn't like he could bring her back, but he didn't even get the chance to say good-bye to her. He didn't have the chance to make sure she knew he loved her. Oh, he was pretty sure she knew. But now she was gone. He wanted to tell her one last time, just to make sure. He wanted to tell her that he loved his life with her, that she'd given him two beautiful kids. That even though she was gone he had many, many wonderful memories she'd supplied him. He wanted to kiss her one last time. To hug her. To let her know he had no regrets about their lives together. None. He really wouldn't change anything.

Nothing except the day she was killed.

* * *

Larry didn't even notice that Tom had gotten up. Hadn't even noticed that he had walked right by him and out the door. Larry was brought out of his daydream by the creaking sound of the door. He noticed Tom's hand on the door as it was shutting.

And he hadn't shared anything whatsoever about God's love. He hadn't come there to see him, of course, but he never should have let the opportunity pass by. God had

72

placed Tom in Larry's sphere of influence today for a reason. And Larry had failed.

Larry decided to wait out the driver's sleep. He'd come to share the word and if that meant he had to wait a while, he'd wait.

Then he got frustrated at himself. He always, *always* brought a book along with him everywhere he went just in case he ever found himself in a situation where he was waiting with nothing to do.

Just like now.

And he didn't have a book.

As it happened, the door creaked again as it opened. He hoped it was Tom coming back-maybe he'd just stepped out to get a drink. But to Larry's great surprise, in walked Steven.

"Steven," he said, quite shocked, "what are you doing here?"

"Larry," he answered, "how many times do I have to remind you?" Steven grabbed the chair in which Tom had sat and pulled it over next to Larry, intentionally extending his dramatic pause.

"Apparently," interjected Larry, impatiently, "you're gonna have to do it once again. Now."

Steven laughed at the fun he was having at his friend's expense. He sat down and made himself comfortable. He then reached his hand over and put a firm grip on Larry's shoulder. "You are my friend and I'm here to help you. If you're going to do this, then I'm going to do it right along with you. I'll lend whatever paltry strength I may have to your cause."

Steven removed his hand from Larry's shoulder and returned it to his lap. He appeared as content as could be and like he was settled for the long run.

"So, what'd you bring for lunch?"

* * *

After an hour of waiting, the doctors ran Steven and Larry out. Mike, the driver, never woke up. So Larry and Steven never got the opportunity to share Christ with him. Larry was a little upset, but Steven reminded him, once again, that it was all on God's timetable, not Larry's.

What the two men didn't realize was that Mike wasn't just sleeping, he had slipped back into a coma. The doctors couldn't explain why, but he had.

Instead of going back to the school, however, Larry went home. He had no afternoon classes on Thursdays and so decided to putter around the house and get some things done. The school was a little relaxed about office hours during the summer. As long as you came in and were available for students some of the time, you were generally okay. Classes were longer in the summer and most students didn't have a desire to stick around and chat with the instructors when class was over anyway. They had their own schedules to keep, and that usually consisted of fun.

Larry hadn't been home more than about fifteen minutes when the doorbell rang. He'd barely had the chance to change clothes and then pick up the old mail and newspapers from off the couch. He wasn't expecting anyone and no one really knew he was here.

Making his way to the door, he set down the stack of mail on the kitchen table. He peeked out the window and saw a young man in a very nice looking three-piece blue suit. He had black hair parted neatly on the side and slicked back so that every hair was in perfect place. In his right hand he held a cigar, about half smoked.

He looked familiar, but Larry couldn't place him. He had the appearance of a salesman, but didn't have a briefcase or sample or anything.

Opening the door, he greeted the man.

"Hi," returned the young man. "My name is Ben Chapman. We met the other day. Do you have a moment you could spare?" He placed the cigar back in his mouth as he extended his right hand to Larry. It was his usual opening line on cold calls. He got more of a kick out of it than any of his potential customers because only he understood the irony behind his statement.

"Well," started Larry, taking the proffered hand and gently shaking it, "what's this all about? Do I know you from somewhere?"

"We met the other day," said Ben, not mentioning the fact it was at Gracie's funeral. "I mentioned something about time to you."

Ben removed the cigar from his mouth once again. He

74

looked for a moment at the cigar and, realizing that he was nearly finished anyway, tossed it aside. Larry watched in disbelief as the cigar burned away in his grass.

"This is going to sound very strange," said Ben, "But listen, you're a Christian, right?" The question surprised Larry, but answering it was easy.

"Most certainly."

"And you believe that, God has a purpose for everything, right?"

"Yes."

"But you don't always understand why things happen, right?"

"Yes."

"What if I told you that you could see Gracie again?" Larry was stunned. "And I don't just mean in a picture or movie or anything like that. But really touch her, hold her." Larry shook his head to get the cobwebs out.

Now he remembered the guy.

"You're the guy from the funeral, aren't you?" Larry asked. "The one who gave me the card—which I seem to have lost."

"Look," Larry continued, "I don't really know what you're after, but my wife is dead." Larry had been in fistfights as a kid-had won some and lost some. He'd never hit anyone in his entire adult life. However, the way he felt at that moment, he was about to hit this man standing in front of him. He balled his fists beside him.

"I know. I know. Just hear me out. I don't usually come straight out and tell people like this, but I just had this feeling about you. I got it during your wife's funeral. I can't explain it." Ben ran his fingers through his slicked hair and looked down at the ground as he tried to put together his next words. He hadn't noticed Larry's fists.

Was this guy nervous? He sure acted like it. Larry's rage subsided somewhat and he studied the man. What could he be nervous about?

"There is a way you can go back in time and relive a part of your life. No drugs, no machines, no tricks. And it doesn't cost you any money."

"What did you say your name was again?" asked Larry, uncurling his fists.

"Ben Chapman. But my friends call me Big Ben. You're

welcome to call me that."

"Ben...wait! Aren't you the same guy the paper did the story on? Written by Tom Morgan?" Then it hit Larry. Tom had been telling his friend Mike some time travel story. The connection couldn't be coincidental.

"Yes," he answered, "that's me."

"So how's it supposed to work then?"

Big Ben was visibly uncomfortable. Larry didn't know if it was because he was outside, if it was because he was nervous about the time-or lying, or if it wasn't because he hadn't invited him inside. He knew that many salesmen believed if they could just get through the door, then the sale was made.

"There's no hocus pocus involved, if that is what you mean," said Ben. "This is real."

"You said it didn't cost money. There must be some fee attached?"

"Oh, there is," he answered quickly, "I'm not trying to keep any hidden costs from you or anything like that. But it's a simple fee. Basically, the time you take comes off the end of your life."

Larry thought for a moment. He saw his daughter's car pull into the driveway. The girls obviously noticed the nice BMW parked on the street in front of the house and were now both eyeballing the stranger as they slowly drove up.

"So, if I travel back for, let's say, a week, then a week comes off the end of my life? I die a week earlier?"

"Not just a week," corrected Ben, "but a week and a half. The fee is time and a half." Ben now noticed the girls as the doors opened and slammed shut.

"This all sounds so outrageous," said Larry, "let me think about it."

"No problem," said Ben, pulling a card from out of his vest pocket. "Here's my information again. Hang on to this one. You want to talk, just drive on up and see me. No appointment needed." He began to walk away as he talked. Larry guessed he was trying to avoid the girls.

"Thanks," said Larry. As he turned to walk back inside, he noticed the girls walking through the grass to the front door-something they never did. They always went through the back door. They arrived next to Larry about the same time that Ben arrived at his car.

"Who was that, Daddy?" asked the oldest.

"Just some salesman, Becky" he answered.

"What did he want?" asked Cindy.

"What do salesmen always want?" he asked, mock sarcasm in his voice. "He wanted to sell me something." Larry moved further inside the door, motioning for the girls to enter behind him.

"What was he selling?" Cindy looked back at the BMW, now pulling away.

"What's with the twenty questions?" said Larry in a playful tone. He shut the door behind Becky as she entered. "He was a salesman selling something. We really don't need anything, do we?"

"No," replied Cindy, "but he sure had a nice car. At least we know he wasn't a used car salesman."

The three laughed as they made their way inside. Larry had some serious thinking to do. It really all sounded like a crock, to him. Some kind of sham. This Big Ben obviously was a salesman and like all salesmen, there had to be some trick to it. What was the old adage? If something seems too good to be true, it probably is. Something like that. Of course, Big Ben had said it wasn't free, but Larry didn't see how that could work. Taking time off the end of a person's life meant that he'd have to know when that person was going to die.

It just didn't seem real.

Yet, it would sure be nice to see Gracie one more time.

* * *

Tom was waiting in Big Ben's driveway when the BMW drove up. He'd been sitting there for just over an hour, hoping Big Ben would return soon.

As he watched the BMW come to a halt, he waited until he knew it was Big Ben in the car before he exited his own. Stepping out, he walked hurriedly to Big Ben, reaching to open the door for him but not getting there quite in time.

"Hey Tom," he said, stepping out of the BMW. "I'm surprised to see you here. What's up?"

"I want to go again."

"Go?"

"Yeah. You know. I want to travel back again." Tom's

eyes glazed over as he remembered the details of his trip. "I just can't believe how incredibly fantastic - and how real it all was."

"Oh, it was real," said Big Ben, "real enough for you to touch and taste and do all over again."

"You're telling me."

"So what do I need to do to go again? Do I need to sign the papers again or can I just go?"

Big Ben looked at Tom with what could have been a look of concern on his face. "I don't know Tom, it all seems kind of sudden. Are you sure?" he said. "It was only yesterday when you took your first trip."

"Yes, I'm sure," Tom answered. "I slept better last night than I've slept in a long time. Actually, should I say last week?" Tom laughed at his own attempt at humor. Big Ben didn't laugh.

"Well," said Big Ben, "It's your life. You're a grown man. Follow me. We'll draw up a new contract."

* * *

Tom was so excited that he couldn't make himself sleepy. He desperately wanted to go to sleep, but even fake yawning couldn't produce a real yawn. For the last hour he'd been watching some infomercial about drug induced fitness or some such.

It wasn't working.

So he popped in the tape. It automatically started playing as he reached for the VCR remote and returned to his spot on the couch.

"No securities, no stocks, no bonds. Nothin' but a miserable little $500 equity in a life insurance policy. You're worth more dead than alive." Mr. Potter's voice. So full of contempt for George Bailey.

Tom hit the rewind button, let up at the perfect time. "No securities, no stocks, no bonds. Nothin' but a miserable little $500 equity in a life insurance policy. You're worth more dead than alive."

Who would pay his death bill when he was gone?

"No securities, no stocks, no bonds. Nothin' but a miserable little $500 equity in a life insurance policy. You're worth more dead than alive."

No one had come to see him after the accident.

"No securities, no stocks, no bonds. Nothin' but a miserable little $500 equity in a life insurance policy. You're worth more dead than alive."

The remote slipped out of his hand. This time George stormed out of Potter's office as Tom drifted off to sleep... and to...

Friday, July 28

The next morning Larry was waiting at the church when Brother Joe arrived. It was a few minutes after eight.

"Good morning, preacher man," he said as Brother Joe opened the door.

"Good morning Larry," he replied, "what brings you here so early?"

"Got a few minutes?"

"I've always got a few minutes for you, Larry. Why aren't you waiting inside?"

"Barb asked me to," said Larry, speaking of the church secretary, "but I figured I could get a good few minutes of quiet time out here."

Brother Joe stopped.

"I hope that's not all the quiet time you plan to spend today," he said to Larry.

"Of course not," Larry laughed. "You know me better than that." They continued through the front entrance hall and into the office area where Barb wished everyone a good morning, Larry for the second time. Larry followed Brother Joe past the minister of music's office-sound already pouring forth-and into the back office.

"Have a seat," said Brother Joe, putting his few books down on the desk. "I'm going to get some coffee. You want some?"

"Nah. Thanks though." As Brother Joe walked back out of the office, Larry sat and looked around. He'd been in the preacher's office several times before. The first few times felt somewhat like he remembered being in the principal's office in grade school. After a few times, that feeling passed. He never really minded the preacher stepping out and leaving him there because it always gave him the opportunity to study the books on the shelves. Brother Joe had a pretty extensive library, mostly books regarding scriptural study.

80

There were also books about other religions and self-help books with a Christian bent, but not many. There were about two dozen Christian fiction books, among them were a few Larry had recommended. Frank Peretti's *This Present Darkness* was one that had turned into one of Brother Joe's favorites. He had told Larry that it really supported or reinforced his opinions on the importance of prayer.

Brother Joe returned with a cup in his hands and up next to his mouth, blowing gently inside.

"I always manage to nuke it too long," he said, momentarily halting his blowing. "So what's on your mind this morning, Larry?"

"Ahhhh, something I'm a little hesitant to talk about" Larry began, "but because it's kinda, I don't know, out there." Brother Joe closed the door behind him and sat in the chair opposite Larry. The two chairs in front of the desk faced each other for the very reason that Brother Joe did not like to have the desk between him when he was having a conversation with someone.

"Well, just say it like it is," he said. "We'll figure out together if it's 'out there' or not."

Larry shook his head not sure whether to go on or not. He took a deep breath and formulated his first question.

"Do you believe in time travel?" he asked.

"Time travel?"

"Yeah. Like traveling back to another time in the past."

"That is 'out there,' isn't it?"

"Yeah. It is."

Brother Joe sipped his coffee as he thought for a moment. "I must confess I've never really thought about it before."

"C'mon now," interjected Larry. "You mean to tell me you've never thought it would be cool to go back to that fantastic summer after 10th grade? Or to go back and replay the ballgame where you missed that catch?"

"How do you know about that?"

"You've only used it to illustrate about a half dozen of your sermons.

"Really?" said Brother Joe, slightly surprised. "A half dozen? Guess I'd better come up with something different.

"But to answer your question, I'd have to say no that I probably don't believe in time travel."

"But why not?" asked Larry.

"Well. Why not?" repeated Brother Joe. He reached over to pick the Bible up off his desk and set the cup of coffee down at the same time. He leafed through the pages as if somehow he thought the verse would leap out at him. "Why not?" he repeated.

"I don't know," he finally said as he snapped his Bible shut. "I don't know. I'll have to do some searching and some praying to give you scripture support, but it just doesn't seem like it would be right. If we try to undo our wrongs like that, then it would seem to me as if we're playing God. I mean, you and I both know that God has an appointed time for everything."

"Yeah," responded Larry, "The Byrds even sang about it."

"Plus," Brother Joe continued, "and I'm not an expert here, but I don't think the science or scientific research supports time travel of any sort. I'd guess there are all sorts of science fiction theories, but to my knowledge, nothing concrete."

Larry nodded.

"Why do you ask about this?" asked Brother Joe.

"Okay, see, you shouldn't have asked that," said Larry, smiling.

"Not following you here, Larry."

"If you hadn't asked, I could have left and just maybe left you with the idea that I was working on my next novel."

"The thought did occur to me some."

"See. Now I have to tell you the truth...because you asked." Larry took a deep breath, slowly blew it out as he stared at some of the books on the shelves behind Brother Joe's head.

"Some guy came to my house yesterday and offered to sell me some time. Sounds weird, I know. But even weirder was that he *knew* things."

"Time share salesmen aren't that unusual," said Brother Joe.

"Not a time *share* salesman," said Larry, returning his gaze to the preacher. "He offered to sell me back some time. It's tough to understand, but I think the gist was that I could revisit a time in the past by sacrificing some time from the end of my life."

"Meaning?"

"Meaning I'd die earlier than intended."

Brother Joe sucked in air through his teeth. "Now see, that's what I'm saying-just doesn't sound right."

"Not even if it's real? Which I'm not sure it is, but just, ya'know, what if?"

"I just think...stay away from it. Even if it is real."

Larry looked away again, this time to a picture of Jesus on the Cross, an artist's vision of it anyway. He had figured Brother Joe would say that...but Larry was the one who'd just lost his wife.

* * *

Tom awoke with a start. Immediately, he fumbled for the phone. Blurry eyes barely able to make out the numbers on the phone, punched them hurriedly.

The phone rang several times and an answering machine picked up.

Mike's voice.

That didn't mean anything, though. What time was it? 8:00 a.m. He called information and asked them to patch him through to the hospital. He had a phone book, but he was too fuzzy headed to a)find it and b)use it.

Tom asked the operator to connect him to the Intensive Care Unit. When the ICU nurse answered, he asked if Mike was still there.

She answered that he was, and wasn't going to be moved out of ICU just yet, probably not until he came out of the coma to stay.

Tom hung up the phone without saying thank you or good bye.

He looked around. He was back on the couch where he'd fallen asleep several days ago-no, last night. It had only been a night, but felt like more. He was hungry.

He'd tried to stop the accident from happening. But nothing changed. Maybe not nothing. He couldn't tell, didn't know. But the accident had still happened and Mike had still been put in the hospital and he'd still be relatively unhurt.

He hadn't touched Mike this time. But it didn't matter.

The lady still died.

Mike still went into the hospital.

Nothing changed.

* * *

It was by chance that Steven happened to see Larry drive into the faculty parking lot. Steven was on his way back from the library and saw Larry pull in. He returned to his own office, put the books down he was carrying, checked his email real quick-nothing urgent-and made his way to Larry's office.

The door was unlocked and slightly open so he knocked, pushing the door open a little more. He stuck his head in and said hello to Larry who was shelving books.

"Hey," said Larry. "Come on in."

"How's it going?"

"Good, good." Larry moved behind his desk, sat in his chair and leaned back. He began to swivel side to side ever so slowly. Steven took the cue and sat down in the chair beside the desk, not the one on the other side. That was the one students sat in.

"I know that look, Lar," began Steven. "What's on your mind?"

Larry stopped swiveling and sat up straight. "What do you think about time travel?"

"Ooohh. Time travel. Pretty cool, I think," answered Steven. Larry had used him for feedback while he had worked on his last novel, a sounding board of sorts. While he didn't know where Larry was going with this, he thought it might be the same sort of thing.

"What would you do if some guy came up to you and said he wanted to sell you time and that it wouldn't cost you anything but time off the end of your own life?"

"What? Like, I'd die early, or something?"

"That's exactly it!" Larry sounded excited that Steven had gotten it so quickly. Steven was pretty excited, too. He wanted to know more about what Larry had in mind. "But, there's more to it than that."

"Of course," said Steven, "There'd have to be."

"Why?"

"What do you mean, 'why?'"

"Well, why would there have to be?"

"Well," said Steven, slowly. He genuinely wanted to be a help for his friend. If anything he could say now could help Larry write a better book, then that was what he wanted. "If it doesn't cost any money, there has to be *some* cost. Right? I mean, we can't get anything for nothing, right?" Steven waited for the expected response.

"But I already said that you'd die early. Why does there have to be more than that? Isn't that enough?"

"How is it interesting if there is no cost. Only one thing in life is free, right?"

"How is dying early not a cost?"

"Well," said Steven, enjoying the role he was playing, "If I travel back a day and die a day earlier, then basically, that's free. I haven't given anything up. Not really. If I travel back and spend a day with George Washington, I still live that day of my life. It just happens to be somewhere else. Like a vacation."

"Hmmm," said Larry. "I see what you're saying."

"So what is the something else?"

"What?"

"You said there was more," said Steven.

"Oh. Right. Yeah, well the time that comes off the end of your life is half again as much as -"

"Time and a half," interrupted Steven.

"Yeah," said Larry, somewhat surprised. "Time and a half."

"Now, that is interesting," finished Steven. "So," he continued after a few minutes of silence, "Who's going back in time?"

"Wouldn't it be something if we could go?" Larry asked.

"Yeah, it would be."

"Where would you go?"

"Shouldn't that be when would I go?"

Larry laughed.

"Okay," he said, "when would you go?"

"I don't know. So many places-I mean times. The time of Christ pops immediately in my head. The American Revolution. Wouldn't it be great to actually see George Washington?" Larry said nothing, but nodded his head. Steven continued, "Or maybe go back to the Second American Revolution, tell Stonewall Jackson not to get out front. Maybe he would not have been shot."

Larry sat silent.

"Wonder if it would change anything? Stonewall was such a man of God, wouldn't it be great to walk in his shadow for a few days, too?"

Change.

Change.

Larry had never considered actually changing anything. Could he change anything? If he went back and saw Gracie, would it change anything? Could he tell her not to leave the house that day? Could he actually finish the phone call he'd tried to make several times and tell her about his novel? Could God's plans be changed? Were they indeed God's plans? Maybe God planned for him to travel back, maybe that actually was the plan.

"When would you go?" asked Steven, still fishing for info on the new novel. He could plainly see that Larry was still lost in the ideas generated by the conversation. Many times when Larry was like this, the answers he got to his questions weren't easily decipherable. But they had done this so often with his last novel, Steven came to expect answers like that. It was part of Larry's creative process. As an art teacher, he knew that everyone had a process for their creativity. Steven was happy to play a part in his friend's.

"I dunno," said Larry, his voice barely a whisper. "Maybe tonight."

This was another of those answers.

* * *

The two men agreed to meet at the hospital where Steven said he'd help Larry pray for the recovering man. Larry still was uncomfortable using his name, but Steven used it all the time now.

Larry's class ended at 12:15 and he was to go straight to the hospital. Steven was going to pick them up something to eat. They'd eat in the lobby and then go upstairs and pray.

Larry entered the lobby area, looking around for Steven.

Not seeing his friend, he sat down.

Not sixty seconds later he saw Tom getting off the elevator.

"Tom," he called out to him. Tom stopped and looked

over at him. Larry waved and Tom shuffled over near him. Larry noticed that Tom looked very tired. As if he hadn't slept in a few days.

"Hello, Mr. Pace," said Tom, offering his hand.

Larry stood, shook Tom's hand, and sat back down.

"You don't look so well, Tom." Larry hoped Tom would sit next to him. He really wanted to ask him some questions about this time traveling idea.

"How's Mike?"

"He's slipping in and out of consciousness. The doctors say that when he's conscious, he's not aware of anything going on around him. Said we might could talk to him, but it was anybody's guess whether he was hearing or not."

"Do you think he hears you?" asked Larry.

Tom thought for a moment before answering.

"Yeah. I do."

"Tom, I've got an off the wall question for you. Do you mind if I ask you something personal?"

In his mind, Tom sighed. He really didn't want any personal questions, but he still felt like it was his fault this guy's wife was killed and the guilt was killing him. So he sat in the chair directly across from Larry and leaned toward him, feigning interest in whatever Larry might ask.

"Tom," Larry began, "Do you know a guy named Ben? He goes by Big Ben."

Whoa! This was not the question Tom expected. It threw him for a loop. He remembered Larry fishing the last time he saw him here, what, four or five days ago?

"Yeah, I know him. I did an article about him. You read that, huh?" But then Tom realized he had used Ben's real name: Ben Chapman and not the Big Ben alias.

"I think I did read that. He was in on robbing the bank several years ago, wasn't he?"

"It was never proven," answered Tom, sounding more like Big Ben's lawyer than a newspaper reporter.

"You think he did it?"

"Doesn't matter what I think," said Tom, trying to recover the non-biased newspaper reporter image and tone, "it was never proven and that's really all I think about it."

"I'd bet if the time travel thing is true, he did it."

"What do you mean?" asked Tom.

"Ah, now don't pretend, Tom. After everything else that's

gone on, don't try to hide the truth now." Larry sounded like a father scolding a good son who'd just been forgiven for a bad deed, but was making that mistake again.

"I heard you talking yesterday-"

"Yesterday? Where did you see me yesterday?" Tom couldn't remember seeing him yesterday.

"Right here, Tom. You were telling Mike about some time travel thing. I couldn't be sure, but Big Ben came to see me yesterday afternoon. I thought you'd surely turned him on to me."

"Yesterday?" It felt like days since Tom had seen Larry here at the hospital. It couldn't have been yesterday.

"But I didn't tell Big Ben anything," answered Tom. "He just, knows. I don't know how he does it, but he knows."

It was Larry's turn to be surprised. He thought for sure that Tom had immediately run and told Big Ben that Larry was a sale waiting to happen.

"You didn't tell him to come see me?" Larry asked.

"Nope. Don't think I've ever mentioned you to him."

"Does it work?"

"Does what work?"

"Time travel? This thing that Big Ben's telling me about. This thing he keeps trying to get me to buy."

Tom wasn't sure what to say. Yes! It worked. It worked and it was great! But Big Ben had been pretty adamant about him talking about it. But he didn't know if that just meant for the newspaper or could he tell others. He told Mike, but he didn't really think that Mike heard him, in spite of what he told Larry.

"Yeah. It works."

"Really?"

"Yeah."

"Do you know how far out that sounds, Tom?" asked Larry.

Tom arose and quickly moved to the chair next to Larry. He leaned in close to him, but his excitement was obvious.

"Yeah, I know how far out it sounds. And I know that you could probably use this against me or something about the death of your wife and get me put away forever.

"But let me tell you, I've done it twice now. It is so real. I mean, I felt like I was really there. When I woke up the memory was fresh. It was a fifteen-year-old memory, but suddenly now it was just days old. I mean, I was there. I could feel, touch, smell, hear. Everything. I was there. I don't know how, but I was there."

Tom relaxed back in the seat.

"I tried to change it, too."

"What do you mean?" asked Larry.

"I tried to make it not happen."

"What not happen?"

"Your wife. The accident. The second time I went back. I tried to leave Mike alone; I shut up talking and let him drive. Didn't want to distract him when your wife pulled out. I thought..."

"Obviously, it didn't work."

"Yeah."

"But," continued Larry, "do you think it could change? I mean, do you think you could change what happened?"

"Geeeeez. I don't know." Tom stared at the floor in front of him.

"But I tell you what," said Tom, leaning close to Larry again, "change or not, I'm going again."

"Back to the accident?" asked Larry, quite surprised.

"I don't know about that. It's so painful I don't know if I can do that a third time. I just mean I'm going back again. I'm going back to a happy time. It's incredible."

"What's incredible?" said a booming voice suddenly right next to them. Tom and Larry both looked up to see Steven standing next to them.

"Hey Steven," said Larry, standing to put his arm around his friend.

"I gotta go," said Tom, also standing.

"Wait, Tom. This is my good friend Dr. Steven Dale. He's an instructor down at the college. Steven, this is Tom Morgan. Remember," Larry tried to jog his friend's memory. "I told you I'd met a guy who was in the car with the driver? This is him."

Recognition came to Steven's face as he realized who Tom was.

"Tom," said Steven, shaking Tom's hand. "It's a pleasure to meet you."

"Same here," replied Tom. "I gotta go, though. Gotta get to work."

The two friends watched as Tom walked through the

89

hospital front doors.

"What's incredible, Larry?" asked Steven.

"This whole thing is," he answered. He wasn't ready to talk about time travel to Steven again. Not yet. "Gracie died. The driver is in ICU. And this guy's walking around practically unhurt."

"Yes, that is incredible. But I sense God's hand on it. Don't you?"

Larry paused. What would God think about time travel? He laughed, remembering a common Christian catch-phrase: what would Jesus do?

"What's funny, Lar? You don't think God has His hand on this?"

"No. I mean, yes, of course I do. It's just...I mean, don't you think it's a little funny that Gracie died and the other two are obviously going to live. Gracie, the woman who has worked nearly all her life doing God's work. And then this kid, who seemingly wouldn't know God if he walked right up next to him."

"God works in mysterious ways, my friend," said Steven, trying to stay upbeat about the whole thing. He didn't know what it was like to lose a wife, but he could imagine that it would be very easy to let depression hit.

"Now come on," he said, "let's go pray for Mike."

* * *

The prayers had been good. Steven did most of the praying that day. Larry seemed to have something on his mind. Steven guessed it was the whole talk of Gracie. But Steven didn't mind the praying. Never did.

After they finished, the two left and Steven said he was headed back to the university. Asked if he was going, Larry said he was headed home.

After a short drive back to the university, Steven walked into the building where his office was and nearly bumped into-

"Brother Joe!" he said, surprised to see the preacher on campus and there at that building. "What are you doing here?"

"What? Don't you think a preacher can appreciate an institute of higher learning?"

"No," said Steven, "that's not what I meant. I guess I just don't think I've ever seen you here on campus before. Please, come on up to my office."

"Well," Brother Joe looked at his watch. "Okay, but only for a few minutes." He followed as Steven made his way to his office.

"What does bring you here?" he asked as he walked.

"Actually, I was looking for Larry Pace. Have you seen him today?" Steven stopped, key in the lock, just having turned it and unlocked the door.

"Sure. I just saw him. I was with him up at the hospital."

"The hospital? Something wrong, or ..."

"Nothing wrong. We were praying for the recovery of Mike."

"Mike? Oh. Yes."

"Now it's my turn to ask if something's wrong," said Steven.

"Wrong?"

"Yeah. You're up here looking for Larry. To my knowledge, that's not something you commonly do. Is something wrong?"

"I don't know. Probably not. He talked to me this morning."

"Yeah?"

"Yeah," answered Brother Joe. "And I've done some praying and searching the scriptures and just wanted to talk some more to him."

"What about?"

"Well," Brother Joe started. "I'd rather not talk about it not just yet. I want to have a chance to talk to Larry first. I hope you understand."

"Certainly," answered Steven. He pushed the door open and walked in, showing Brother Joe to a seat near the door. "Larry's my friend, though, and if something's wrong, I definitely want to be able to help. But I wouldn't ask you to betray any confidence at all. I can wait. Most importantly, I can pray. Right?"

"Right." Brother Joe looked around the office. He couldn't remember ever being in Steven Dale's office before, a fact which he wished he'd correctly months—if not years ago.

"That's nice work up there," he said, pointing to a group of illustrated images hanging on Steven's wall.

"Yeah," said Steven. "I call that my wall of honor. I pick one piece each semester from my drawing class to go up there. I've been doing that for the last ten years, so you should see one up there for each semester I taught that class."

"Interesting."

Brother Joe continued to scan the room. There was a single bookshelf with a handful of books, mostly about the subject of art or related to art somehow. The rest of the office was filled with art supplies and materials. Brother Joe didn't know what half of the things were, but he could tell they were used in the art classes.

"Hey!" he suddenly said, causing Steven to jump ever so slightly. "You said that Larry was headed home. Do you mind calling and seeing if he is there? I'll just head over there if he is, but I don't really want to go chasing all around the place if he's not."

"Sure," said Steven, picking up the phone. "That's no problem at all. I've had Larry's number memorized for years."

Steven punched the numbers on his phone and then sat back as he waited for the ring. After a few rings, the answering machine picked up and began to repeat the message.

"He's not there," said Steven. "The answering machine's picked up."

"Well, shoot."

"I'll leave him a message-Hey Larry! This is Steven. Hey, we just finished lunch, so you may not even be home yet. When I came back to the office, I found Brother Joe up here looking for you about a conversation y'all had this morning. Give him a call when you get in."

Steven hung up the phone and Brother Joe stood.

"I'd better go, Steven. Thanks for trying."

"No problem. Hang out a while."

"Thanks for the offer, but I had better get on back to the church. See you tomorrow."

"Tomorrow?"

"Yes. Clean up day at the church."

"Oh. Yeah. No problem. I'd forgotten briefly. I'll see you

tomorrow."

* * *

The tires on Larry's pickup crunched gravel as they pulled up the long driveway. The massive house impressed him. He didn't know much about architecture or styles of houses or anything, but the columns on this one made him think it was old.

The gravel drive widened as it neared the front of the house becoming a small gravel parking lot. The BMW he'd seen Big Ben in yesterday was parked neatly near the front of the door, as if there were lines to keep it in an appropriate parking slot. Larry pulled up next to the BMW, but not too close. He didn't want to open his door into the car or, most importantly, he didn't want to set off a car alarm. He thought surely a car that nice had one of those zone sensor alarms, the kind that would scream "back away from the car" at you if you got too close.

He shut off his engine and exited his truck. Walking slowly to the front, he noticed a beagle sleeping next to the door. The beagle, upon hearing Larry, stood and barked. In between barks, however, he wagged his tail. He was accustomed to strangers and obviously found most of them to be friendly. Larry talked to the dog as he approached, causing the bark to lessen and the tail wagging to increase.

He knocked on the door and looked down as he wiped his feet on the mat. Checking the mat to see if he'd left any dirt, he read the big red lettering "welcome again." Larry laughed. Pretty funny for a guy who sells time. He wondered if he'd be back again. He wondered why he was there. This all seemed like such nonsense. He wrote stuff like this in his stories. It was science fiction. He didn't believe it. As interesting as it all was, it was still just fiction.

Larry turned to walk back to his truck, but just as he'd taken the step off the front porch, the door opened.

"Hello Dr. Pace," said Big Ben, cigar firmly clenched in his teeth. "I was hoping I'd see you."

"Just hoping?"

"No." he continued. "I knew." Big Ben opened the door and stepped aside, making room for Larry to enter. "But never you mind," he said, "come on in and let's talk some business."

"As you know," Big Ben continued, "I'm in the business of selling time, not wasting it."

"I'm still not sure I believe all this," said Larry.

"You don't have to believe it," answered Big Ben. "Faith is the assurance of things hoped for, the conviction of things not seen. You're here, aren't you?"

"That's scripture," said Larry. "Are you a believer?"

"Is it?" asked Big Ben in surprise. "A believer in what? This cigar? My car? That time travel is real? In God?" Big Ben led Larry through some sliding doors and turned on a light. The room inside was filled with clocks of all sorts.

Big Ben turned to Larry just as the two of them crossed the threshold. He leaned so close to Larry that Larry could smell the cigar on his breath.

"Does it matter what I believe in? If you can see...what's her name? Gracie? If you can see Gracie again, do you really care what I believe?"

"I'm not here to argue with you. All I said was that I'm still not sure I believe this works."

"Yes. And I responded that you're here." Big Ben stepped further into the room, motioning for Larry to follow.

The entire room was sunken and a sundial sat in the center of the room. A recliner sat immediately in front of the sundial. On the seat of the recliner lay some paper and a pen. Larry couldn't make out the writing on the paper.

"Nice collection of clocks," said Larry, trying to shift the subject and break the tension he'd caused.

"Thank you," returned Big Ben. "But it's more a collection of time than clocks. Each of these clocks come from a different time, not just a different place, but a different time."

"How did you ever manage to come upon the sundial?"

"Oh, you know what this is?" asked Big Ben.

"Sure. I mean, I don't know much about it. Celtic, isn't it?"

"Yes," said Big Ben, surprised. "It is indeed. The Celts knew more about this stuff than any historian ever gives them credit for."

"Oh, I don't hold much stock in history today. Too much politically correct info being added for the mere sake of political correctness. Whatever happened to unbiased history?"

"Yes, well, have a seat and we'll work out the details." Big Ben picked up the paper and pen in the chair and motioned for Larry to sit where they once were. After he'd sat, Big Ben offered him the paper and pen. Larry took it and began to read.

"You're welcome to read it all," said Big Ben, "but I assure you it is a pretty standard contract."

"When we spoke the other day," continued Big Ben as Larry read, "I explained to you how this all works, right?" Larry nodded and Big Ben continued, "And you understand it all, right?"

"I understand the way you say it works," said Larry, looking up from the papers in his hands. "But I still don't get how you're saying this all really works."

"I'm not trying to tell you the technical details of how it works, Larry. That's unimportant. The important thing is that is does work, and the procedure for it is easy."

Larry was indeed looking for an explanation of it all. He wanted the details. But Big Ben wasn't giving them.

"You say the details are unimportant," said Larry. "Why? Is it because if it gets out, folks will hone in on your business? Right now you're the only thing going."

"Well," began Big Ben as he sat on the stair next to Larry, "yes and no. Yes, in that I don't really want a lot of locals trying to do what I do. Because it is a business that is profitable for me."

Larry immediately thought about the bank robbery. Still unproven, it sounded as if Big Ben did indeed play a part in it.

"And no," Big Ben continued, "because, well, I'm not the only one doing it. I'm the only one you know, and I'm certainly the only one in these parts. But I can assure you, I'm not the only one."

This revelation surprised Larry. A time-selling network? How long had they been around? Now that he was thinking about it, he studied Big Ben. Just how old was he?

"So, what do you say, Larry? Would you like to see Gracie again tonight?"

Larry said nothing. He still didn't think it could happen. But he wanted to see Gracie. He was desperate to see her.

So what if he made a fool of himself? It wouldn't be the first time. If he could really see her again, it would be worth the risk.

"Yeah," he finally said. "I do."

"Great." Big Ben smiled. "All you need to do is sign here at the bottom. Make no bones about it, Larry, this is a legitimate and legal contract. How long do you want?"

"I want one day."

"One day? Only one day? You could spend an entire week with her."

"I want one day."

"Very well," sighed Big Ben. "Then you must know the cost is a day and a half. It comes off the end of your life. You'll die exactly thirty-six hours before you were intended to die."

"Also, before you sign the bottom line," said Big Ben, "I must warn you of a few things." Larry grinned inwardly. Here it came. Here came the part where he was warned that none of this stuff might happen. He resisted the urge to look around for a 'Smile. You're on Candid Camera' sign.

"What's that?" Larry said.

"Well, time travel is very addictive, very much like a drug."

"So," guessed Larry, "there's a drug to take?" He immediately assumed that all the time travel nonsense was a drug induced hallucination. How it could be so specific, he couldn't begin to guess.

"Not at all. Why does everyone thing that when I mention the addiction? What I mean is simply that you'll enjoy it so much that you'll want to do it again and again and again. I know you teach numbers, so you know yourself it wouldn't take long to add up. Like drugs, abuse of this can kill a person pretty quickly."

"So if there's no drugs, what do I do?" Larry still hadn't signed the contract. The pen in his hand was poised to sign, but he continued to ask questions.

"Larry, it's understandable that you're nervous. But nothing will happen if you don't sign. All you must do is go to sleep tonight. That's it. When you awaken, you will be where you want to be. To return, it works the same way. When you awaken then, you'll have simply slept through the night. You'll be a little confused when you first wake up, but your brain will immediately adjust. It knows."

Larry signed. He handed the contract and pen back to Big Ben. He had paid no money, had issued no collateral of property or person. On the outside this whole ordeal seemed really to cost him nothing.

Big Ben examined the contract quickly, smiled, and offered his hand to Larry. Larry smiled and chortled. He couldn't believe what he'd just done. But he took Big Ben's hand and shook it. It's quite possible this guy was making a big fool of Larry.

Larry looked around the room at all the clocks. He didn't see any video cameras, but that didn't mean they weren't there. They could be easily hidden these days. He didn't know what his being a fool could actually do to hurt him...being a fool was just being a fool.

Larry sighed and arose from the chair.

"I think I'm supposed to thank you about now, aren't I?" he asked.

"Commonly," said Big Ben. "Many do. But you don't have to. I know you're still not certain. And that's okay. It'll all prove out tonight."

The two men began to exit the room, slowly, as if comfortable and hesitant to leave.

"I would like to ask a favor," said Big Ben.

"What's that?"

"Well, I don't ask all my customers this, but because of your continued uncertainty, I'd like you to call me tomorrow and just let me know how it went. It's not a requirement. I never have to see you again, actually. But I am curious and it'd simply be a favor to me."

"I can't see how that would hurt." Larry tapped his shirt pocket. "I've still got your card in my pocket. Hopefully I can keep up with this one, so I'll give you a call tomorrow morning."

"Sounds great."

Big Ben opened the front doors for Larry as they walked out. He reached down to pet the beagle as Larry continued off the front porch. The beagle wagged its tail as Big Ben stroked its head. Larry entered his truck and cranked the engine. Before he backed away, however, he took one last look at Big Ben, now squatting and petting his dog. He didn't have the look of a lunatic. He sounded just as sane as the next man. And what else does he do to earn money? If time travel costs no money, how can he afford such a big house and nice car? What does he do to earn good old all-American money?

Larry quickly lost those thoughts as he pulled back out onto the highway. The sun was setting and he was anxious to get home and get to bed. He was ready to try it out, to test it. He wasn't really tired, but he was going to go straight to bed.

* * *

*L*arry tossed his keys on the table as he entered the house. He was trying to think of anything that would make him sleepy and that might make him fall asleep faster. If simply going to sleep was how time travel worked, he'd hit the sack immediately. The girls were both in the living room, but called out to him as he passed through.

"Dad?" said Becky. "Are you okay?"

"I'm fine," he answered.

"Where've you been?" asked Cindy. "We fixed dinner. We waited for an hour and a half before we ate."

"That's fine," he said. Both the girls had gotten up and were slowly walking to the kitchen to see him. Larry, however, had moved on through the hall to his bedroom.

"What's up with him?" Cindy asked her older sister quietly. Becky just shrugged. Not knowing exactly what to do, both girls simply stood in place.

"We made a plate for you, though," yelled Cindy down the hall.

"That's fine," came her dad's voice.

"Do you want me to heat it up for you?"

"No." Larry walked back into the hallway. He'd changed into his pajamas already.

"Where've you been, Dad?" asked Cindy again.

"Nowhere." Larry opened the freezer door.

"I put the plate in the refrigerator, Dad," said Cindy. She was surprised to see him looking in the freezer for the leftover plate.

"Okay." Larry pulled out the half gallon box of ice cream and sat it on the table. He turned to the cabinet and got out a bowl and a spoon. Opening the box, he dipped several spoons of ice cream into the bowl.

"Are you okay, Dad?" asked Becky.

"Fine," he said.

"Dad," she continued, "Why are you eating ice cream? Did you eat supper already?"

"I'm tired and maybe this'll help me sleep. I'm going right to bed."

"It might also give you a stomach ache," said Cindy, remembering hearing that very thing from her Mom and Dad whenever she did the same thing.

"I'll be fine," said Larry.

"That's an awful big bowl, Dad," said Becky.

Larry stopped dipping.

"Would you girls quit mother-henning me? I'm hungry and didn't have supper. I realize that ice cream may not be the best thing for me to eat, but I think it'll help me sleep. I usually get sleepy after eating ice cream. I just want to eat this and get to bed."

Both girls were stunned by his reply. Neither could see any reason for him to be so sharp. Larry stuck the spoon in his mouth, closed the box of ice cream and returned it to the freezer.

While his back was turned, Becky motioned for Cindy to have a seat at the table. Clearly they were going to join him and continue to question him as he ate. Something was up and they intended to get to the bottom of it.

Larry turned, momentarily saw his girls-now seated at the table- picked up his bowl and made his way down the hallway once again. The eyes of both girls widened in complete shock. They couldn't believe that their father was not going to eat at the table.

"You girls be sure to lock up before you go to bed," he said over his shoulder. Then added "good night" just before he shut his bedroom door.

Neither Becky nor Cindy said anything for the longest time. They were stunned.

"What just happened?" Cindy asked her sister.

"I have no idea."

"I can't ever remember not getting a goodnight kiss from Dad," said Cindy after another few minutes of silence.

"Me either."

"And if ice cream's his meal, Why didn't he pray?" asked

Cindy.

"Well," answered Becky, trying to give her dad the benefit of any doubt, "we don't know that he didn't. He could be praying in his room now."

Cindy got up suddenly from her chair and stormed down the hall. She put her ear to the door to listen. Becky laughed to herself. She'd done the very thing before. Cindy's ear was near the crack of the door, hoping that more sound would make its way through to her.

Cindy looked back down the hallway to her sister at the table and nodded. She couldn't hear her father saying anything. She did hear the occasional clink of the spoon against the bowl.

"Dad!" She knocked. "Can I come in?"

"No. I'm trying to go to sleep."

"Dad, I can still hear you eating ice cream. Becky and I want to talk to you." She had to bring her sister's name into it. She felt it would give her plea some strength and it also gave her a little confidence to know that her sister stood with her, even if she just only used her name.

Leaning close to the crack of the door again, she heard the bowl hit the nightstand beside the bed.

"I'm finished now and I want to go to sleep. I'll talk to you both in the morning at breakfast. Whatever it is, it can wait till tomorrow. Now, good night."

Her father had dismissed her. He was done. The conversation was finished. She should leave the door now and get back to whatever it was she was doing.

Cindy walked slowly back to the kitchen and returned to her seat across from Becky. Becky was shaking her head in disbelief.

"I've never ever seen Dad this way," she said.

"You don't think it was something we did, do you?" asked the younger girl.

"No," said Becky, "because we've not done anything." But Becky's voice didn't sound so sure.

"Dad's never done anything like this before," said Cindy. "Not that I can remember, anyway."

"Me neither."

"What should we do," asked Cindy.

"Pray," answered Becky. "It's the only thing I know to do."

* * *

When was the last time he'd written anything? When was the last time he'd done any work? When was the last time he'd been paid? Had that been the last check, or was he due another? Tom had stopped by the office today, but Marty, his editor, wasn't in. To top it off, no one knew when he was coming back in. Or at least they claimed to not know.

So Tom had checked his mailbox-nothing in it-and hung out for a few minutes. He'd hopped on the internet to check his email and look at the sports.

There was nothing on his email but spam. He didn't even smoke, why would they send him four to five emails a day on how to quit smoking?

He once considered smoking because all the cool newspaper editors in the old movies smoked. Of course, everyone cool in the old movies smoked.

Finally, he'd skimmed the sports section, particularly looking for news about the upcoming college football season. Anything about the Southeastern Conference schools he would read through fairly completely. He not only wanted to know about his team, but about the competition, too.

When he got home, all he'd wanted to do was sleep. He wanted to travel again. But he'd slept so much that he couldn't. So after an hour of tossing and turning, he got back up.

He thought he'd write some...and that's how he found himself at his computer. He grabbed his laptop and headed to his spot in the living room. He clicked on the TV, flipped a channel or two, and then turned it back off because it was distracting. His brain was moving at a million miles an hour and he couldn't focus. He needed to work, to write something. Not just because he needed to do something to try to earn some money, but also because he needed it to exercise his brain, to make it tired so that he could sleep. And he needed it to distract him from obsessing about time traveling.

He opened his laptop then set it aside as it powered up. He was hungry, but didn't feel like going out. Making his way to the kitchen, he opened cabinets looking for something substantial. Finding nothing much more than potato chips, he grabbed a jar of peanut butter-the crunchy kind-and a spoon and sat back down. He always kept peanut butter around, usually two to three jars just to be safe.

He returned to his seat and the laptop to his lap and opened the peanut butter. Dipping the spoon in the jar, he took a big bite of peanut butter.

He then realized he had nothing to drink.

He double-clicked on his writing program, allowing the program to begin opening, and set the laptop back down. He hurried to the refrigerator and grabbed a beer. He hurried back to the couch, returned the laptop to his lap, and let out a yell of victory as he did it all before the program could open. He frequently reveled in the fact that he was faster than his old computer, but he wouldn't tell that to anyone except Mike. He often told Mike that his laptop was now so old that he'd have to pay a charity to get them to take it.

He scanned through his most recently opened documents, all of them stories of one sort or another at various beginning stages, but none of them called out to him. He popped open a blank page and thought he might write on this whole time travel thing. He wondered why Big Ben hadn't gone public with it. The whole idea was something 99.999 percent of the population thought was hogwash. Even he had thought so until he actually took the plunge and tried it. What a revolutionary industry it could create. Big Ben could be charging a lot of money. Thousands would pay to do what Tom had done. So what if you lost time off your life. What sort of cost was that? People will pay good money for almost anything.

Heck, maybe Big Ben was charging for it. Maybe Big Ben searched for high dollar customers, let them try it a time or two to get them addicted, then charged them outrageous amounts of money. How else could he afford that big house and all that property?

Unless the stories about the robbery were true. Tom still wasn't sure what he believed about that. Big Ben never confessed to stealing the money, not even during his interview for the paper.

He wrote all those thoughts down, but really couldn't figure out exactly what he would do with it. Tom never was really into writing in a journal even though he told himself often that he should. Preserve all his thoughts and ideas for future generations. Plus, Big Ben had warned him that all of the time travel stuff was personal, not for publication.

He picked up the remote control on the cushion next to him and turned on the TV and VCR. He hit the play button expecting his usual scene. Instead, the beginning of the movie started.

Tom glanced around the room wondering if anything had been taken. Momentarily he thought someone had been in his apartment.

Then he remembered falling asleep while watching it. It must have played out through to the end and then automatically rewound.

He didn't really feel like watching the entire movie, so he hit the fast-forward button watching all the actors move in super speed until they came to the part he wanted to see.

"No securities, no stocks, no bonds. Nothin' but a miserable little $500 equity in a life insurance policy. You're worth more dead than alive."

Tom wondered if anyone would have come to see him if he'd been the one in ICU instead of Mike. Mike's family were there frequently checking on him. And there was that weird family of Christians who kept going to see him. Tom didn't know if they wanted him to slip up and say something so that they could sue him or what. But it was just weird that they kept coming up there.

But even that family had each other. They'd lost their mom, but they still had each other.

"No securities, no stocks, no bonds. Nothin' but a miserable little $500 equity in a life insurance policy. You're worth more dead than alive."

If he went, who would care? Mike's death would affect a great deal of people, himself included. That Mrs. Pace's death had apparently affected a lot of people, too.

Who would be affected by his death?

He couldn't think of anyone. Mike, maybe.

Oh yeah. There was the preacher who came to see him. Maybe he would care. But he was paid to care, so he didn't count. It was his job.

This wasn't what he expected his life to be. This wasn't what he'd planned for all those years.

Tom put his face in his hands and wept.

"No securities, no stocks, no bonds. Nothin' but a miserable little $500 equity in a life insurance policy. You're worth more dead than alive."

It wasn't long before sleep overcame his anguish, and like he had done many times in as many days, Tom cried himself to sleep.

* * *

Larry knew he'd cut his daughters short. But it couldn't be helped. He had to get to sleep. He had to try it out, to test it. It still seemed to be more fiction than truth.

He convinced himself that he wouldn't be upset when he woke up in the morning and nothing had happened. He told himself he wouldn't be angry. Sure, he might still feel like the fool he was thinking himself to be, but he wouldn't be angry. There's a big difference between being angry and being a fool.

And he might be disappointed.

At this point, he was fully expecting to go. He *wanted* to go, whatever or however it was that it worked, he wanted it all to be true. He'd worry about all the other stuff later.

If it was true, he had to do it.

As he lay awake in the bed, his mind raced through all the possibilities of what real, true time travel could bring. Endless!

Historians would benefit greatly if it were all true. To be able to go back and witness the signing of the Declaration of Independence or the battle of Gettysburg or the invasion of Normandy Beach or any number of events.

He wondered if it was possible to take something with you. Taking a digital video camera would be amazing. To get Pickett's Charge on video would be an incredible historical achievement. Larry knew this and he was no historian.

He yawned and stretched. Turning over to his stomach, he pulled the pillow up under his face and tucked his arms under the pillow so that his elbows were out to either side. For some reason, he preferred to sleep with his hands up above or around his head and face even though the doctor had told him before this wasn't a good idea. Something about the circulation of his blood in his shoulders which then in turn brought on arthritis ... or something.

Gracie usually told him not to sleep that way because he had a tendency to drool when on his stomach. He didn't mind drooling so much, not really. What really bothered him was the thought of sleeping in hotels on pillows that others could have drooled on. Sure, they change and wash the pillow cases, but drool soaked through to the pillow stuffing. As far as he knew, hotels didn't wash the pillows.

Gracie always slept on her side, one or the other. She never slept on her stomach, and rarely slept on her back. And she had to have a second pillow pulled up next to her stomach, a habit she'd acquired when she was pregnant with Becky, their first child. It had been so comfortable, she said, that she just continued to use it.

It wasn't unusual for Larry to reach over in the middle of the night while turning or shifting and pat the pillow thinking it was Gracie.

When they were first married, they slept closer together, cuddling, arms and legs over and under one another. As they got older, they each seemed to need to sleep a particular way so as to minimize back or neck or whatever pain. Their bodies didn't seem to be able to take the weight of an arm or leg on top of them or the lump of one under them.

That and the girls' infrequent bad dreams caused them to have an occasional surprise guest in their bed. So they'd come to sleep in their own way, keeping contact with a foot to a leg or hand to a hip or head or leg. The contact might not be as intense as when they were young, but the contact was still there. It was contact that expressed a deep love without saying any words. The love might have gotten older, but it was just as deep as ever.

Larry shifted again, turning onto his back. He tossed his right arm over his face, putting his eyes in the bend of his elbow. The flesh of his arm was cool and felt good on his eyes and forehead. He often lay like this when he had a headache.

"Would you like bacon and eggs this morning?" asked Gracie. She grabbed his arm, pulled it off his face and put it down on her pillow, laying her head on it and pulling up closer to his chest.

"Yes. I would love bacon and eggs," he said.

"Okay," she said, "I'll fix them while you're in the shower."

Larry sat straight up in bed pulling his arm out from under her head.

"Oww," she said. "What's wrong? What'd you do that for?"

Larry turned to look at the voice from the pillow. Though it was dark in his room, the face was easily recognizable.

"Gracie?"

"Yes, dear?"

"Talk about déjà vu," he said. He dropped his feet over the side of the bed, yawned, and rubbed the back of his neck. What an odd feeling, a weird sensation. He'd been here and done this all before.

He felt the bed move as Gracie got out of the bed.

"You get up every morning, dear. Now you grab your shower," she said momentarily from the hallway, "I'll get breakfast started."

Larry watched as her shadow disappeared down the hallway. He rubbed his head again trying to get the déjà vu feeling out.

Making his way to their bathroom, he shaved. He grabbed his robe and hung it next to the shower. He tossed a towel on top of the back of the toilet and hopped in the shower. As he began to rub the shampoo through his hair, it hit him.

If this was a dream, it was incredibly real. All the stuff about time travel. Or wait! Maybe that was the dream and then that would mean that Gracie's death was all a dream, too.

As much as he wished that were so, he couldn't escape the reality in the back of his mind.

If this wasn't a dream, then all that time travel hooey wasn't just nonsense. That meant that he was now somehow back in time.

Not sure exactly what to do or how to react, Larry finished his shower as he normally would. He donned his robe and peeked quickly out the bathroom door. He could smell the bacon cooking in the kitchen.

"Gracie!" he yelled out.

"What, honey?" came the voice from the bedroom door in mere seconds as Gracie reappeared.

"I love you," said Larry, staring intently at Gracie.

"I love you, too," she said, unmoved by his declaration.

"Now get dressed. I've gotta get back to the kitchen unless you want your bacon burned."

Larry quickly threw on slacks, socks, shoes and a tee-shirt. He grabbed a shirt and was buttoning it as he walked down the hallway.

"What's today?" he asked, stepping into the kitchen.

"Wednesday," answered Gracie. "Why don't you come home early today so you can go up to church with me."

"We'll see," he said. He thought back, trying to remember exactly what had happened that Wednesday morning a week and a half ago in real time. What had he said? When had he said it? It all seemed like such a blur to him. He wanted to remember exactly what happened in real time, though.

Real time? Is that what he was calling this now? If that was real time, what was this? Dream time? Travel time? Fake time?

But he knew it had to be that Wednesday because that was the day he'd wanted to do over. Big Ben had told him he'd go to the day he wanted. And while he didn't really want that, he did want it. He might be able to actually spend more time with Gracie and tell her things he didn't the first time around.

He sat down as Gracie put the plates on the table, trying to think of something else to test this.

"Girls!" she yelled over Larry's head. "Get down here! Breakfast is ready."

"I've been meaning to ask," he said, returning his attention to Gracie, "did you and Betty ever get things straightened out?"

"No," said Gracie, sitting next to Larry. She sighed. "God's been talking to me about that. I think I ought to go see her today."

Larry suddenly remembered that's where Gracie was headed when she was killed. Why had he forgotten that? Wasn't it important? She'd already been to church and left Maggie in charge. She was on her way to see Betty.

"No!" he said suddenly. "Just talk to her at church tonight. Don't make it a special point to go see her. You just catch her at church and say what you've got to say."

"What've you got to say?" said a sleepy voice just entering the kitchen.

"Good morning, sleepyhead," said Gracie to their eldest

107

daughter as she sat down at the table.

"Where's your sister?" Larry asked Becky.

"She's sleeping, Dad. Have a heart and let her sleep. It's summer! What's she gotta get up for?"

"It wouldn't hurt her to get up with us and eat breakfast," said Larry. "Spend some time with her family. That's not a terrible thing, is it? Time spent with your family is very precious, don't you think?" Since when had he become the time salesman? He sounded like he was trying to make a time sale of his own.

"I'll get her up when you leave, dear," said Gracie, not exactly siding with their daughter, but doing her best to play mediator. It was something she'd become very good at over the years.

"Fine," said Larry. "I can't win against both of you." He took a big bite of bacon and eggs, chewed for a moment and then remembered where they were before the interruption.

"Let's get back to Betty," he said. "If you go see her, you're admitting to her that she is right. And you know good and well she is not."

"I know she's not," said Gracie. "But it's not a matter of who's right and who's wrong. It's a matter of what's right and what's wrong. Don't you agree?"

"Humph," he said. "Maybe." How could he tell her that she would be killed in an accident if she went? What could he say to her to convince her not to go? He knew very well that he believed the Christian thing to do was to go talk to Betty face to face.

Why couldn't he just come out and tell her the truth? That'd he'd traveled back in time to keep her from being killed in an accident.

Yeah. Right. She'd either laugh him off or have him in a straightjacket in no time flat.

"Well," he continued, "you never know what's going to happen. Accidents happen every day."

"Oh please," she said, a bite of bacon still crunching in her mouth. "You know good and well I am not going to stay in this house afraid of what might happen to me if I set foot outside. I'm no paranoid Patty. Seriously, Larry."

That didn't work. He could just tell her not to go. He was the man of the house, after all. It was God's directions that she listen to him because he was the leader of the house.

But no, he couldn't just forbid her. That was not the way their relationship had worked all these years. To try to do so now would only cause hurt feelings and maybe harsh words.

"Well," he began, "what if I just forbid you to go?"

Becky's eyes widened over the rim of her glass of milk as her mother almost choked on her eggs. Once she'd forced her eggs successfully down her throat, Gracie broke into a terrible fit of laughter.

"Larry," she said through laughing breaths, "what has gotten in to you this morning?"

Larry said nothing. Obviously that tactic wasn't going to work either. He thought about faking anger, but decided that wouldn't really do anything either. He decided to test it another way.

"Becky," he said, "how much did I tell you I got for my novel?"

"What!?" Becky reacted in surprise. "Did you sell it?"

"Larry?" Gracie too, acted surprised. "Have you heard from your submissions?"

Larry desperately wanted to tell Gracie that he'd sold his novel. That all those months of her proofreading and giving feedback had paid off and that a publisher finally wanted to buy his novel. But he couldn't do it. What proof did he have to show her? He tried to make his mouth form the words, but he couldn't. And he didn't know why.

"No," he said, though not wanting to and nearly gritting his teeth. "I was just trying to wake Becky up." Maybe the reason he couldn't tell her was that it hadn't actually happened in this time. Real time, yes, but this time no.

"Well," said Becky, "it sure worked. I was all excited there for a minute. Don't do that to me so early in the morning."

"Have faith, Dad," said Gracie, "it'll happen. God will bless you because you've been faithful to Him. Just continue to do so."

As the three finished breakfast, Gracie cleared everything away behind them. Nearly zombie-like, Larry returned to his bedroom and finished preparing for work. Ever bone in his body screamed at him to stop! Screamed at him to simply stay where he was and enjoy Gracie.

As he brushed his teeth, he struggled to recall Gracie's last day. What had they talked about that morning? Hadn't he actually teased Becky about his book? Wasn't he in fact surprised when he got word of the sale? Had the words simply repeated themselves over this time without him giving much thought to it? He couldn't be sure. He couldn't actually remember what had happened that day. He remembered, but the couldn't remember the specifics and now that it was happening again, he wasn't sure what had happened then. He was too confused. The two memories were now tied together as one and he didn't know which was which.

When he finished tying his tie, he made his way to the back door, on his way picking up his lunch nicely prepared by Gracie and waiting for him on the table.

He stopped at the door where she had followed him, same as she did every day. He turned and looked deeply in her eyes. It felt like forever since he'd seen her. Sure he'd stared at her pictures, but here she was living and breathing. And he didn't want to leave.

Maybe he should fake a heart attack?

But Grace kissed him and hugged him and then ushered him out the door wishing him a good day the same as she did every other morning. In moments he was sitting behind the wheel of his truck driving to work, still in a daze.

After parking, he started walking towards Steven Dale's office, but before he could knock on the door he remembered that in this time Steven was away on a mission trip and wouldn't return for a while.

He shuffled on down to his own office. There were no messages on voice mail and no email messages of note. Only some spam from university employees about this or that school event and selling cars and couches. He really wished they'd clamp down on that junk.

He didn't want to stay in his office. He wanted to go back home and spend time with Gracie. He didn't really care what they did. It would be okay with him if they just sat next to each other and watched TV.

He decided to wander downstairs to see who else was there and to check his faculty mailbox. He bumped into a student who had taken his class last year and wanted to know what Larry would be teaching this year. Larry recited his class assignments to the student and the student replied they'd be sure to sign up for such and such a class. Larry assured the student he'd look forward to having him in the class again.

The door to the office was locked, but Larry, like all the full time faculty, had been issued a key for convenient access. The secretaries often operated on a time schedule known only to them and to keep the faculty from complaining, the department had simply issued keys, because of their irregular hours.

Larry grabbed the stack of mail from his box and locked the door on his way back out. He'd no more than taken a few steps away when the secretary entered through the side door. Larry smiled and said good morning, but proceeded to his office.

He checked email again. Nothing. Everyone else on campus was probably still just getting in and drinking coffee. The emails wouldn't start for another twenty minutes or so.

Flipping through the mail, he spotted the envelope. How could he have forgotten it? He'd been so wrapped up in his desire to go back home and spend time with Gracie that he'd forgotten about the envelope.

He excitedly tore it open. His own excitement surprised him. He already knew what it was going to say, but he was tearing at it as if he had no idea. Could it be a rejection? Might traveling back in time change the publisher's decision?

He read quickly.

No. Not a rejection. It was exactly the letter he was anticipating.

The letter thanked Larry for his submission and proceeded to tell him that his manuscript had made it through many levels of readers and that to get this far was nothing short of a miracle. It said that Larry had been placed on a certain level regarding pay and promotion based on the publisher's sales expectations, and that he should be expecting an advance in the next thirty days and a call from the marketing department to schedule book signings and other promotional opportunities.

Lastly, it welcomed Larry into the publisher's family.

He leaned over and held the letter in the sunlight shining through the window. He needed to make sure there was enough light so that he didn't mis-read it.

Nope. He hadn't misread.

He folded the letter and put it in the left breast pocket of his coat. He patted it to ensure it was firmly planted and wouldn't fall out.

Larry immediately picked up the phone to call Gracie. He punched in the first six numbers and then stopped.

He wasn't going to call her and he knew he wasn't. He'd planned to surprise her, to pick her up and take her out to eat. He'd forgotten, of course, that it was Wednesday and that the two of them always ate at the church.

He couldn't call her, could he? Even if he really wanted to, he wouldn't be able to bring himself to do it.

He stared at his computer before realizing it was time for his first class of the day to begin.

He picked up his textbook and notes and made his way across campus to his first class. He'd been teaching this stuff so long, he felt, that he could do it without any notes or a textbook. Or at least with his eyes closed. But he took the books and notes anyway, lest the students accuse him of making this stuff up.

He droned through his class and the one that followed, thinking of nothing more than getting home and seeing Gracie. He'd told her how much he loved her this morning and so he knew she knew. Of course, he already knew she knew, but this way he knew he'd told her.

Once back in his office, he'd punched the numbers to their home several more times, never managing to punch that seventh and final number. He wanted to do it, but he couldn't. It was unexplainable. Why couldn't he punch that number? If he could just get Gracie on the phone, he could tell her to stay put, that he was coming home and he had a big surprise.

But he couldn't do it.

He couldn't remember what time he'd left the office the first time—in real time—but he was intent on leaving it early and catching Gracie at home this time. He was going to see her again. And it wasn't going to be in a casket.

As he gathered his things together, he struggled to remember what time he'd left that day. Didn't he, in fact, leave early in order to try to surprise her?

But what time?

And what time had she left the house?

It was all he could do to keep from speeding on his

112

way home. The speedometer crept up several times and Larry had to lift his foot off the gas to keep it down. It was during times like this he wished his little truck had cruise control.

His heart sank as he pulled into the garage and saw his wife's car wasn't there. He'd missed her again.

He hurried inside, thinking one of the girls might be around. He yelled as he entered, but no answer came.

He quickly checked the answering machine to see if she'd left a message. The light was steady. He then decided he would drive over to the church and catch Gracie there before she left for Betty's. Or maybe she'd listened to him today, listened to his warnings-even if they were vague-and instead opted to see Betty tonight.

As he pulled out of his driveway, he noticed the police officer in his rearview mirror. For the second time in just a matter of minutes, his heart sank. The first time around he'd suspected something had happened to one of his daughters. But now he knew the news the officer carried.

Larry stumbled through the rest of the day much as he did the first time around. Everything seemed the same, yet the pain seemed fresh and new.

Finally, that night, he tucked his girls in, kissed them goodnight and sat down on the couch to rest. In moments, his closed eyes and exhausted body allowed sleep to catch up with him.

Saturday, July 29

*L*arry awoke the next morning without the sound of an alarm. His body simply jerked him awake. He sat up and reached for his shirt to unbutton and remove it. Gracie had always told him not to fall asleep on the couch, but it happened occasionally anyway.

He began unbuttoning...his pajamas?

He yawned and rubbed his eyes. How'd he get to his bedroom? He'd gone to sleep on the couch, that much he remembered.

Wait.

Larry jumped out of bed, opened the door to his bedroom. Why was it shut?

He hurried down the hallway to find the girls busily making breakfast. Both girls were dressed in t-shirts and shorts, hair pulled back in ponytails.

"Morning girls," he said, rushing around the table and staring into the living room.

"Did one of you girls pick up my clothes this morning?" he asked.

"What clothes?" asked Cindy stirring eggs in a frying pan.

"The ones I left there last night when I fell asleep."

Cindy and Becky exchanged glances. They both remembered Dad coming in and heading straight to his bedroom where he'd changed into his pajamas, the same pajamas he was still wearing.

"You changed in your bedroom last night, Dad," said Becky. "You made a bowl of ice cream and shut your door."

"Yeah," added Cindy, "and you didn't even kiss us goodnight."

"Didn't kiss..." Larry began.

"No," Becky said, reinforcing her sister, "not even a

114

hug!"

Larry put his hands on his face and closed his eyes. He shook his head and hurried back to his bedroom.

Sure enough, there was the used bowl from the ice cream sitting on his night stand.

"Then that means..."

It worked! He'd traveled. He didn't know how he did it or how it worked, but it did. He'd relived Gracie's final day. It hadn't changed anything, but he'd had the chance to kiss her again that morning and to tell her he loved her.

Larry could hear the girls calling him from the kitchen as he quickly hopped in the shower.

Becky walked down the hallway to check on him and heard the water running.

"He's in the shower already," she said, running to the kitchen.

"That explains why he didn't answer, then," said Cindy.

"Not really. He's just acting too weird."

The girls continued to work on breakfast, preparing three plates. Cindy even got her father's Bible from the bookshelf and placed it near his plate. She put his keys on top. Larry usually got his Bible himself to read to them every morning over breakfast, but the girls were doing everything they could think of to get their dad to sit still for a moment.

Larry dressed quickly. He was still tying his tie as he emerged from his bedroom. Both his daughters were seated at the table, food untouched.

"Looks like you girls did a great job on breakfast," he said, rubbing his tie on his chest and stomach to ensure it was free of wrinkles.

"Thanks, Dad," said Cindy, smiling from ear to ear.

"I'm sorry that I don't have time to sit and enjoy it," he said, grabbing his keys off his Bible on the table.

"What?" said the girls in unison.

"What do you mean you don't have time, Dad? Where do you have to go?" asked Becky.

"I've got to get to work," he said.

"On Saturday?"

"Is today Saturday?" Larry stopped and looked at the calendar.

"It usually comes after Friday, Dad," retorted Cindy.

"Shoot!" he said. He began to remove his tie. Why was he thinking today was Thursday?

"See," started Becky, "you've got time after all."

Larry tossed his tie over the back of his chair. Keys still in hand, he started for the back door, grabbing a banana as he went.

"There's still a lot to get done today," he said. "You girls go ahead and enjoy breakfast. I'll see you later today."

The back door nearly slammed just as Larry finished his sentence. It was clear to the girls he was in a hurry to get something done, but they had no idea what it was.

"He didn't offer to pray for breakfast," said Cindy.

"He didn't kiss us goodbye," said Becky.

"He didn't even take his Bible," added Cindy.

"He always kisses us goodbye," said Becky.

"He always takes his Bible with him," added Cindy.

The girls sat in silence for a few minutes not really knowing what to say to one another.

"We've got to get to the bottom of this," said Becky, suddenly breaking the silence. "This is so unlike Dad that it really has me worried."

"Okay," said Cindy. "But what are we gonna do?"

The two thought for a moment.

"Okay, how's this sound," started Becky. "We finish eating, clean up, then we follow Dad."

"Follow?"

"I know it sounds a bit melodramatic," said Becky, "but maybe we can figure out what's got his attention."

"It's certainly not us."

"It's certainly not," confirmed Becky.

"There's no way we can catch him or keep up with him now, though," said Cindy. Her sister smiled a sly smile.

"No. There's not. However, where has he gone every morning since Mom was killed?"

"The hospital!"

"That's right. He's usually there for at least thirty minutes. That gives us plenty of time to get into place and get ready to follow him when he comes out of the hospital.

"We can see what's up with him then."

"Good idea, Sis!" said Cindy.

"C'mon. Let's pray and eat and get going."

* * *

Tom awoke with a start. This time he knew. He'd traveled and he was back to real time. He recognized the feelings and recognized how his senses reacted.

He immediately picked up the phone and dialed the operator and asked her to connect him to the hospital. He knew his laziness would be reflected on his phone bill once it came in, but he was in too much of a hurry to bother with finding the phone book, assuming it could even be found.

Once connected, he asked for ICU and then asked about Mike. Yes, the polite nurse said, he was still unconscious. Was there anything else he needed?

Tom said no, nicely, but slammed down the phone. It fell off the stand next to his bed and into the floor. He kicked the phone as he got out of bed.

He'd done everything he could possibly think of to change the outcome of the accident. He couldn't exactly remember what he'd done this time. He was beginning to get confused as to which memory was the real time. He couldn't even think straight.

But he did know who could give him the answers, and he was going to go straight to him and get them. He didn't care what time of the morning it was.

* * *

Larry's mind was beginning to clear now. His girls had helped shock him back to reality. Big Ben had told him that there would be some disorientation at the beginning and end of his time travel trip, but it was still somewhat surprising to him.

Since it was Saturday morning and not Thursday, traffic was very light on the roads. He didn't even try to hold down his speed as he usually did. He was in such a hurry to tell someone about this.

Minutes later, he whipped his truck into Steven's driveway, squealing his tires ever so slightly and pulling all the way up the drive to the back of the house where the carport was.

Steven was out back puttering around with his lawnmower. When he saw Larry pull up, he smiled and waved.

Larry hopped out of his truck, barely shutting the engine off. He left the door open as he nearly ran to meet his friend.

"Good morning, Larry," said Steven, pushing the lawnmower away as if to suggest he was done with it.

"Steven!" began Larry excitedly. "You'll never guess what happened to me last night."

"What?" asked Steven, catching the excitement from Larry. He'd always said that Larry's excitement about anything was contagious. He'd tried to talk Larry into becoming a minister once before. It was his belief that Larry's natural excitement about God would be such a real and honest testimony to all those who heard him. And because Larry was so real and honest, folks would be drawn to have what he had. The perfect ingredients for a minister.

Or so Steven thought.

"I traveled in time," said Larry. After his announcement he merely crossed his arms across his chest, smiled and stepped back to wait and see what Steven would say.

"Traveled in time?" asked Steven. He motioned for his friend to take a seat in the iron lawn chair beside him. "Want some lemonade?"

"That would be great," said Larry, sitting in the offered seat.

Steven walked the few feet over to the back door of his house, cracked it open just enough to stick his head inside. "Christy? Larry's just come over. Would you mind fixing us both a glass of lemonade?" A short pause. "Thanks, honey."

Steven closed the door and walked around to the other side of his lawnmower where another lawn chair sat. He grabbed the back of it and dragged it over to the shade near Larry. While it wasn't burning hot this early in the morning, sitting in the shade was still more comfortable than in direct sunlight. It was July in Alabama after all.

"Obviously, Larry," he started, "I've got to hear more about this. What exactly do you mean?" Steven sat down with a sigh. He always enjoyed being a sounding board for his friend's ideas. Obviously, Larry was intent on time travel as some sort of theme for his next novel. Steven wanted to give him the best possible devil's advocate that he could.

"While I slept last night, I traveled in time. That's simple enough, isn't it?"

"Well it all sounds well and good, but what happened?" asked Steven. "I mean, what did you do?"

"I just went to sleep as usual. Then when I woke up, I was back."

"You mean like a dream?"

Larry grimaced, "Not exactly like a dream. Even though it sounds like it. It was genuine time travel. I was there."

"Where'd you go?"

"Last week," answered Larry. "Although I guess technically the question should be 'when' did I go."

"But the answer to that would be last night, wouldn't it?"

The two sat in confused silence for a moment.

"That's not important," said Larry, breaking the silence. "I went to last week and I was here in this town."

"Was it a choice you made? I mean, if you had a choice, why would you only go last week and go here? I mean, why wouldn't you go to visit George Washington, or the crucifixion, or something like that? Or even go to try to stop Hitler?"

"What?" said Larry, surprised. "Don't you remember what happened last week?"

Steven sat still for a moment trying to think of something, some plot point or story turn that his friend has already given him, but he couldn't remember anything.

"Larry," he finally admitted, "I can't remember. Can you remind me?"

Larry stood suddenly, obviously upset. "My wife died last week!" he yelled.

Christy walked out the back door at just that moment but not in time to catch the words, only the tone. She laid her own tone on thick to help lighten the situation. "Fresh lemonade for you boys," she said. "I'd like to tell you it was freshly squeezed, but that wouldn't be exactly the truth."

She handed the lemonade first to Larry, still standing, and then to Steven. "Y'all want anything else?" she asked, and then without pause, "Larry, you need something?"

"No thanks," he said and sat back down. The irritation she saw in him visibly subsiding.

"Well, just holler when you need a refill," she said as she

reentered the house. She tried to make eye contact and some sort of communication with Steven before she went inside to get some clue as to what was going on, but it couldn't be done. Larry was too keyed in to the way they communicated like this and had his eyes on them both. Not that he was intentionally watching for some secret communication, it was just a matter of knowing someone so well for so many years and subconsciously anticipating something.

"Steven, why are you being so insensitive?" he asked the second the door closed.

"I'm sorry, Larry," he offered, "I really didn't mean to be insensitive. I thought you were talking about some new novel idea. You now have me thoroughly confused. Did you have some sort of dream last night? I don't understand."

"No," he said. "I time traveled. Really and truly time traveled."

"Okay, Larry," started Steven after a big gulp of lemonade, "Bear with me. Are you talking about a novel you're working on or not?"

"No."

"You're not working on another novel?"

"I am," he said, "of course. But I haven't mentioned it to you yet and this time travel thing has absolutely nothing to do with it."

"Larry," Steven said, shaking his head as if to clear the confusion, "are you telling me that the living, breathing Larry Pace sitting in front of me now...traveled back in time?"

"That's what I'm saying. That's what I've been trying to tell you for the last five minutes."

Steven sat stunned. Was this some new tactic, some new ploy to get a reaction out of Steven? Larry was studying him intently, watching for a reaction. Was it all just part of the research? Steven was afraid to say anything, not sure what to say or which direction to go. Surely his friend didn't believe he *really* time traveled. Did he?

Then he really became worried. What if his friend really did believe he time traveled? What if Gracie's death had so affected him that he was slightly off kilter now and not even realizing it? But not Larry. Someone else maybe, but not Larry. Larry was a rock.

"Larry," he started slowly, munching on a piece of ice,

"before I go on, I have to-I must-get this straight. This is no joke, you're not looking for my reaction, and you're not bouncing ideas for your novel off me. You're telling me that you went back in time?"

"Geez, Steven, how many times do I have to say it. Yes. Yes. Yes. I traveled back in time! And it was just like being there the first time all over again."

Steven visibly slumped in his chair. Seeing this, Larry stood up.

"Wait. I know what I need." He dashed to his truck where his door was still open and leaned inside. Steven craned his neck to see what Larry was doing. After a few minutes, Steven called out to him.

"What are you looking for, Larry?"

"My Bible," Larry answered. "I always bring it with me, but I can't find it."

"I'll grab mine," said Steven. He stood and opened the door. Larry mumbled some response with an affirmative tone, but Steven couldn't hear the words.

Once inside, Steven quickly found his wife. His voice was urgent.

"Christy, listen. No questions, just do this. I'll explain everything later." Christy had no time for a verbal answer, only a nod as Steven continued. "Call Brother Joe. Tell him to get to the house immediately. It's about Larry. After you do that, honey, pray. Just pray."

Steven kissed her squarely on the lips, not a passionate kiss at all, but one that communicated more than words could have. It told her that he loved her and appreciated her and that he was the luckiest guy in the world to have her. It was a "thank you" for trusting him and loving him enough to do the things he'd just asked her without playing twenty questions. That was enough. As Steven picked up his Bible and headed back out the door, she was punching the number for the preacher.

Larry was still in his truck when Steven returned. Rather than sit, Steven made his way slowly to Larry's side.

"What's wrong?" he asked.

"I know my Bible has to be here somewhere," he said, "I always bring it."

"Well, don't worry about it, good friend," said Steven, "I've got mine. Here ya go." Whatever it was that Larry wanted,

Steven planned to stall him until Brother Joe arrived.

Larry sighed. He opened and closed his glove compartment even though he never put his Bible there. With some resignation, he stepped out of his truck and took the Bible from Steven.

"Fine," he said, "Your Bible will do." He placed the Bible firmly in-between both his hands; the right one looked as if he were taking the oath in a courtroom.

"This will prove it to you," said Larry. "I've got my hand firmly on the Bible. I swear to you that what I'm telling you about time travel is the truth. It's not something I made up. It's not for a novel. It's the truth. It happened to me."

The breath was sucked out of Steven's lungs. As far as he knew, Larry had never lied to him. Why would he start now? And he certainly wouldn't place his hand on a Bible and then swear. And why was he even doing that? Swearing on the Bible was also way out of character for Larry. If Steven recalled, they'd even had a discussion once in which Larry said he was torn over the idea of courtrooms using it. On one hand he was for it and on the other he was against it. Why the sudden need to use it himself?

"Larry. That's a lot to take in. Let's sit back down and talk about it."

Without looking back, Steven began walking back through his carport to the lawn chairs. He intentionally left the Bible with Larry thinking that would encourage him to follow. And it did.

Steven sat back in his chair and took a sip of lemonade while Larry slowly ambled back.

"This is just incredible, Larry," said Steven, still unconvinced. "How'd it all happen?"

"Exactly as I've been telling you," Larry answered. "I just went to sleep, I traveled, and I woke up."

"Did your body actually travel...y'know, phase out or something?"

"I don't really know. I went to sleep and when I woke up, it all felt real. Then I went to sleep again and woke up this morning, just a little while ago. I couldn't actually tell you. Maybe it is some sort of dream state."

"Could it have been just a really vivid dream? I mean I don't know much about it, but we could do some research and--"

"No! Absolutely not." Larry's voice was laced with small hints of anger.

"Sorry," said Steven, "I'm just trying to understand it all, Larry. I mean, imagine yourself in my shoes, what you'd be thinking if I told you this story."

"You're right," said Larry. He quickly shoved the Bible back at Steven. "Here, and thanks. I needed it to prove to you that I wasn't kidding. I've got to go, though. I've got a lot to do today."

"Oh?" said Steven inquisitively, "You headed up to the church work day?"

"The church--? Shoot! No, I flat forgot all about that."

"Yeah, me too. Until the pastor reminded me." Steven stood and placed his hand on Larry's shoulder. "C'mon," he said, "we'll head up there together. I'll ride with you since you're parked behind me."

"No," said Larry, "I can't. Not today."

"What? Larry, when was the last time you missed a church work day? You're practically the foreman out there." Steven chuckled at his own humor, attempting to get Larry to lighten up a bit. It wasn't exactly true, but Larry did have almost as perfect attendance at the work days as he did at the church services.

Larry turned, ignoring Steven's comments.

"I can't," he said, "I've gotta go."

"You can't go so quickly," said Steven, "You've dropped this bombshell on time travel on me and now you're running off before I can get the full story."

"Sorry," came Larry, rolling the window down and closing the door at the same time. "I'll catch you up on it all soon! Promise!"

Steven said a silent prayer that the preacher would pull in behind Larry and block him in, keep him from leaving. But he knew it was an impossibility. There hadn't been enough time for the preacher to make it this far yet, not even if he sped. And Brother Joe never sped.

"Well, hey look" started Steven, continuing to make light of the situation. "Take care of your business and then come by up at the church. I know we could sure use your help."

"We'll see," answered Larry.

"Okay then," returned Steven. "God is good. See ya."

"Yeah. See ya."

* * *

Becky and Cindy made several trips around the parking lot looking for their Dad's truck. Even though they hadn't spotted it, they mutually decided that he was still likely to keep with his schedule and was inside praying even as they parked and walked.

As they entered the front doors of the hospital, Becky asked one of the volunteers she knew if she'd seen her dad this morning. The volunteer said she hadn't, but said Becky knew how that was-she was in and out and all over the place this morning.

Becky knew. She thanked the girl and hurried over to the elevator where Cindy was standing with the door open.

"She hadn't seen him," said Becky as she entered.

"Do you think he's here?" asked Cindy.

"I don't know," Becky answered. "But where else would he be? He's been here every morning that I know of since mom died."

"Since she 'died?'"

"Yeah. Why do you say it like that? What do you mean?"

"Well," started Cindy, "we've been saying since she was killed. But you said died. What's changed?"

Becky shrugged. "I don't know. I have no idea why I said it like that."

"I think I do," said Cindy.

"What? Why?"

"I think it's about forgiveness."

"Are you saying that I don't have forgiveness in my heart?" asked Becky, hurt coming through her voice. She'd always wanted to be the example for her little sister.

"No. I'm saying exactly the opposite. I'm saying that I think you've forgiven the driver and have moved on. To say Mom was killed is very accusatory, don't you think? I mean, it sounds a lot different saying Mom was killed than saying Mom died."

The elevator dinged and the doors opened. Both girls stepped out and slowly made their way down the hall to where Mike had been and to where they expected to find their Dad. Before either girl could open the door, Becky reached out and grabbed her sister by the arm.

"Is that bad?" she asked? "Do you think it means that I don't care about Mom?"

"No," Cindy replied, "I don't think that at all. I think it means you have a much more forgiving heart than I do. Or than Dad. I think, right now, that that's a very good thing."

"And it makes me proud," Cindy continued, "that you're my big sis." She grabbed her sister and squeezed her in a big bear hug. "Now c'mon, let's go see what's wrong with Dad."

Cindy reached her hand down to the big handle on the hospital room door. She'd been to this room several times before, but she was never as nervous as she was then. She pushed the door open.

"Huh?" said Becky. "Where's Dad?"

Mike lay still in the bed, monitors still attached and still reading all the vital and necessary signs of life. The girls entered and closed the door behind them.

"What if he's already come and gone?" asked Becky.

"That would almost be impossible. Dad wouldn't do a drive-by prayer, would he?"

"Anything seems possible with him these days."

"You're right there." Both girls sat in a chair, looking at the sleeping figure on the bed.

"Wait! What if he hasn't been here yet? What if we actually beat him here?"

"I didn't drive *that* fast, Cindy!"

"I'm not trying to say that, but what if he stopped to do something else before coming here?"

Cindy threw up her hands in surrender. "Oh! I don't know. But we're here, so let's pray for this guy."

The sisters both bowed their head where they sat and began to pray. Certainly they prayed for Mike who was in front of them. They'd prayed for him many times before. They prayed for his recovery and they prayed for his salvation.

But today they also prayed for their Dad. Something was going on in his life that was having a negative effect on him and they could see it plain as day. If they couldn't talk to their dad directly, they'd go directly to the source of everything: God.

As they prayed, Mike moved his hand. Ever so slightly

did it move. But it was enough to catch the attention of Cindy who sat closest to him. Not sure whether she was seeing things or not, she stopped praying and stared up at Mike.

His eyes were open. Just barely.

"Becky!"

Mumbling a few words in order to finish the thought of her prayer, she looked up at her sister to see what she needed. "What?" she said in a near whisper to indicate that she wasn't finished praying, and to subtly suggest to her sister that she had been rude to interrupt her.

"Look!"

Becky followed her sister's pointing finger to see Mike's open eyes. He smiled. It was a faint smile. One that might not have been noticed had they not been staring straight at him and had they not been in the room so many times before that they'd memorized his face.

Becky reacted without hesitation.

"Go get the nurse, I'll call Dad," she said.

Cindy darted out of the room to the nurse's station. Becky dialed the numbers to the house so quickly she couldn't remember if she'd punched them all. The answering machine kicked on about the same time as Cindy reentered with a nurse in tow. Cindy glanced at Becky and although no words were spoken, she asked her sister if their dad was home with nothing more than a look. Becky shook her head to let Cindy know he wasn't there. The nurse began to talk to Mike as Becky left her message.

"Dad. This is Becky. Pick up if you're there. Cindy and I are at the hospital and you should get up here immediately!"

Cindy made her way slowly over to her sister as she left the message. Becky hung up the phone and Cindy hugged her.

"Where could he be?"

* * *

Big Ben had acted as if he expected Larry. Even at this early hour-and on a Saturday-he was dressed in a suit and tie. He eagerly ushered Larry inside and immediately placed a cup of coffee in his hands. Once the two were

126

seated back in the "clock" room, Big Ben quickly pelted Larry with questions.

"Well," he started, "I expected a phone call, not a personal visit. But I do appreciate your time to come over. So, tell me about it. What did you think?"

"It was," Larry began with a deep sigh, "it was more than I ever could have imagined possible. I mean, I was right there. I could smell her, I could touch her, I had a conversation with her. It was almost as if nothing had ever changed. It was so real."

"Oh," answered Big Ben, "it was very real."

"But," said Larry, blowing on the coffee, still too hot for his lips, "how can that be? If she's dead, she's dead. How can she be alive? How can I talk to her and touch her? I don't get it."

"Does it matter that you don't get it?" asked Big Ben.

"Well, yes," Larry started, "oh, I don't know. Not really, I don't guess. I mean, I like to know how things work."

"That's the mathematician in you," said Big Ben. Larry laughed.

"Maybe so," he said, "maybe so."

"But hey," said Big Ben, "I bet there are a lot of things in your daily life that you use and don't fully understand how they work. You don't question the microwave oven or the cellphone, you simply use it."

Larry nodded. Big Ben was right.

A quiet stillness settled over the room as Larry sipped his now barely cool-enough-to-drink coffee. Big Ben was already refilling his cup, the pot sitting at the top of the steps near the entrance. As he started his second cup, he could see that the wheels of Larry's mind were turning. Big Ben knew that many of the more intelligent people who traveled were overwhelmed with so many questions and possibilities. Time traveling was one of those childhood fantasies people write off as fiction so that when it proves true, many of their illusions are shattered. To coin a common phrase, it rocks their world.

Some cannot mentally handle it.

"When will I die," asked Larry, without breaking his trance-like stare at the sun-dial in the middle of the room.

"You don't really want to know that, Larry," answered Big Ben. "Oh, it's okay to ponder that question without really seeking an answer. It's one of the first questions everyone has when the reality of time travel is realized. It's natural. But it's not a question you really want to know."

"No," he answered with a sigh, "I guess you're right." Then he looked Big Ben straight in the eyes. "But still..." Larry's voice trailed off. "Do you know?" he asked.

"I don't have it committed to memory if that's what you mean," Big Ben answered. "I couldn't give you the date this very instant. But it is information that is available to me should I see any fathomable reason to need it."

"How many times can I do this?" asked Larry.

"What?" asked Big Ben, "come visit me?"

Larry laughed. "No, not visit you. How many times can I travel back in time?"

"Oh, as many as you want," answered Big Ben.

"Really?"

"Well, so long as you have time remaining."

"You mean as long as I'm still supposed to live that long?"

"Yes."

"Makes sense." Larry took a bigger drink of his coffee. It was still hot, but not hot enough to burn his tongue anymore. He'd only barely noticed how quickly Big Ben had been drinking his own coffee until he poured his third cup.

"But remember, I warned you-" Big Ben began before he spotted Larry watching him pour the coffee. "You want some more?" he asked.

"No thanks," Larry answered, "I'm fine."

Big Ben set the pot back down and again immediately began to sip the very hot coffee. Larry wondered if his tongue was burnt raw or if he'd drank his coffee so hot for so long that it didn't matter.

"You were saying?" said Larry.

"Hmm?" asked Big Ben, a confused look on his face.

"You were about to warn me of something."

"Oh!" said Big Ben, suddenly remembering. "Remember I warned you that it was addictive, like a drug."

"I don't think you told me that," said Larry, a bit surprised. "Are you trying to say that this feeling I have to do it again is because of some addictive nature of the travel?"

"Well," Big Ben began, "yes and no. It's difficult to explain because it is not a drug. It's not something you ingest and then physically require more of it to satisfy you. It's more of a... a ... mental or emotional addiction. Physically, you're the same as you ever were. Mentally, or maybe, more appropriately, your soul is experiencing a longing for it. In some people, that longing gets unbearable and they find themselves having to travel again and again.

"So while you can travel as much as you like, I warn you to be careful and not get dependent on the euphoric feeling it gives you."

Big Ben took another swig of his coffee. He felt good he'd warned Larry about the addiction. He was actually beginning to like Larry and almost felt sorry for him.

Almost.

"What's the maximum length one can travel?" asked Larry, not batting an eye to the addiction idea.

"Most of my customers either get a day or a week," answered Big Ben. "Obviously, you can get any amount, but those are the two most common requested amounts."

"Yeah," said Larry, catching Big Ben's reference to him as a customer, "but what's the maximum?"

"The most I've ever sold is a month," answered Big Ben.

"Yes, but what's the maximum?"

"I'm not sure what you're getting at, Larry. Tell me exactly what you want to know."

"You don't understand maximum?" chuckled Larry. "I'm only wondering if there is an upper limit to the amount of time one can travel."

Big Ben set his now empty coffee cup down. He'd finished three cups before Larry had even finished his one. Big Ben reached into his inside coat pocket as he talked and pulled out a cigar.

"That's an odd question, Larry," he said. "But I guess it shouldn't surprise me coming from a mathematician, what with you being interested in numbers and all.

"To be honest with you," Big Ben continued as he ran the cigar under his nose and sniffed-He'd seen the move on some movie, one that he no longer remembered-it was now simply a habit for him. "I'm not really sure. What do you have in mind?"

"I don't know that I really have anything particular in mind. I just thought it curious that if I wanted like a year, could I take it?"

"Whew," said Big Ben. "A year? Do you realize that means you'd lose a year and a half of your life? Five hundred and forty seven days you'd never see."

"Forty seven and a half."

"Huh?"

"Five hundred forty seven and a half days would be the payment," said Larry.

"Oh," said Big Ben, laughing. "Still, that's a long time."

"If I did that," asked Larry, "would my body age while I slept?"

Big Ben guffawed, "Larry, I honestly don't know."

"Can you die while traveling?" asked Larry, not blinking an eye.

"Do you mean can you be killed in the past?"

"No. What I mean is: let's say that I'm supposed to die in six months. I buy a year's worth of time, but I don't really have that much to spend. Instead of waking up after the travel, would I die? And, would you tell me?"

"I see," said Big Ben. "Yes and no. What would happen is that when you went to buy the time, I'd see that you didn't have enough left. I wouldn't say anything to you because that would be breaking my salesman's oath. What would happen without your knowledge is that your contract would be reworked so that the time fit exactly. If you are supposed to die in six months, then technically your contract could only be for four months even though you think you're getting a year."

"So basically, I can't spend it if I don't have it?"

"Right. Think of it somewhat like a pre-paid calling card. You can call and call and call...until your minutes run out."

"But I'd never know because you're not allowed to tell me."

"Right. And to all on the outside world, you've simply died in your sleep. Ever notice how many people die in their sleep?" asked Big Ben.

The thought had never occurred to Larry. A lot of people died in their sleep. Had *they* been time-traveling?

"What about-" Larry's voice was cut off as a loud

130

thumping came from the front door. Someone was banging very hard and very loud.

"Excuse me," said Big Ben. His teeth clinched down on the unlit cigar.

"Go right ahead," said Larry.

Big Ben made his way calmly out of the room, taking the pot of coffee with him as he left. Larry, still holding his cup, stood to look at some of the assorted clocks on the walls around the room. He was fascinated by the variety. He was never really into clocks all that much himself. He liked them with big numbers, that was it. He didn't care if they were digital or not, as long as they had big numbers so he could see them easily.

Seconds later he heard loud voices from the foyer. He couldn't make out what they were saying, but he thought he recognized the voice.

He inched his way over to the doorway, still looking at the clocks on the wall in case anyone spotted him from outside the room. His curiosity overwhelming, he peeked out.

In the foyer he saw the reporter Tom Morgan talking with Big Ben, who looked slightly uncomfortable that Tom was here. Larry had a guess as to why, but couldn't be sure.

"Hey!" said Tom, spotting Larry in the doorway. Larry took a step back, but realized he'd been caught watching. "Mr. Pace! Is that you?"

Larry leaned out, exaggerating slightly to make it look as if he were more in that out of the doorway. "Tom? What are you doing here?" Larry knew, though. And he knew that Tom knew why he was there also.

"Same as you I guess," he answered, not hesitating to suggest why both men where there. He pushed his way past Big Ben "Did you go?"

"Did I go where," answered Larry, pushing the ruse as far as he could.

"Did you travel back in time?"

"Tom!" said Big Ben, "these are not things to talk of like this." Tom turned to look at Big Ben.

"Why not?" Tom asked. "I know you talked to him. Heck, if he hasn't gone already, maybe I could help you get some commission."

"Commission?" asked Larry.

"Gentlemen!" said Big Ben, taking control of the conversation running wild. "Let's all have a seat in here and we can have a nice conversation."

Big Ben led Tom into the room where Larry waited for them. Larry offered his hand to Tom as the two entered and they all had a seat.

"What sort of commission?" asked Larry.

"Larry," Big Ben began, "I'm a businessman. What did you think I got out of this all? I never charged you a single penny."

"I don't have any idea," said Larry. "And to be honest with you, I guess I'd never given it any thought whatsoever. The whole rest of it-time travel-was just so far out that I don't guess I even considered what you got out of it. I think I've been more wrapped up in what it would cost me.

"So what do you get out of it?" Larry finished.

"As our excited friend here mentioned," said Big Ben, "I get a commission. My commission is in time."

"Can you be a little more clear?" asked Larry. "All the time references can be a little confusing."

"Really," Big Ben said, slightly perturbed, "it's none of your business. If you're satisfied with the dealings as is, that should be sufficient."

Big Ben paused long enough for the reprimand to sink in, but not long enough for Larry-or Tom, for that matter-to recover and answer.

"But because I have great respect for you, I'll tell you." He removed the cigar he'd stuffed into his shirt pocket and stuck it unlit into his mouth. "All it means is that I get a block of time added to my travel account. Whenever I travel, I use my commission instead of my own life's time."

"So you travel, too?" asked Larry.

"Sure I do," he answered.

"But all your time is free, based on what you sell?" said Tom, not really to anyone, but more musing to himself out loud. "So the more you sell the more you can travel and not have it come off the end of your own life."

"That's exactly it," said Big Ben.

"But how do you pay for all this?" said Larry, looking around at the room full of some obviously very expensive clocks, and subtly indicating the bigger home around it.

132

"Now, Larry," he began, "did you read the article that our friend here penned?"

Larry looked slightly confused for a moment, then he realized Big Ben was referring to the newspaper article about the time he did in jail.

"Are you saying all the speculation is true?" Larry asked innocently enough.

"I didn't say that. But, if you were to ask anyone, that's where they would say I got my money, wouldn't they?"

"It was never proved," said Tom, repeating the conclusion he'd offered in his column.

"No, it wasn't," agreed Big Ben. "But the public majority believe it, don't they? So I might as well be guilty in the court of public opinion."

"Well," said Larry, using that tone of voice that indicated you were about to hear something contradictory to what was just said. His students heard that tone more than anyone else. "Public opinion doesn't put you in jail. At least it's not supposed to. In this country one is supposed to be innocent until proven guilty."

"True," said Big Ben, "very true. At least it's supposed to be that way."

"But now," said Big Ben, shifting the conversation, "you gentlemen didn't come here to discuss the private details of my life. We had business transactions and you've got questions."

Tom was first to speak, barely allowing Big Ben to finish. Larry had already asked the most pressing questions he'd come with, and in no way had any difficulty deferring to Tom's questions.

"I've tried to change the outcome," said Tom, "but each time I return, nothing's happened."

Though he didn't voice it, the thought of changing time had crossed Larry's mind more than once. If he could change the outcome of Grace's death, he'd do it instantly. He'd even tried somewhat, but couldn't be sure whether he actually gave an effort or whether he just thought about it.

"Tom," began Big Ben, "I thought we'd had this discussion once before already."

"Not that I recall."

"Hmmm. Well, maybe not. And I apologize for that oversight. It's not among my standard lines as most are content to simply revisit. But no, Tom, you can't change it."

"Why not?" asked Larry.

"Why not?" repeated Big Ben, slightly surprised that Larry was asking it.

"Sure," said Larry, emboldened by the idea. "This whole idea of time travel seems so far outside the realm of accepted believability anyway. I mean, the overwhelming majority of people would think the three of us sitting here are certified for the loony bin. Time travel? Yeah, it's possible as the three of us can attest. Okay, so if it's possible to do something that we really think is impossible, why not change it? We think that's impossible, but is it really?"

"Yeah," echoed Tom.

"You don't understand," said Big Ben, "it *can't* be changed."

"But why not?" continued Larry. "I know how it was when I traveled. I was there. I felt, I breathed, I tasted, everything I do in real time. Can't I be killed?"

"No."

"No? Why not?"

"Larry, Tom, you can't change time. You can't change what's happened to you. What's done is done."

"Ben," said Larry, "you're only telling me it can't be done but you're not telling me why. Until you can actually tell me why, I'm thinking you're trying to hide something. That maybe it can be done but there are consequences."

"I'm not hiding anything. It's impossible to change time," said Big Ben. "It's impossible because it's all part of a grand plan that can't be changed."

"Grand plan?" asked Tom. "What do you mean?"

"You mean it's all part of God's plan?" asked Larry.

"I didn't say God," said Big Ben.

"No, but that's who you meant."

"I'm not certain I believe in God, anyway" said Tom.

"Don't believe?" asked Larry, feigning more surprise than he really felt. "Why? Even Satan believes in God. Isn't that right, Ben?"

Ben made no move to attempt to answer that part of Larry's question.

"It's part of an ultimate plan, you may ascribe it to whomever you choose," said Big Ben, "makes no difference to me. It's not my plan, that's for certain. However, it can *not* be changed. Period.

"Imagine it more like a video tape," he continued. "You can watch it over and over and over and over again, but it never changes. No matter how many times you watch it, it remains the same. You can't change it...but you can live it again. And again and again if you wish. But you cannot change it."

Big Ben's voice trailed off. Larry couldn't decide what sort of emotion it was that Big Ben's voice contained. On one hand it almost sounded as if he was arguing a point that he himself didn't believe in one hundred percent. On the other, it nearly sounded like Big Ben might have believed it, but wished it otherwise. Maybe there was something in his own life that he wanted to do over. Maybe he'd tried to do some part of his life over himself, only to prove what he was arguing. The fact of his argument, Larry reasoned, didn't mean that he liked it.

For Tom, the instant he heard "video tape" he thought of all the hours he'd sat in front of the television watching *It's a Wonderful Life* over and over and over again. The movie never changed, yet the circumstances behind his watching was frequently different. Heck, you could even say that he sometimes watched it from the couch and sometimes from the chair. And even sometimes from the floor. The video tape never changed. And never would no matter what conditions he changed around it.

"But what if I want to try?" asked Larry. Out of the corner of his eye, he spotted Tom perk up to the question. Tom obviously wanted to change something. Larry had a pretty good idea what it might be.

"Hey!" he said, suddenly. "What happens if we work together to cause a change? I mean, how many of your other customers know each other and have some sort of relationship to one another?"

"Doesn't matter," said Big Ben. He spoke slowly. "You... can...not...change... time. It's impossible."

"Y'know," said Larry, responding in a calm and assured voice even though Big Ben's reflected that he'd obviously reached the end of his patience. "All things are possible through the God that created me."

Big Ben rolled his eyes.

"What?" said Larry. "You don't believe?"

"Larry," said Big Ben, "and Tom, you as well, if you insist. I'll sell you the time you want. I've issued you the required warning and I've told you that under no circumstances can time be changed. You're welcome to travel back as much as you like and I'll be happy to sell that time to you. But please, I find that I'm now tired. If you want to make a purchase, let's do so. I don't mean to be an inhospitable host, but I must lie down. It's still very early for me."

Larry and Tom looked at one another. Neither spoke, but it was clear what the two where thinking. Larry had germinated the idea that maybe the two of them could work together to change something. Big Ben had a good idea what that something was, and he could see their minds were made up.

He produced two pieces of paper, one contract for each man, and let them sign again.

* * *

Steven knocked on the hospital room door and slowly pushed it open at the same time. He'd driven faster than he knew he should have, but the sound of Becky's voice told him she was both scared and excited. She was scared because she didn't know where her dad was. She was excited because Mike had just regained consciousness. He wasn't so much concerned about her excitement as he was about her fear.

He saw both girls sharing a single chair in the far corner of the room. Their eyes were fixed on Mike as a nurse took additional readings from assorted monitors to which he was hooked. As the door pushed open further, Becky spotted him.

"Dr. Dale!" she cried as she nearly leapt from the chair. She ran to him and threw her arms around him. Steven gave her a big hug. Becky and Cindy were both almost like his own children.

The nurse turned quickly when Becky hollered. She'd heard "doctor" and wanted to see which one. Not recognizing Steven, she immediately got back to work.

"I don't guess you've talked to your dad in the last few minutes, have you?" Steven asked. The question was aimed at both girls.

"No, we haven't talked to him since he left this morning," answered Cindy. "Dr. Dale, we're really worried about him."

"Yeah," he said, "I kinda got that from the phone. I came as soon as I could."

"I'm gonna have to ask y'all to hold it down," said the nurse, "or just take your conversation to the waiting room. There's really only supposed to be two of you in here at a time anyway."

"Okay," said Steven, "Sorry about that. We'll go outside." At that, Steven and the girls turned to exit the room.

"Wait!" came the voice from the bed. The trio stopped and looked back at Mike. The look in his face told them he did not want them to leave. "I want to talk to you," he said.

"Not right now," said the nurse.

"Five minutes be okay nurse?" asked Steven.

"That should be fine," she said.

"Mike," Steven said, looking directly at Mike. "We'll be back here in five minutes." Steven gave him a big smile and ushered the sisters out of the hospital room.

"What's up with your dad," he asked once they were outside and the hospital door was closed.

"We don't know," said Cindy. "That's what we're hoping you can help us with."

"You said you don't know where he is. When was the last time you saw him?"

"Oh," said Becky, "we saw him this morning, but he was not his usual self."

"He didn't even tell us goodnight last night," said Cindy, slightly in a huff.

Steven chuckled at her consternation, but knew that to these girls who'd just lost their mom, they needed some stability in their lives. Or at least the sense that their dad was stable and not also about to leave. Not that they were insensitive to their dad's loss, but they needed him. Steven knew that.

"Cindy," he said, trying to sound reassuring though not completely convinced himself, "I'm sure your dad just got in a hurry this morning. I also saw him this morning and-"

"You did??" The sisters said in unison. "Where?"

"Actually, he came to see me. Talked about time travel

or something like that. I had initially assumed it was for a new novel he was working on. Do you know if he's started work on a new novel?"

"Time travel?" asked Cindy.

"New novel?" asked Becky.

"Nevermind," said Steven. He could see by their eyes that they had no idea what he was talking about. He decided it was better not to confuse them even further even though he felt Larry's whole time travel conversation was somehow at the bottom of all his sudden weirdness.

"He came by to see me briefly this morning. He didn't stay long and he didn't tell me where he was going. He did tell me where he was *not* going, though. I reminded him that I would see him at work-day at the church this morning and it had completely slipped his mind."

"That's when I knew, girls," Steven finished, "that something else was going on with your dad. To my knowledge, your dad has never missed a church work day because he forgot!"

"But where did he go?" asked Becky.

"I don't know," Steven answered. "I wish I could tell you. I'm wishing now that I had followed him this morning when I could sense something wrong. But I didn't..."

"You can't blame yourself," said Cindy. "How could you have known?"

"You're right, of course. But still... We'll get to the bottom of this. I promise. I'm going to go look for him now."

Before that last word had escaped from his mouth, the door opened and the nurse walked out of Mike's room. Steven remembered he told Mike he'd come back in and say something to him. While he really wanted to get out and look for Larry, he knew he had to go back in and say something.

The trio edged their way back in, slowly making their way toward Mike. Even though Steven had been the last one in, the sisters had walked so as to maneuver him to the front. Steven smiled again as he approached Mike.

"We're sure glad to see you awake," he said, reaching the side of the bed.

"I know." Mike spoke slowly and softly, the voice of one that hadn't been used in some time and was out of practice.

138

"Do you know where you are?" Steven asked.

"Yes."

"You don't know us, though, do you?"

"Yes. No. I don't know your names."

"My name is Steven Dale. I teach art at the university. This is Becky and Cindy Pace." Steven pointed to each of the girls in turn as he introduced them.

"What do you remember about the accident?" Steven asked.

"No," Mike said, "I know you."

Steven stopped. "You know me?"

"I mean I don't know your name, but I know you." Mike looked at the sisters. "And I know them."

"How do you know us, Mike?" asked Steven. He reached behind him and pulled a chair up close to Mike. He didn't want to tower over Mike while standing, but mostly he wanted to get closer to as to ensure he heard it all correctly.

"I've seen you." Mike continued to speak in a soft voice, weak from disuse.

"You were a student? You've seen me at school?" Immediately Steven began to search the index files of his brain trying to place Mike. Many students came through and were simply passing through. They did as little as they could get away with, received their grade, and moved on. The students who stood out were few and far between. But search as he may, he couldn't place Mike.

"No," he answered. "Here. I've seen you here."

"I'm not sure I understand what you're saying Mike." Steven turned to look at the sisters. Neither of them appeared to understand either.

"I've seen you here and I know what you've been doing."

"Doing?" Steven asked.

"He means praying," Cindy said. "He's seen us praying." Steven knew that's what he meant, but he wanted Mike to say it with his own voice, weak though it was.

"Is that it, Mike?" asked Steven, "You've seen us praying?" Steven had an idea where he thought this might be going, but it was too bizarre for him to voice out loud.

Mike shook his head. He had indeed seen them praying. "And I've seen the angels."

"Angels?" asked Becky?

"Yes." Mike answered slowly and deliberately. He wanted to be sure he was understood. Yet Steven couldn't decide whether this was some unconscious-induced hallucination or whether he'd really seen what he claimed. He believed in angels one hundred percent without a doubt, and he believed that they walked among and around us every day. Steven believed that with all his heart.

But he'd never seen them. What was that about faith being belief in things unseen?

"Tell me about them," said Steven.

"They were with you when you prayed," said Mike. "At first I didn't see them. But then I saw them. They stood over you. Like they were standing guard or something.

"That's when I knew you were praying for me."

"Could you hear what we said?" asked Steven, remembering that he had prayed aloud once or twice with Larry, but most of the time they'd prayed silently. He knew simply from his experience with folks in the hospital before that sometimes people can hear you even when they're in a coma or seemingly unconscious. He was a firm believer in talking to those people in order to offer encouragement, even when there was no response from them.

"No," answered Mike, "I couldn't hear you. But they told me what you said."

"Who told you?" asked Steven.

"The angels!" insisted Cindy. "The angels told him what we said!" She'd become excited that the angels had been there and was, even now, glancing around hoping to catch a peek at one. Steven knew what Mike was meaning, but he wanted him to repeat it so there would be no misunderstanding.

"The other man," continued Mike. "He came every day. He cried a lot. He was angry at first. But then he changed. Where is he?"

Steven knew Mike meant Larry. He wasn't about to tell him he had no idea where Larry was, not now that Mike was conscious and not in front of Larry's frightened daughters.

"He'll be here soon," Steven said, "I'm sure."

Almost as if on cue, the hospital door opened and everyone turned to look. Brother Joe walked in wearing a big smile.

"Hello everyone!" he said. "I see the gang's all here."

Steven noticed he had a way of making everything feel complete even though it was obvious Larry was still among the missing.

"Brother Joe! Isn't this just fantastic?" said Cindy.

"Fantastic? Of course. It's an answered prayer," said Brother Joe. "All answered prayers are fantastic."

"That's not him," said Mike, looking at Brother Joe.

"No," answered Steven, "that's not the man you're looking for. The man you want to see is Larry. This man is Brother Joe. He's the preacher at our church."

"Mike," Steven continued as if Brother Joe had never entered. "You said you'd seen us praying. Do you know what we were praying for?"

"Yes."

"What?"

"You were praying that I would recover and if I recovered you wanted me to meet Jesus Christ."

Becky began to cry. It was a soft sobbing, but enough to cause Mike to look at her, taking his attention off Steven.

"The man, Larry," Mike continued, "knew I would recover. He did not pray for my recovery. He prayed only for me to meet Jesus. At first I didn't think I would recover. I thought I would die. But then, he had such confidence that I would recover, that I began to believe it."

"Mike," began Steven, taking on a very serious tone. "Do you know who Larry is?"

"The only thing I know is that I killed his wife in that car."

Steven closed his eyes, if for no other reason than to hold back the tears. He sighed. "How do you know that," he asked.

"I don't know how I know," Mike answered. "But it's true, isn't it?"

"Yes, Mike," said Brother Joe, stepping up near Steven and slowly edging him aside. It wasn't a rude gesture, but one that said 'I'm here now and will take the ball now. You've had it, now it's my turn to run with it.' Steven wasn't the least bit bothered by it. In fact, he was relieved. It was, in Steven's mind, Brother Joe's strength. "It is true," Brother Joe finished.

"I want what he has," said Mike. His voice sounded defiant, as if he were rejecting something else in making this statement.

"What do you think he has?" asked Brother Joe.

"I'm not sure," began Mike, now not so defiant, "but I want it. What could possibly make a man pray for the life of someone who killed his wife? Whatever it is, I want it."

"I've known Larry for a long time, Mike. I know exactly what he has that makes him like that. Larry is-"

"I want it!" Mike interrupted Brother Joe before he could finish.

"Great!" said Brother Joe. "Let me tell you about Jesus Christ."

With that, Steven turned to the girls and the three walked outside the hospital room once again. Steven quietly shut the door and wrapped the girls up in his arms as if they were his own children.

"Do you think he really saw angels?" Cindy asked, her voice slightly muffled because she was squeezed up next to him.

"I do," answered Steven. "Don't you?"

"Yes," said Becky, "I do. How else can you explain all that he knows?"

"It's a miracle!" said Cindy.

"It's what we've been praying for, isn't it?" asked Steven.

"Yes," said Becky. "Well, most of the time. Today I was praying mostly about Daddy."

"Well, of course," said Steven. "But it's what we've all been praying about mostly when we come here. God answers prayers."

"God is so good," said Becky.

God is sovereign, thought Steven. It was the answer he'd have given had Larry spoken the first line and was the answer -under normal circumstances- Larry would have given in response. For now, he had to imagine the response of his friend. A friend yes, but at this time he had no idea where he was.

* * *

Tom keyed into his apartment and swung the door wide. He left the keys in the lock and the door open as he entered. He was completely and utterly depressed.

He wanted to be optimistic. He wanted to think that tonight's foray into the past would somehow change things. But Big Ben had stated categorically that there was nothing he could do to change the past events of his life.

Yet he couldn't imagine that possible. If you could actually travel back in time-if time travel was a reality-and it was because he'd done it-why couldn't you change it? He wasn't willing to accept the idea that it couldn't be changed. Not yet. It might be true, but he wasn't willing to accept it.

That was why Larry's idea to work together excited him. Might it be possible for two working toward the same results at the same time? Maybe they could actually change something? Might it cause some wrinkle in time? It seemed to Tom as if it had to be possible. It just didn't make any sense otherwise.

Leaving the door open, he made his way on the path to his spot on the couch. Picking up the remote from the cushion, he clicked the TV on and began flipping channels. He wasn't normally much of a channel surfer, but every now and again, he went through a thoughtless flipping session.

He was having one such session. Still, he was depressed. The thoughtless flipping did nothing to cheer him up.

Holding the remote tightly, Tom felt his finger slowly inch toward the "play" button. It wasn't something he thought he was consciously aware of, but he must have been to have noticed it. Thing was, he didn't recall willing himself to press the button. But, the button was pressed regardless, and the scene began as if on cue. Tom wasn't ready to believe it was his cue, but it was his finger. Hadn't Big Ben told him there would be side effects? Maybe a thumb with its own mind was one of them. Or maybe, Tom from some point in the future had traveled back to this time and was now controlling his actions. Possible, except why in the world would a future Tom want to return to this part of his life when there were so many much better times?

Okay, so he knew he was getting a little loopy, but that didn't stop him from watching *It's a Wonderful Life* yet once again for the umpteenth time.

"No securities, no stocks, no bonds."

Initially he'd thought he could change his life by changing the past. But if he couldn't change the past, then he was doomed to this failed life.

"Nothin' but a miserable little $500 equity in a life insurance policy."

Big Ben had said that time travel was like watching a video tape. Tom knew video tapes pretty well. He had his collection of them (which was beginning to become obsolete because of DVDs). They never changed...unless you recorded over them or maybe if you spliced into them. Wouldn't changing something in a time travel session be like recording over them, making a new recording?

And in all seriousness, who would pay his death bill when he died? That had really started to bother him the past few days. Is that something the government would pick up? Had he paid enough taxes throughout his life to have enough in his "account" to get him buried? What happens to someone when they don't have the money to get buried? What is a pauper's grave? He'd heard the term frequently during his lifetime, but what did it mean? No casket? Cremation, while cheaper than a casket, was still expensive.

"You're worth more dead than alive."

A better person would find out what would happen and try to solve it now, before they died. But he wasn't a better person. What good had he done? He'd made a mess of his life, and ruined a few others in the process.

The old phrase "history was doomed to repeat itself" made a lot more sense to him now. History is just like a video tape. We can't change it.

What exactly did Big Ben mean when he said it was all part of some grand scheme? Larry was sure it was the plan of God, but what had God really done for Tom? Hadn't he called out to Him before only to be ignored? What did God know or care of him? And yet, Larry seemed to have some sort of peace about it all. After all, he'd just lost his wife and was now a single father taking care of two girls and yet he never acted as if he were angry at Tom.

Tom knew that had the roles been reversed, he'd have been piping hot. He would have probably said so many nasty things to him.

But Larry hadn't done that. Why not?

But still, Larry wanted to change time, so he was really no different from Tom. If Larry believed God was in charge of it all, why would he want to try to change it? Wouldn't that be sacrilegious or something? Trying to change what God had already planned? Wouldn't that be like trying to play God? If God were real, what would he have to say about all that?

Plus, if God were real, he'd have nothing to do with someone like Tom. He'd abandoned all things right and decent when he cheated on his wife and then left her with their young child.

"No securities, no stocks, no bonds. Nothin' but a miserable little $500 equity in a life insurance policy. You're worth more dead than alive."

Worthless was really what Mr. Potter meant. George Bailey's life was worthless. It was a shame that Tom's life couldn't be like George Bailey's. But George was a fictional character in a movie. Tom was a real live breathing person. His life really was worthless.

* * *

Brother Joe and Steven waved goodbye to the girls as they drove out of the hospital parking lot. Both girls were smiling, but the men knew it covered up the fears in their hearts about their dad.

"Okay, so where do we go from here?" asked Brother Joe, ever ready to tackle a situation head on.

"Work day, I guess," Steven answered. Brother Joe slowly put his hand on Steven's shoulder and grasped it in a massaging grip, very much like a father to a son.

"Steven," he said, "I'm all about doing the work of the Lord, you know that. I believe it's important. No, I believe it's integral to our duty as believers. However, we've got a friend and brother in need and it's also our duty to look for him, to find him and to minister to his needs, whatever they might be."

"Yeah," said Steven, "you're right. I was just testing you, of course."

"Of course."

"We'll look for him until lunch time and then head back to the church. If we haven't found him by then, he doesn't want to be found."

"You don't think he's suicidal, do you?" asked Brother Joe.

"No, no, I don't, not at all. He's got some odd notion that he's time traveled. It's not just some make believe plot line he's working on for his next novel either. He talked to me about it before but I thought he was grilling me with ideas for his next book. Apparently I was wrong. But he's not suicidal, of that I'm sure."

"He's talked to me of the same thing," said Brother Joe. "Time travel, I mean. I also thought it might be for his next novel. He asked me my thoughts on it and I told him I thought it would be wrong, but I had to do the research to come up with some scriptural support. I didn't want my answer to just be what *I* thought to be right or wrong. I wanted the answer to come from scripture."

"As it should," answered Steven. "I wish I had thought to do that when he talked to me."

"Don't worry about it," said Brother Joe, "as I said, I was just offhandedly commenting. Sincere, sure, but deadly serious, no."

"So," began Steven after a short pause, "do you think it's true? Do you think he really could have time traveled?"

"No," answered Brother Joe, "I don't. For Larry's sake, I wish I could say yes. Every part of my sane being screams it's all science fiction, the same stuff Larry writes." Brother Joe closed his eyes and shook his head slowly. "But then that verse out of Matthew, chapter 19, I think, keeps popping up in my head. Y'know... with people it is impossible, but all things are possible through God?"

Steven laughed. "Yeah, it's kinda hard to argue with stuff like that. Especially if you believe it."

"But even if it was true, I still can't accept it as being good," said Brother Joe. "There is something inherently wrong about trying to play God in a time travel fashion. I can't see there being anything good about it. Can you?"

"To be honest with you, Brother Joe, I haven't thought on it that much. The way you put it, though, I'd have to agree with you. I just don't know how or what Larry's suggesting he's into, though."

"Let's take my car," said Brother Joe, "I can bring you back here when we're through."

"Why don't we both just drive up to the church and I can leave my car there."

"I'm afraid if we head to the church now, we'll get

caught up there and not look for Larry," said Brother Joe. "Someone will have a question or some problem and we'll get sidetracked."

"Good thinking," answered Steven.

The men took Brother Joe's car and drove to all the spots they thought Larry might possibly be: his home, the bookstore, campus, the library. They even drove by the church on the odd chance that he might have come on to the church work-day. But they didn't find him anywhere.

Finally, just after noon, they gave up and headed to the church. Larry's daughters were both there, but still no sign of Larry.

"Well, do you want to try to catch him at home this evening?" asked Steven as the two men got out of the car.

"I can't," said Brother Joe, "I have the Howard memorial service tonight. We'll catch him first thing in the morning. Bring him into my office when he gets here. We should have plenty of time before the service."

Becky walked up to the two men as they made their way into the church's fellowship hall. "Well, did you find him?" she asked.

"No," said Steven, "Sorry Becky. We looked everywhere. Wherever he is, he doesn't want to be found."

"This is just not like Dad at all," she said.

"We know," answered Brother Joe, "that's why we've been looking for him." Brother Joe placed both his hands on Becky's shoulders and looked her straight in the eyes. Steven noticed that he really had a way about him that seemed very fatherly and very in control. He could put nearly anyone at ease.

"But listen, Becky," Brother Joe continued, "I've known your father for a long time. And while it is unlike him to act the way he's acting, we've also got to try to understand that this is a man who just lost his wife. The pain he is feeling must be incredible. I can't imagine what it would be like to lose my own wife. I'm sure it's just some odd way that your dad is handling his pain. We've never seen it, I suspect, because we've never seen him in such pain before."

"I hope you're right, Brother Joe," answered Becky.

Steven hoped he was right, too, but was not about to voice that concern in earshot of Becky or her sister.

* * *

Larry knew that there must have been several folks worried about him right now. He'd left his daughters at home that morning with barely a decent goodbye. He'd gone to see his friend Steven only to leave fairly abruptly when it didn't seem Steven understood anything he was saying. He wasn't exactly mad at Steven, how could he be? He really hadn't given him the opportunity to understand because Larry wasn't patient enough to explain it sufficiently. He wanted Steven to understand immediately.

But Steven himself put it all in perspective when he asked Larry how he'd feel if he were in Steven's shoes.

Larry knew exactly how he'd feel: he'd think Steven was fit for the funny farm is what he'd have thought.

It was the whole time travel thing that was doing it. No one would believe it unless they actually did it themselves, of that he was sure. But the haunting question was why would someone want to do it? What would cause someone to want to travel back in time?

Larry didn't think just anyone would go. Or maybe they would. But what reasons would they have?

Why was Larry doing it?

He knew why.

He was doing it do see Gracie again. She was taken from him so suddenly that he didn't get to say good-bye to her. And it wasn't fair. He didn't get to cherish those last hours with her. Obviously, he hadn't known they would be his last hours with her or he would have done things differently.

But would he really?

And yet if he was doing this whole time travel thing simply to spend time with her, why was he thinking of how he could change it? Big Ben had told him emphatically that it could not be changed. Time was as it was, period. Should that actually be time is as time is? It was confusing.

Still there was a whole host of intelligent science fiction authors who believed time could be changed, or so they purported in their novels. Larry was inclined to go along with them. It might not necessarily be a good thing to change time, but you could change it.

Change was possible, but the ramifications could be deadly serious.

And Larry himself couldn't see any reason why it couldn't be changed. He wasn't a scientist and certainly not the smartest guy in the room...but he wasn't an idiot, either. If you could travel back in time, why couldn't you do anything to change the outcome of something or some time in the past?

And what would happen if he did change it? What happened if he managed to be successful in his attempt? What happened with Gracie? What was going on with her now? Was she in heaven already or was she just in some sort of temporary place? All his life he'd heard "they're in a better place" when folks would refer to someone who'd just died. But were they really already there? How could anyone be sure of that? And if they were already there, how could he see her when he time-traveled?

Larry's understanding of death was that they simply went to sleep and wouldn't awaken again until Christ came back. He wasn't sure enough to bet the farm on it if he were a gambling man, but he felt fairly confident in that understanding.

What would happen if he could change it where she survived, how would that affect where she was now? Would this time, now-the real time-be simply a memory? Would he even be able to remember this? Would the changed time replace the old real time?

It was all beginning to confuse him so much that he couldn't think straight. But he didn't care that he didn't understand it and it didn't matter that Big Ben had said there could be no change. If a person could actually travel back in time, surely they were able to cause a change to occur somehow, someway.

At least put it this way: If it could be done, Larry would find a way to do it.

Snapping out of his daydream, Larry gently shook his head and focused his eyes. He'd come to the city park to get away from all his usual places so that he could think. He knew that there would likely be people looking for him, but he was okay. He had actually seen Brother Joe's car drive by twice and Larry knew Brother Joe should have been at the church work-day. There were many reasons he could think of for Brother Joe to not be at the church now. Looking for Larry was one of them.

If that's what he was doing, Larry appreciated the concern, but he was okay. He just needed a little space and a little time.

Yeah. Right. When had he ever needed time before? Whenever he'd heard that in the past, Larry always assumed someone was just feeding him a line. And even though he'd just thought the same thing, he knew it was a line.

The truth was he was focused on changing time and that wasn't something he was real comfortable talking about right now. How could he explain changing something to folks who didn't believe in that something to begin with? If you didn't believe in something, there was no use even bringing up how to change it.

Larry opened the bag on the bench beside him. He'd stopped by a Subway on his way to the park and picked up lunch. He just wanted to stay away all day and not worry about anyone else. He wanted to steer clear of any and all conversation until it was time for him to go home and go to bed.

And to travel again.

What he really wanted to do was to go home and go to sleep right now. But he was afraid if he did, the girls, or something or someone else would wake him up. Saturdays were busy days around the Pace home and with his being out of pocket, it was likely to be even busier. He wasn't really sure how being awakened would affect his time travel. If he were awoken during the middle of his sleep, would his travel be cut short? Would he pick it back up when he fell asleep again? Why hadn't he thought to ask Big Ben those questions?

There were so many things Larry didn't understand. But, he knew it worked. Just like so many things in the Bible, Larry didn't have to understand it, all he had to do was have faith that it was real.

He decided the park might not be the best place for him to hide out. He was surprised his truck hadn't been spotted yet.

He finished his sandwich and tossed the trash into the can near the bench as he made his way back to his truck, slurping his drink. He liked to eat on the ice after he'd finished a fountain drink, especially if it was crushed ice.

He decided to drive to the river just a few minutes away.

Near the bridge was a marina that was infrequently used and another city park that was used even less frequently. The only thing Larry remembered of the marina was the time that the replica of Christopher Columbus's ship docked so all the local school kids could come see. Ever curious, Larry took a trip to see it as well, and was surprised at how small it was. Columbus was a brave man to have ventured across the Atlantic Ocean in a ship like that.

Larry drove along the marina, looking for signs of activity. He saw none, as usual. He continued along the small road until he came to a parking lot near the shoreline.

Parking, he exited his truck carrying only the cup with ice in it. Shaking it every few steps, he brought the cup to his mouth to grab a fresh bite of ice. The ice nearly gone now, he stopped next to a trash can as he finished what was left. Depositing the cup in the trash can he sat on a small bench facing the water.

The bench was backed up and chained to a large oak tree less than five yards from the water. During the hottest hours of the day, the large branches shaded the bench. The shoreline had been reinforced with large rocks along the edge to help prevent erosion. Generally, the rocks were used to let people get their feet wet without sinking them down into the Alabama mud.

Larry heard voices off to his right and suddenly noticed a large gathering down at the pavilion. He immediately recognized a collection of international students grilling hotdogs and hamburgers, playing soccer and generally having a good time. Any other time, Larry would have ventured down to join them. He was pretty sure that one or two of them at the minimum had been students of his.

He searched to his left looking for another seat further away, but decided that they were having so much fun and focused on their own activities that they would never notice him. He'd noticed that most international students were that way anyway: in instances where most Americans would approach and speak, most international students would not.

Ignoring the noise, he shifted to the center of the bench and rested his head back against the tree. He stretched both arms out on the back of the bench and crossed his legs, right over the left. He used to come often, but it had been months since he was last here. He tried to remember the specifics, but couldn't.

Wait. He was with Gracie. They were also trying to escape that day. Something had happened at church that upset Gracie and the phone had been ringing off the hook with both gossipers and folks genuinely concerned about Gracie. Grace didn't want to talk to any of them, but she wasn't one who could let the phone ring if she was there. She felt not answering the phone was a form of dishonesty. Larry had tried to assure her in multiple ways that it was in no way dishonest to let their answering machine get it. After all, their message said they "couldn't get the phone" not that they "weren't home."

After an hour and twenty minutes of taking calls from concerned friends and ... others ... from church, Larry grabbed her by the arm and pulled her out to the car and the two drove around for an hour before stopping at the park.

Neither of them had ever been to the spot before and so were surprised to find the bench there. Oh sure, they'd been to several of the summer festivals the city held there, but they'd always sat way up near the stage, which was always a good distance from the water. Water and electricity don't mix well, and musicians generally want to be as far away from the water as possible.

"Dr. Pace?"

Larry jumped a little, the voice catching him completely off guard. His head scraped against the trunk of the tree where he had leaned back.

Sitting up, he rubbed the back of his head as he turned to look at the voice. Standing a few yards back and holding a Frisbee, which she had obviously just retrieved, was a small Japanese girl. And although Larry was warm in his shirt sleeves, the girl had on a light jacket, zipped up about half way.

"Yes," said Larry, as he stood.

"Hi. I thought was you. I'm Eiko. I took your class." She bowed slightly at the waist as she said hello. Not enough to really be a bow, but enough for an American to notice that that part of her culture hadn't gone away during her stay here.

"Yes," Larry said, though not really remembering her,

"How are you?"

"Fine."

"What are you doing out here?" asked Larry.

"International Student party," she answered. "You can come."

Larry smiled. "No thank you," he said. "I'm just out here trying to think by myself for a little while. Thank you for the invitation, though."

Eiko returned the smile and bowed slightly again as she said goodbye. Larry searched his memory, but couldn't place her. He'd met so many international students at the university, but they almost never came to see him once the semester was over. Sure, he'd see them on campus occasionally, but that was it. He was accustomed to waving at students he couldn't remember, and it always made him squirm a little when they asked him if he remembered them. He realized years ago that often the impact he made on the lives of students was greater than the impact students made on lives of teachers.

As she walked away and back to the group eagerly awaiting the return of their Frisbee, he caught movement out of the corner of his eyes just another few yards away. The movement was coming his way.

He turned and saw a man approaching.

Tom Morgan.

But how could he have known where Larry was? Chance?

As he neared, Larry could see an incredible grin on his face.

"Tom?" said Larry, "what in the world are you doing out here?" Larry took a few steps toward Tom and extended his hand.

"The same thing you are, I'd bet," answered Tom, taking Larry's offered hand and shaking it.

"I highly doubt that," said Larry, as he chuckled lowly.

"What? You mean you're not out here to escape it all?" asked Tom. It was Larry's turn to grin. He was indeed out here to escape, but he was willing to bet they were escaping completely different things.

"Well," Larry began, "yes, and no. I'm more out here to be alone with my thoughts than to escape."

"That sounds like escaping to me," said Tom.

"Humph. Well, maybe. If I stayed at home, the phone would be ringing with folks asking why I'm not where I'm supposed to be and my daughters would be asking me a million questions that I'm just really not prepared to answer yet."

"Time travel, right?" asked Tom. He circled the tree and sat down on the bench Larry had previously occupied. Larry noticed he was careful enough to sit on one end, leaving plenty of room for Larry to sit again, although not in the center as he had been earlier.

"Yeah," answered Larry, as he sat on the opposite end of the bench. "That's just a tough one to explain."

"I haven't told anyone about it," said Tom, "have you?"

"Yeah," answered Larry, "yeah I have. I don't have many secrets in my life, really. But my explanation didn't exactly go the way I expected it to go."

"Sounds like my entire life," guffawed Tom.

"Huh? What do you mean by that?" asked Larry.

"Oh, just ignore me."

The two men sat in silence for a few minutes. Larry couldn't tell by the tone of Tom's voice whether he really wanted to be ignored or whether that was an open door for discussion. Larry decided not to press that direction, but he couldn't sit quietly with Tom at his elbow.

"So, Tom," he started, not able to stay quiet for long. "Why do you time travel?"

"Same as you, I guess."

Larry laughed. "You're at least ten years younger than me, we can't do *everything* for the same reasons!" Larry's laughter was contagious and Tom laughed with him.

"I don't know," said Tom. "I haven't been doing this as long as you think. I've only done this since your wife-since the accident."

"Really?" asked Larry, truly surprised. "You're right. I did think you'd been doing this longer. What made you go the first time?"

Tom sighed a long, deep sigh. So deep that his lips pursed as if he were really forcing the air out of his lungs. Larry had hit some nerve, he could tell, but maybe not a bad one.

"Y'know," Tom started, "the first time I really wanted to set things right."

154

"Things?" asked Larry.

"Yeah. Y'know, with the accident and your wife and all. As I said, my life hasn't really gone the way I expected it to go. Most of it has been my fault. Mostly I've just screwed up my own life. But after the accident I came to the realization that I was screwing up the lives of so many other people.

"I don't know," he said after a short pause, "I just thought I could put your life back the way it should be before I messed it up."

"I see," said Larry. "You said 'the first time.' Why did you travel after that?"

"Man," Tom sighed again, not as deeply this time, but with more flair. "You go right for the hard questions, don't you?"

Larry laughed again, "It's the teacher in me."

"After I realized what a cool thing it was, I wanted to remember if I was ever really worth anything. When I went to sleep, I wanted to go to a time when I thought I might have meant something." Tom's voice trailed off as he remembered the trip.

"And?" Larry said, after a few moments of silence.

"Ahh," Tom picked back up, "my life has pretty much always been the same. Worthless."

Tom sat up on the edge of the bench, picked up a stick near his feet and propped his elbows on his knees as he fiddled with the stick.

"My life is nothing like yours," he said, finally.

"Mine?" asked Larry. "What could you possibly know about my life?"

"Well, you just lost your wife because of some idiot- that's me and not Mike-and you hold conversations with the guys responsible. You even pray for Mike every day. That's just plain not right. It's not normal."

Larry grinned. "There is nothing I am that I can take credit for," he said. "Anything and everything I am is purely because of God's grace."

"There you go with the God stuff again."

"Tom," he began, his voice taking on the tone of a lecture, "You yourself just said there was something different about my life. All I'm doing is telling you what it is."

"Okay," Tom replied, "then if you're so caught up in all the God stuff, why do you time travel?"

155

The question gave Larry pause. He hadn't expected Tom to turn the question back around on him. He had expected what he'd gotten, but not to have the question thrust upon him.

"Well, you may not believe me," Larry began, "but that's just what I was out here asking myself. What really, am I trying to accomplish by time traveling? At the bottom of it, I want to think that maybe I have some sort of death wish, or suicide mentality. Y'know, the time travel is addictive and I continue to do it and then bam! I'm dead because I traveled so much.

"While I'm not afraid to die, I certainly don't want to bring it on before my time. Which leads to the other question: *can* I bring it on early? If I believe all this 'God stuff,' as you put it, don't I believe that God has the appointed time and place for me? Can paying for time-travel really shorten my life, make me die earlier than what God had planned? And what happens to the changes - if we can indeed make them - or to the people whose lives are affected?"

Larry left the question hanging. Tom was staring at the stick in his hand, turning it over and slowly peeling the bark away.

"Those are some deep questions," he finally said.

"Yeah," laughed Larry, "that's why I'm out here."

Tom laughed, tossed the stick toward the river, but it fell short, being too light and small to make that short distance.

"What about your family, Tom?" asked Larry. "Don't you have family around here? It distresses me to hear anyone say they are worthless."

"Nah," he answered. "My parents died when I was in college and I'm an only child. Dad moved the family down here from upstate New York and so any extended family I have are all still up that way. I don't really know any of them."

Tom reached to the ground and picked up another stick. Larry could tell there was something left unsaid and so he kept quiet hoping Tom would continue. There was something soothing about sitting on the edge of a river with no real noise of modernity swarming around you.

"I've got an ex-wife and a kid, too," he finally said. "I don't ever see them, though. I agreed to it that way when

156

we divorced. I didn't want to have anything to do with her or the baby. I didn't even try to get visitation rights."

It became clear to Larry where Tom must have thought his life had messed up. Divorce is never easy on anyone, despite the way Hollywood always dresses it up.

"Do you want reconciliation now?" asked Larry.

"Are you kidding?" said Tom. "Even if I did, she would never in a million years consider it. I did her wrong in a multitude of ways. Heck, if I was her I wouldn't take me back. Let's just say that I was very incredibly mean."

"Fair enough," said Larry, deciding once again not to press the issue.

"But y'know," said Tom-he paused and closed his eyes as if seeking information hidden deep inside-"you never really answered my question, I don't think."

"You mean why I travel?" Larry asked.

"Yeah."

"I think I did," answered Larry. "The real answer is that I'm not sure."

"So you're beginning to question whether God is real or not?" asked Tom.

"Absolutely not," said Larry. "I know He's real because I've turned my life over to Him. But my belief doesn't stop me from ever having the same sort of questions you have. Tom, I'm just loaded with questions."

Once again, the two men sat in silence.

"Do you think it'll work?" asked Tom after several minutes.

"I don't know. But I am ready to try it."

Tom didn't have to explain that question to Larry. He knew Tom was asking if he thought they could change history together. Larry had answered him honestly. He didn't know and he was ready to get to sleep now.

* * *

When Larry returned home, both his daughters were waiting for him in the living room. It was obvious by the untouched plate of food at his regular spot on the table that they had both expected him to be there for supper. He had no idea how long they had waited, but they had eaten and had cleaned up afterwards, leaving only his untouched plate on the table.   If nothing else, it was a means of communicating to their dad without saying anything.

Neither of his daughters heard him enter and tiptoe to the doorway that connected the kitchen to the living room.

"Evening girls," he said. Both girls jumped at the sound of his voice.

"Daddy!" they answered in unison and jumped up to see him. Both girls made a mad dash for him almost as if they were racing.

"Where have you been?" asked Becky, "We've been so worried about you." Both girls grabbed him around the waist and squeezed. They nearly knocked him over.

"Ooofff," he said as they squeezed the breath out of him. "Not so hard, girls. You're not ten anymore."

They relaxed their grip and each girl grabbed a hand as if to pull him into the living room. He pulled his hands back out of their grasps, staying in the doorway.

"Uh-uh, girls. I'm going straight to bed," he said.

"What? To bed? Again?" asked Cindy. "Already?"

"It's 9 o'clock," he answered. "It's not too late for any sane human being to hit the sack."

"Daddy," began Becky, "there's so much we need to ask you. Can't you come in and sit with us for a few minutes?"

"No." His answer was firm. "You don't understand," he said, "I'm anxious to get to bed. I want to go to bed right now. I need to go to bed right now. I *will* go to bed right now."

The two girls couldn't believe what they were hearing. Where had he been? What had he been doing all day? So many people had asked them those questions at the church work day, and they were both embarrassed because they had no idea how to answer.

"Dad," said Becky, beginning to visibly show some anger, "you've been acting too weird lately and we feel like you owe us an explanation."

"Becky, hon, I appreciate your concern, but I'm fine." Larry turned and moved into the kitchen. He took the keys out of his pocket and started to set them on the table but then thought better of it. If he knew his daughters-and he did-they could very well take his keys and hide them from him in an attempt to keep him at home. He stuck them back in his pocket.

"There are some things," he said, and then stopped himself before he said something more he'd have to explain, "let's just say there are some things I have to work through."

"But you're wrong about one thing," he said, turning his back to them and moving down the hallway to his bedroom.

"What's that?" said Cindy.

"I don't 'owe' you anything. I am still the parent around here. I've always been open and honest with you both, but there are some things I have to work through on my own and just because I don't feel like discussing them with you at the moment doesn't mean that I owe you anything."

Cindy had had enough. "You're not the only one who lost something," she said angrily. "We lost our mom, too!"

Larry stood silent for a moment, stunned not only at the words she'd spoken, but the tone she'd taken with him. He couldn't recall a time since before she was about ten years old that she'd ever spoken to him that way.

"Go to your room," he said, sounding much angrier than he really was. Cindy stood wide-eyed as Becky looked at her in shock. In shock both at the way she'd spoken to their father and in shock at what he'd said to her.

"Go to my room?" Cindy asked. Her tone this time held not an ounce of disrespect, instead it was fully posed as if she was unsure exactly what she'd heard.

Larry stood silent for a moment staring from one daughter to the other.

"You're right," he finally said. "Do whatever you want. I'm going to *my* room. Which is what I'd wanted to do from the minute I walked in the door." He walked down the short hallway to his bedroom door.

"Goodnight, girls," he said, not looking back at them. "Be sure to lock the doors before you go to bed." With that, he closed-and locked-the door behind him.

Changing into his pajamas, he grabbed his Bible to read before closing his eyes. He turned off the light, hopped in bed and pulled the covers up. He reached over and turned on the light on his nightstand. He pulled his Bible up on his lap as he inched up into a sitting position.

Without opening his Bible, Larry looked at the empty spot next to him. Even though she wasn't there, Larry could feel Gracie's presence. Reaching over with his right hand, he placed his hand on the pillow where her head would have been.

He began to cry.

Larry pulled her pillow up next to him and squeezed it into his chest and face, his tears soaking the pillow.

"I'll see you in just a few minutes," he said into the pillow. "I'm going to change what happened and you'll come back to me."

Larry sobbed. It was a soft sob, but one of true heartfelt pain. And even though he sobbed into the pillow, his daughters standing just outside the door could barely hear him. Quietly reaching to the doorknob, they tried to turn it and discovered it was locked. Giving up for the night, they returned to the living room where they, too, sobbed into the arms of the other.

* * *

Exhausted from sobbing, Larry turned over on his stomach and pulled Gracie's pillow up under his face and squeezed it up close to him.

"Would you like bacon and eggs this morning?" asked Gracie.

Startled, Larry opened his eyes to find it was Gracie he had wrapped up in his arms and not her pillow. He sat straight up in bed, causing his arms to be pulled quickly away from Gracie.

"Oww," she said. "What'd you do that for?"

The light was off in the room, but Larry didn't remember ever turning it off.

"What time is it?" he asked, stumbling-no, falling out of bed to get a good look at their alarm clock.

"Well, seeing as how the alarm just went off, I'd be willing to bet it is 6:30. Now answer my question or I'm just going to lie right here in bed."

"What question?" Larry asked, getting up off his knees and sitting on the bed. He wiped his eyes with the palm of his hands. Had he really fallen asleep? He couldn't remember even being close to sleep.

"Would you like me to fix you some bacon and eggs this morning?" Gracie repeated.

"Yes. I would love bacon and eggs," he said.

"Okay," she said, "I'll fix them while you're in the shower."

Larry turned to look at Gracie.

"Gracie?"

"Yes, dear?"

"This is just plain strange," he said. "Talk about déjà vu."

He felt the bed move as Gracie got out of the bed.

"You get up every morning, dear. Nothing strange about that. Now you grab your shower," she said momentarily from the hallway, "I'll get breakfast started."

Larry shaved and showered. Opening the bathroom door to release all the pent-up steam and to clear the mirror, Larry yelled out the door.

"Gracie!"

In just a few seconds, he heard her voice from the bedroom door, "what do you need, honey?"

"I love you," he said, peeking around the corner to see her standing in the doorway with a spatula in her hand.

"I love you, too," she said. "I've got to get back to the kitchen unless you want burned bacon. Now get dressed and come on to the table."

Hurrying to his closet, he grabbed a pair of slacks and a shirt and quickly dressed. He was buttoning his shirt as he walked down the hallway to the kitchen.

"What's today?" he asked. He wanted to make sure it was the right day. He wondered if time traveling this way could ever send you back to the wrong day. In so many movies and books about time traveling, hitting the correct day in the past often made for many plot points. But there were no dials or gadgets to depend on the way he was doing it. At least none that he knew of.

"Wednesday," Gracie answered, pulling the bacon off the skillet. Her back was to Larry as he pulled a chair out from under the table to sit down. "Will you come home early today and go up to the church with me?"

Was this the opportunity to change things? Had she asked him that before? If so, then it was his fault for everything that had happened. He could have come home and stopped the accident from ever happening.

"Why yes, dear," he said matter-of-factly, "I think I

would love to do just that."

Gracie turned and looked at him over the rim of her glasses. She had that don't-get-smart-with-me-mister look on her face.

"What?" he said defensively.

"You're being smart, aren't you?" she asked.

"Of course not," he answered. "I think it would be a good thing for me to come home and help you out at the church."

"What are you gonna do about your classes?"

"Ohh," he said, feigning deep thought. "I'll just give them some homework or something and let them do it on their own time."

"Well," she began, "I'll call you today at lunch." Gracie put a plate on the table in front of him and one at her place. She went back to the stove and brought back two more plates and set them in the girls' spots.

"Girls!" she yelled over Larry's head. "Get down here! Breakfast is ready." Gracie sat down across from Larry.

"Oh!," she said as she snapped her fingers. "I forgot. Actually, I'm planning to go see Betty today. God's really been dealing with me about her and I've decided to go see her."

"I thought y'all had that all straightened out," said Larry, trying to suggest to her not to go. She was headed to Betty's when she was killed.

"No," she answered, "we-I never did."

"It's not just you," said Larry, "remember what you always tell me: it takes two to argue. I think you should just wait and talk to her after church tonight."

"Catch who after church," said a sleepy voice just entering the kitchen.

"Good morning, sleepyhead," said Gracie to their oldest daughter as she sat down at the table.

"Where's Cindy?" asked Larry.

"Sleeping, Dad," Becky answered through a yawn. "You should just let her sleep. It's summer!"

"Well, it wouldn't hurt her to get up and eat breakfast with her family. You just never know when it will be your last meal with someone you love."

"I'll get her up when you leave, dear," said Gracie, ever playing the role of the mediator.

162

"Fine," said Larry. "I can't win when y'all gang up on me." He took a big bite of bacon and eggs.

"Dad?" said Becky, looking at him as if he'd lost his mind. "Prayer?"

"Oh!" said Larry through his mouth stuffed with food. "I forgot. You pray."

"Don't talk with your mouth full, dear," said Gracie, "it's a bad example for the children." Gracie winked at Becky as Becky giggled.

Becky said a short prayer asking for blessings on their food and their day while Larry finished up the bite he had in his mouth.

"Amen," he said. "Let's get back to Betty. If you go see her, you're admitting to her that she is right. And you know good and well she is not."

"I know she's not," said Gracie. "But it's not a matter of who's right and who's wrong. It's a matter of what's right and what's wrong. Don't you agree?"

"Humph," he said. "Maybe. You just never know what's going to happen. Accidents happen every day."

"Oh please," she said, a bite of bacon still crunching in her mouth. "You know good and well I am not going to stay in this house afraid of what might happen to me if I set foot outside. I'm no paranoid Patty. Seriously, Larry."

"Well," he began, "what if I just asked you nicely not to go?"

"Larry," said Gracie, "what has gotten into you this morning? Why are you wanting me to ignore what God is telling me?"

Becky looked from parent to parent during the exchange while eating her breakfast. Both his daughters had always been very in tune with what was going on with their parents. Larry figured all kids were that way, but really noticed his.

"No," he finally answered, "of course not." Larry took another bite of food to give himself time to think before he spoke again.

"I just wonder," he continued, "if this is the best way to respond to what God is telling you to do."

"Well," she said, "I'm not going to pull a Jonah. I'm not running from it."

Larry struggled to remember the exact words of their conversation before. It struck him as odd that he could

163

remember the conversations pretty clearly, but then he couldn't remember the exact words. He was often that way in real-time, too, remembering conversations, but not exact words.

After they'd finished breakfast, Gracie cleared away all the plates and cleaned up while Larry returned to his bathroom and brushed his teeth and finished his final preparations to go to work.

He thought momentarily about just staying home with Gracie and spending time with her. If he stayed, maybe he could convince her through the course of the day just to stay with him and wait and see Betty later.

But then he remembered the plans he'd made with Tom and decided he couldn't throw those out the window. If he did, he'd never know whether it could be changed or not. He had to follow through with the plan, even if that meant leaving Grace for now.

When he returned to the kitchen, Gracie stood holding his lunch for him near the back door. She followed him through the utility room the same as she did every morning he went to work. The same as she'd been doing since the day they were married.

Larry opened the door to leave and stopped. He turned to Gracie and looked her deeply in her eyes. He didn't want to leave, but he was counting on this plan to work and he'd have her back again.

"I love you," he finally said.

"I love you, too," she said. She kissed and hugged him and then ushered him out the door.

"Have a good day," she said. "I'll call you at lunch time to find out exactly what time you'll be home."

After a short drive to the school, he moved like a zombie through the parking lot. He made his way to his good friend Steven Dale's office and knocked on the door. After waiting for a moment, he remembered that in real time, Steven was still off on a mission trip.

He'd come to rely so heavily on their friendship and his Christian encouragement, it was almost depressing when his friend was unavailable.

Entering his own office, he found there were no messages of importance for him either on his email or his voice mail. It was this way nearly every morning as he was one of the

164

first to arrive on campus and the communication and spam systems hadn't had a chance to kick into gear just yet.

He walked downstairs to the department office to see who else had arrived and to check his faculty mailbox. The office door was locked and the lights were off. As he fished for the key on his key ring, a student entered through the side door.

"Good morning, Dr. Pace," said the student.

"Good morning," Larry returned, not immediately remembering the student's name.

"I want to take another one of your classes in the fall," said the student, "do you know what you'll be teaching?"

Larry went down the list of classes he was scheduled to teach. The student stated he'd be taking one of them. Larry said he'd look forward to having the student in class again.

Larry grabbed the stack of mail from his box and locked the door on his way back out. He'd no more than taken a few steps away when the secretary entered through the side door. Larry smiled and said good morning, but proceeded to his office.

He sat at his desk and began flipping through the mail that had come through departmental office. Even though he had his own post office box on campus, many people simply sent him mail care of the department.

Then he spotted it.

It was such an exciting moment for him but he kept forgetting it because of all that was going on with the whole time travel thing and Gracie. It was hard for him to understand how he could be so excited this third time, but he was. It still felt like the first time.

He tore the envelope open even though he knew the contents already. He examined it and found it to be exactly as it had been the previous two times. Still, though, he was excited. He'd written, and now sold, his first novel. He wasn't trained to do it, he'd never even been in a book or writing club before. Sure, he knew folks who claimed to be writers, but most of them did more talking than writing.

He folded the letter and put it in the left breast pocket of his coat. He patted it to ensure it was firmly planted and wouldn't fall out.

Larry immediately picked up the phone to call Gracie.

He punched in the first six numbers and then stopped.

He wasn't going to call her, was he?

Yes, he would! He would force himself to do it and that would prove that time could be changed and he wouldn't have to wonder through the rest of the day.

So he dialed the numbers again, this time punching all seven. He began to sweat a little, but it confused him. He wasn't afraid to call his own wife. He wasn't nervous to talk to her.

No, he was sweating because he anxiously thought it would work and that he would be able to change things and he was excited about it.

The phone rang.

Larry loosened his tie.

"Hello" said the voice that picked up.

Larry hung his head. It was his voice on the answering machine instructing him that no one could come to the phone and to leave a message.

He hung up without leaving a message, disappointed. Where could Gracie have gotten to so early?

His disappointment didn't last long, though. Instead it turned to excitement. The first two times Larry had not been able to complete the call. He couldn't even dial the last digit on their phone number. This time he had, so he had changed time! It could be changed!

He was so excited he wanted to tell somebody. But a glance at his clock quickly reminded him it was time for the first class of the day to begin.

He picked up his textbook and notes and made his way across campus to his first class. He'd been teaching this stuff so long, he felt, that he could do it without any notes or a textbook. Or at least with his eyes closed. But he took the books and notes anyway, lest the students accuse him of making this stuff up.

He blazed through his first class and the one that followed, thinking of nothing more than being able to fix time and to have Gracie alive again. He was anxious, but the clock was dragging as time seemed to move so slowly.

When he arrived back in his office, the light on his phone was flashing indicating someone had left a message. It was Gracie. She told him that she did indeed want him to come home early and join her. She was stepping out now, but she would be back in time for when he returned and they could go up to the church together. She thanked him for offering to do that and said she loved him and would see him at home.

He hung up the phone quickly. He was more excited than ever now. He looked at his watch. It was 12:45. It was going to work! He couldn't believe it. What would Big Ben say to all this?

Tom Morgan had told him he didn't arrive at Grady T's until around 2 that afternoon. Mike had been there waiting on him when he arrived. It wasn't until after they left that the accident had occurred.

Larry grabbed his keys, his gradebook, and his lunch and headed out the door. He took the steps two at a time. He missed the last one and his foot twisted and he fell into the door, slamming his shoulder into the wall.

It hurt like fire, but he was thankful otherwise he'd have fallen headfirst out into the first floor hallway.

He hurried out to his truck, tossing his lunch and gradebook in before him. He cranked the truck and pulled out of the parking lot. Tom had given him directions to his apartment to pick him up. He knew exactly where the complex was. Fortunately, Tom lived only three or four minutes from campus.

Larry struggled to hold his speed down in his excitement to reach Tom's apartment. His tires squealed more than once as he took a turn a little too fast.

He pulled into the apartment complex and threw his truck in park. He jumped out and hurried up the steps to Tom's door. He knocked loudly, almost afraid Tom wouldn't be there.

The door opened and Tom stood holding a remote control in his hand.

"Dr. Pace?" he asked as he opened the door for him to enter.

"Yes," said Larry, "you know me, right?"

"Yes," said Tom, still sounding slightly confused.

Larry looked around the apartment. Tom was a genuine slob. There were clothes, books, magazines, cds, dvds, games, you name it spread all over the place. Larry noticed a single clear pathway from the door where he was standing to the couch. And, intersecting with that path was a pathway from the couch to the kitchen. The kitchen floor was relatively free of clutter, but the cabinets and counters were not.

Larry noticed an odd smell, but wrote it off as old pizza as evidenced by the dozen or so pizza delivery boxes laying here and there.

"Do you remember our plan?" asked Larry.

"Yes," said Tom, slowly realizing what was going on. "It's still foggy, but I do remember."

Larry noticed the television was on and stole a glance.

"Hey!" he said, "*It's a Wonderful Life* is on."

Tom looked back at Larry like he was an idiot.

"What?" said Larry, "I love this movie."

"You love this movie?" asked Tom.

"Sure," Larry answered, "who doesn't?"

Tom pressed a button on the remote and the screen froze in place. George Bailey was frozen with a cigar in his hand in Mr. Potter's office.

"It's my favorite movie of all time," he said. Tom pressed another button and the television flicked off. "Most of my friends won't even watch it at Christmas. But c'mon, let's go down and meet Mike."

Tom grabbed keys from off the top of his microwave and followed Larry out the front door.

"Y'know" started Larry as the two men hurried to his truck, "that movie is all about the positive contributions a single man's life has on the world."

"I know," said Tom.

"Well," continued Larry, "the other day you mentioned to me how your life was-how did you put it? I think you even used the very word 'worthless.'"

"Did I?" asked Tom.

"Your words, not mine," Larry said.

"And your point is what?" asked Tom as he opened the passenger door to Larry's truck. Larry opened his own door and scooted in behind the steering wheel. He didn't want to answer while they were half-in half-out of the truck. Tom might not hear him.

"George thought his life was worthless, but God-through the angel Clarence-helped him see how wrong he was."

Tom sat silent as Larry cranked the truck and began to pull out of the parking lot. Grady T's was close enough they could have walked. Tom had stated he'd done as much his first time around. But neither man wanted to walk out in the hot sun right now and Larry had suggested if they needed to go somewhere else quickly, they'd have the truck waiting.

"Do you know where Grady T's is?" asked Tom.

"Yeah," answered Larry, noting that Tom had changed the subject without answering. "So what do you think about what I said," he asked.

"I'm sorry," said Tom, "did you ask me a question?"

"It wasn't so much a question, I guess, as a statement."

"I heard what you said," said Tom, "but I think you're forgetting that it's just a movie."

"No, I'm not forgetting that," said Larry. "But you'll have to admit that there are a lot of truths in movies."

"There are a lot of falsehoods, too" Tom answered. "I appreciate what you're trying to say, really I do. But let's just get to Grady T's and take care of the business at hand."

Tom had no more completed his statement than Grady T's came into view. The parking lot was mostly empty. It wasn't a big lunchtime restaurant. Come back around 10 that night and the place would be packed.

"I don't see Mike's car," said Tom, scanning the parking lot. As the two men exited the truck, Tom continued to look around as if maybe he'd missed it the first time.

"Maybe you actually beat him here," suggested Larry.

"Maybe," said Tom. He sounded unconvinced.

"I've never been here before," noted Larry as the cold air struck both men when he opened the door to the restaurant.

"Decent place," said Tom, "not the best in town, but not the worst, either."

"Nice fountain," said Larry, pointing to the decorative water fountain just inside the doors. He leaned over the pool below, secretly looking for goldfish. He liked to see the big ones swimming around.

"Hmm. I don't guess I ever noticed it before," said Tom. "This way," he continued and led Larry off to the right and in the direction of the bar.

"What time is it?" he asked Larry as he hiked himself up on one of the bar stools. Larry looked at his watch and took the stool beside him.

"1:10," he answered.

"I think it was about 2:30 when I got here in real time."

"Real time?" asked Larry. He'd toyed with all the potential labels for what really transpired and what was time travel, but never really came to any conclusion he liked.

"Yeah," answered Tom. He looked puzzled. "Y'know, I'm not real sure how to identify what really happened and each trip back. Does that make sense?"

"Unfortunately, it does. I have...I had?...the same problem."

"Hi Tom," said the bartender emerging from a door behind a big wall of alcohol. "Your usual today?"

"Nah, not today," Tom answered, trying to secretly nod his head in the direction of Larry to indicate to the bartender that he wasn't going to drink alcohol because of the man beside him. "Beer-man...uh...bartender, meet Larry Pace-Dr. Larry Pace."

"Dr. Pace," he said. "Actually, I had one of your classes a few years back."

"What grade did you get?" asked Larry playfully.

"I think it was a B," he answered. "I'm not really sure."

"Good," said Larry, "that means I can drink what you give me, right?" All three men laughed. "I'll have a coke," said Larry, "and give it to me straight and strong."

Larry regretted saying it the minute it came out of his mouth. He must have really sounded like a dweeb and probably did nothing to enhance the image of a non-drinker. To say nothing of a believer. I'll have a coke was a strong enough statement alone.

Maybe he'd have to time travel now just to correct that! He laughed to himself and Tom thought he was still laughing about the statement, further heaping coal on the fire.

"Okay," Larry finally said if for no other reason than to shift gears. "So now we just wait. What time were you supposed to meet him?"

"About 2:30, I think. I was late, I remember that much. But frequently Mike's early anyway. He's just that kind of guy."

"Hey beer-man...ah...bartender!" said Tom. The bartender returned with two big glasses of coke.

"Here ya go," he said, "two cokes straight out of the fountain and as strong as we've got."

Larry smiled at the bartender's humor. It was mighty nice of him to cater to Larry's foolish attempt at humor. Heck, though, the man lived off tips, he had to be used to idiots. Being nice to fools couldn't have been easy, especially drunk ones.

"What do you think about time travel," Tom asked the bartender, not skipping a beat.

The bartender wiped a spot on the bar, Larry hadn't seen anything there to begin with, and then tossed the towel across his left shoulder.

"Time travel," he began. "I dunno. Would be fun, I think. I wouldn't mind going to see some cool historical events."

"Like what?" asked Larry.

"Like maybe the battle of Thermopylae."

"Thermopylae?"

"Yeah, you know," said the bartender, "when the three hundred Spartans whipped the entire Persian army."

"That's not a common historical highlight, is it?" asked Larry. He knew a little about the battle, but not much. While he was interested in military history, it was primarily American military history.

"I don't know about how common it might be," answered the bartender, "but all serious students of war know about it."

"Serious?" asked Larry.

"Well, once I was," said the bartender. "I was a history major for a while."

"What happened?" asked Larry.

"I found my calling," he said, spreading his arms as if to reveal the bar around him. "I can mix and serve drinks like no one else in town."

Larry wasn't sure that was something to be proud of, but he sure wasn't about to offer up judgment to the man. If he did, there was no telling what might be included with his next coke.

Tom and Larry continued to carry on the conversation about time travel and to discuss all the interesting historical events one could go see on a time machine. Every now and then, the bartender would poke his head in and offer up some words and then he'd disappear behind the bar periodically. Larry noticed that he'd never really side with either him or Tom regarding what might be the better trip. Instead, he'd actually pose questions to the two that would get Larry and Tom debating again. He wasn't really contributing to the conversation, but he sure was heaping coals on the fire when the debate began to die down. Once he noticed it, Larry found the idea very amusing.

Time continued to tick by, however, and around 2:55 the men began to get very antsy. Tom began to pace back and forth from the front door to the bar. Larry was waterlogged from downing nearly four full glasses of coke. His stomach sloshed when he moved. He realized that had he been an alcohol drinker, he likely would have been pretty drunk at that point.

"Why don't we hop in my truck and go look for him," suggested Larry. "You know where he works, right?"

Larry paced to the door and back once more before answering.

"Yeah," he finally said. "Let's go. He should have been here by now, and I can't take this waiting anymore." With that, he turned on his heel and headed straight for the door. Larry looked over near his glass and searched for a tip. Tom had left none. Larry dug in his wallet and left a tip large enough for the both of them, realizing that the cokes and nearly two hours had been mighty expensive.

Tom was waiting next to the door when Larry finally walked out of the restaurant. Had he been in his wife's car, he could have clicked a button on his key chain and unlocked the doors. His truck, however, wasn't equipped with such modern conveniences.

"Where are we going?" asked Larry. He unlocked and opened his door, clicking the auto-unlock to let Tom open the passenger door.

"Out on Cox Creek," said Tom, "near the mall. We can be there in five minutes."

"Do you know if he has a special way to get here?" asked Larry, inching the truck forward but not committing to a direction.

"I don't really know. I don't think he cuts through, if that's what you mean," said Tom. "I think he takes Florence Boulevard all the way to Tennessee Street."

"Okay," said Larry, turning right out of the parking lot

and onto Tennessee Street. "That's the way we'll go. You keep your eyes peeled for him."

They hadn't gone more than a mile after turning onto Florence Boulevard when the traffic began to back up. Larry was afraid this would cause Mike to take a side street. Larry knew *he* frequently did that when there was a traffic jam.

"You don't think he'd turn off, do you?" asked Larry.

"Nah, I don't think so," answered Tom.

As they inched forward they spotted flashing lights up ahead. All sorts were there: blue ones, red ones and yellow ones.

"There's been an accident," said Larry. "Don't you think I should turn off to go around?" Tom did not immediately answer, and Larry looked over at him. The traffic was momentarily stopped, so he could easily study him without putting them in danger.

"Tom?" he said.

"No," Tom answered, though his mind was millions of miles away.

Larry suddenly had a frightening thought. What if Tom had been pulled away during his travel? What if this were the Tom from the real day, the one in the past? What if Tom of the future, though it wasn't really the future, it was Larry's current time-it all got so confusing-but what if something caused Tom to return and leave out of this time? Would this Tom know him? Would he have any idea what was going on?

For that matter, what if Larry was pulled out? It was still a question he had for Big Ben. What if one of his daughters banged so loudly on his bedroom door that it woke him up? Would that cause him to be yanked back to the time in which he belonged?

"Tom?" he said again, "are you okay?"

"That's Mike truck," said Tom, nodding ahead, "there it is."

Larry's heart sank. He searched the oncoming traffic for the truck. He'd seen it only once after the accident.

"I don't see it, Tom," he said frantically, "where is it?"

"It's behind the wrecker."

"Behind the-" Larry's mind raced, but he couldn't think of any words to say. What could this mean?

The wrecker pulled into traffic going the opposite way

and slowly drove off. The rubberneckers on the other side had caused traffic to remain slow even after they'd passed the scene of the accident.

Then, when they were about three cars from the police officer directing traffic, Larry spotted it. Gracie's car sat half in the median half in the left lane of the oncoming traffic. As far as he could tell, the car was empty—Gracie was not inside. The car looked exactly as it looked after the real accident...except this wasn't the right location. A second wrecker had backed up to the front of the car and a man was working to get it hooked up to pull it away.

Larry rolled his window down as they neared the police officer.

"Officer," he said.

"Move on," said the officer, sternly. "There's nothing to see here." Instead, Larry touched the brake, stopping his truck. He slammed the truck into park, still sitting in the middle of the road.

"Officer," he insisted, "that is my wife's car." Larry pointed to the vehicle. Can you tell me where my wife is?"

The disposition of the officer changed visibly. He walked quickly to Larry's window.

"I'm sorry, sir," he said, "If you'll pull over there the officer in charge will come see you and explain everything."

Larry immediately pulled his truck to the side of the road where the officer had pointed. Looking in his rear view mirror, he noticed the officer had stopped all traffic behind him to allow him to pull over. Larry stopped on the shoulder of the road just behind a patrol car.

Larry and Tom jumped out and walked quickly to the officer standing in front of the patrol car and holding a clipboard in his hand. Larry didn't catch all the words, but he could tell the people with the officer were witnesses to what happened.

"Officer," said Larry, interrupting. "That is my wife's car there." He pointed to the car still in the median. "Can you tell me what's going on?"

The officer set the clipboard down on the front of the car and excused himself from the witnesses. He took Larry by the shoulder and looked at Tom. He couldn't tell who Tom was, but he was accompanying Larry and therefore he allowed him to stay with him.

"Sir," said the officer once out of earshot of the witnesses, "I'm sorry to have to tell you that your wife was killed in this accident here. From all that we can tell, she was killed immediately."

"What about the guy in the Expedition?" asked Tom. The officer looked at him not sure how he knew of the other vehicle or of the passengers in it, but answered anyway.

"He's been taken to the hospital. He's in pretty serious condition." The officer continued to hold his hand on Larry's shoulder as Larry began to cry.

"Sir," continued the officer, "if you'll wait here, I'll be happy to take you where you need to go." He looked over at Tom again, still unsure of his role. "Are you his son?" asked the officer.

"No," answered Tom, "just a friend."

"I'm okay to drive," said Larry, and nodded for Tom to follow him.

"Sir," called the officer from behind them, "it's not a problem at all for us to do this if you'll just wait a moment."

Larry didn't answer nor did he look back. Without a word, he and Tom returned to the truck and pulled off onto a side road to avoid the traffic. Larry circled back around and took Tom back to his apartment.

"We tried," said Tom, as he opened the door. He could only imagine the pain Larry must be feeling, and feeling it all over for a second time as if it were brand new. In a sense, it was new. This wasn't how the accident happened the first time. So, for all practical purposes, it was a completely new death.

Tom was *in* the accident the first time. How could that have happened? How could he not have been in it?

Tom was visibly relieved because in this new reality, the accident wasn't his fault. He wasn't in the vehicle to be a distraction to Mike. It wasn't his fault.

"We'll have to try it again," he offered when Larry didn't respond. "We did change it, because I wasn't in the accident this time. So we've proved that time can be changed or altered. We've just got to figure out how to make it work for us. I wonder what Big Ben will say about this?"

Tom thought the words he said were floating to ears that weren't hearing. Larry sat staring at the steering wheel, seemingly lost in his own world. Tom really couldn't blame him.

But Larry heard every word he said. Before Tom could close the door, Larry looked over to him through eyes filled with tears.

"Think on it," he said to Tom.

"Think on what?"

"Think on what we can do the next time to ensure it doesn't happen," said Larry. "Think on what we can do to make sure we don't fail."

There was an edge to Larry's voice. It sent chills up Tom's spine.

"Yeah," he said. "I will."

Tom closed the door and Larry drove off. Once back at his home, Larry went straight to bed. He didn't remember what he'd done at this moment the first time around, but he didn't care. He was going to sleep so he could get back to his real time and buy another trip from Big Ben. Tom was right: They *had* proved it could be changed. What that meant and what the ramifications of it were, he didn't know. And at this point in time, he really didn't care.

Sunday, July 30

When Becky spotted Brother Joe, tears began to well up in her eyes. She and her sister had come alone to church that morning, the first time she could ever remember leaving either parent at home when they weren't sick. Their Dad had answered the knocks on the door with simple and stern replies to leave him alone.

"I can tell by the look on your face that it's not a good morning for you," said Brother Joe, taking the girl in his arms and giving her a very fatherly embrace.

"No," Becky answered, "it's not. Dad wouldn't even come out of his room for us to talk with him this morning. Just kept telling us to go away. We thought about not coming, just staying there with him. But then both of us realized this is the place we need to be."

"Is Cindy here?"

"Yeah," answered Becky, "she's already in her Sunday School class."

"Good. And you're right that this is where you need to be right now," answered Brother Joe. "Your Dad needs to see that you depend on your relationship with Christ and not your relationship with him. Love your Dad, but your relationship with Christ should always come first. I'd bet he's told you that himself."

"I know," started Becky, "but..."

"But it's a whole lot easier to say than to do, right?" asked Brother Joe.

"Yes," she answered, "it is."

"How's your sister holding up?" he asked, finally releasing Becky.

"Okay," she answered, "about as well as me, I guess. We've really been leaning on each other the past few days."

"Have you seen Steven-Dr. Dale this morning?" Brother Joe asked.

"No," she answered.

"Don't you worry about it. Head on to your class and I'll find him and fill him in." Brother Joe gave Becky another fatherly hug and ushered her on her way. No sooner had she turned the corner than Steven Dale came from the other direction.

"I was just about to look for you," said Brother Joe. "I just saw Becky. Larry's not here this morning."

"Yeah," answered Steven, "I figured as much. I just came from his class and they were sitting patiently without a teacher. I took the liberty of moving them all to Bob's class. Hope that's okay."

"That's fine," answered Brother Joe.

"What're we going to do about Larry?" Steven finally said to break the silence.

"We've got to love him up," said Brother Joe, "but we've also got to point out that he's getting out of line."

"Missing one day of church and a church work day is hardly getting out of line," answered Steven.

"You're right, of course," continued Brother Joe, "But that's not what I'm talking about. I'm talking about what he's doing to his daughters. Would you not agree that he's getting out of line there?"

Steven thought for a moment. Larry was his best friend. He'd known him for many years. Like anyone, Larry had missed Sundays here and there for various reasons. They were never really legalistic about that. They both believed that when the brethren were meeting, true believers had a desire to be there, but it wasn't always possible to be in the church every time the doors were open.

But they also both agreed that it was the way you lived your life when no one was looking that was the true test of Christianity. What did one do behind closed doors? There were many days-and nights-that their families would fellowship with one another. After years of that, you had a pretty good idea of what someone was like.

And Larry had certainly not been himself lately-especially in regards to his actions toward his daughters.

"I don't know how I'd respond or react to the death of Linda," Brother Joe said of his wife. "I can't honestly say how I'd respond. Would I retreat into a shell? Would I push away my friends? Would I be angry at God? I like to tell myself that I'm strong enough in my relationship with God that I wouldn't blame Him. But, I don't know, I haven't walked that path.

"I don't think, though, that I'd make up time-travel stories."

"Yes," said Steven finally, "I agree."

"Then we go see him immediately following the church service. Before anything else. How does that sound to you?"

"Fine," said Steven. "What if he's not there?"

"Then we try again later," answered Brother Joe. "And again later if he isn't there then. And later. We try until we get him. He's our brother and we need to show him that we love him and care about him and want to help him through this time of pain and confusion."

"Okay, then," said Steven, "I'll pick you up at the back door immediately following the service. I'll try to get Christy to come up with something to keep Becky and Cindy busy for a little while after. Maybe we can get them over in the nursery or something."

"Good idea," said Brother Joe. "I'll meet you at the back door after the service."

* * *

Were you a little distracted during the sermon, preacher?" asked Steven as Brother Joe opened the door to his car.

"Could you tell?" asked Brother Joe, very serious about the question. He sat down in the passenger seat beside Steven.

"Nah, not really," laughed Steven. "I was just giving you a hard time."

"Actually, my mind was on Larry," Brother Joe answered, closing the car door behind him. "Don't get me wrong, I was prepared for the sermon, I'd studied and prayed about it all week. But I just kept thinking about Larry. I missed his 'Amens' during the service."

The drive to Larry's took approximately fifteen minutes. For most of the drive, Brother Joe prayed from the passenger seat, prayed earnestly for Larry.

Arriving at Larry's, they spotted his truck still in the

open garage. Steven pulled his car around to the left of the garage. They hoped that Larry hadn't seen them drive up and would answer the knock on the garage door.

Taking a deep breath, they knocked.

They heard Larry's voice from within.

"-forget your keys?" came the question as he opened the door. Larry was dressed in sweat pants, a t-shirt and socks. His hair was unkempt. He hadn't showered yet this morning and showed no sign of even attempting to make it to church.

"My keys?" joked Steven, "why, Larry, you've never given me any. What are you trying to tell me?"

Though Larry hadn't invited them in, they both entered through the open door as if they had been invited.

"Oh," said Larry, "I thought you were my daughters." He looked out the door, searching for his mentioned daughters.

"It's the cream I've been using," said Steven, rubbing his face. "Keeps me young looking."

"It's not doing anything for your looks, though," quipped Brother Joe. Larry stood with the door still open, a bit perplexed that his two friends had entered uninvited.

"Uh," he started, "I'm kinda busy. Why don't you come back later? Where are my daughters?"

"That's why we're here, Larry," replied Brother Joe. "You've been very busy lately and quite frankly, we're worried about you."

"Not like you to miss church, Larry," said Steven. "You didn't even arrange for someone to teach your class this morning."

Larry winced. Obviously, he hadn't thought of his Sunday School class until Steven mentioned it. Steven wasn't sure which was worse: intentionally not calling someone to step in for him, or forgetting about his class completely.

Steven and Brother Joe made themselves at home at the kitchen table. Larry still stood with the door open. He would have been pleased if both the visitors walked right out the door, but they had no plans of doing that.

"Where are my daughters?" Larry asked again.

"Still at church," answered Steven, "they're helping Christy close down the nursery."

"Why don't you sit down, Larry," said Brother Joe. "We

180

just want to talk a little bit."

With a sigh, Larry pushed the door closed with a minor slam. He pulled the chair out at the head of the table, Steven to his left, Brother Joe to his right, and sat down.

"Okay," he said, "What is it?"

"We just want to know what's going on," said Steven. "You're not yourself lately, and the people who know and love you have noticed it and want to help."

"There's nothing you can do to help," said Larry. He closed his eyes and slowly shook his head 'no.'

"Larry," started Brother Joe, "I think all this has to do with your time travel idea. Am I correct about that assumption?"

Larry looked at Steven, a look of shock in his face.

"Steven didn't say anything to me until I said something to him," interjected Brother Joe. "Don't you remember coming to me with questions?"

For a moment, Larry looked confused. All of his days were beginning to blur. Traveling in time had caused his days to run together so that he wasn't sure with any certainty what had happened when. Slowly, he began to nod, remembering the conversation he had with the preacher.

"What you had asked me really threw me for a loop," Brother Joe continued, "and I really just thought you were asking me because you were working on your next book. After I swapped notes with Steven, I figured maybe it wasn't just something you were making up."

"I'm not making it up," said Larry.

"I know," replied Brother Joe quickly. He pulled out his Bible and began to flip the pages. He pulled out an index card on which were written verses. "I spent some time studying the issue, as I promised I would. I told you that I felt uncomfortable about the whole thing but couldn't put my finger on it. You know me well enough to know that I couldn't just leave it at that. So here's what I've found. I'd like to read these with you and discuss them."

Laying the card on the table, Brother Joe flipped to the first passage.

"I started in Ecclesiastes because that's where you'd mentioned something. The New American Standard version of Ecclesiastes 3:1-8 says

There is an appointed time for everything. And

181

*there is a time for every event under heaven-A time
to give birth and a time to die; A time to plant and a
time to build up. A time to weep and a time to laugh;
A time to mourn and a time to dance. A time to throw
stones and a time to gather stones; A time to embrace
and a time to shun embracing. A time to search and
a time to give up as lost; A time to keep and a time to
throw away. A time to tear apart and a time to sew
together; A time to be silent and a time to speak. A
time to love and a time to hate; A time for war and a
time for peace.*

That's pretty powerful stuff, Larry, wouldn't you say
so?"

"Yes," agreed Larry, "but those are the verses I pointed
out to you. The Byrds made a song out of those verses."

"Yes. Okay. But what do The Byrds know?" asked
Brother Joe. Steven started humming the tune.

"Is that it?" he asked.

"I have no idea," answered Brother Joe, who also shot
him a sharp glance.

"Yes, that's it," answered Larry. "It was a popular song
back before our day."

"Okay, so what do these verses mean to you?" asked
Brother Joe.

"Pretty simple, I think," answered Larry. "God is in
control of it all. He's determined when everything will
happen."

Brother Joe sat up straight, as if to declare victory.

"But there has to be more than that," said Larry. "It's
not enough. It's more a series of verses that tell us we have
to pick and choose our actions carefully because everything
should occur in the proper time."

"Okay," said Brother Joe, "let me read further in
Ecclesiastes. Verse 15 says

*That which is has been already and that which will
be has already been, for God seeks what has passed
by.*

How would you explain that one?"

"Time has no real meaning to God," answered Larry.
"Our yesterday is like his tomorrow. He sees it all at the
same time. That's part of his incredible power. To us, last
year is such a long time ago, but to God, it was as only a

minute ago."

"Further in Ecclesiastes," said Brother Joe, flipping the pages, "Chapter 8, verses 6-8 say

> *For there is a proper time and procedure for every delight, though a man's trouble is heavy upon him. If no one knows what will happen, who can tell him when it will happen? No man has authority to restrain the wind with the wind, or authority over the day of death; and there is no discharge in the time of war, and evil will not deliver those who practice it.*

Any thoughts about those?"

Larry sat silent. Brother Joe knew the words were sinking in. He continued.

"And in the New Testament as well, Larry. First Thessalonians chapter 5 verses 1 and 2 say,

> *Now, brothers, about times and dates we do not need to write to you, for you know very well that the day of the Lord will come like a thief in the night.*

That's a pretty common verse. We've heard it often, especially when we're talking about the return of Christ. But it's the first verse in that passage that really struck me. I think it's basically telling us not to worry about dates and times. And what is time travel," asked Brother Joe, "if not a worrying about dates and times."

"Who said I was worrying?" asked Larry.

"No one has to say it, Larry," said Steven, "It's obvious to those who love you. Something's chewing you up."

"You just don't understand," said Larry. "You have to experience it."

"What? Now that sounds like something a drug pusher would say. Hey, try it before you trash it," said Brother Joe.

"I have a couple more, Larry," Brother Joe continued, "let me read them to you."

"You don't have to," started Larry.

"He knows," said Steven, "but we want to."

Before Larry could say another word, Brother Joe was speaking again.

"James chapter 4 and verse 14 says

> *Why, you do not even know what will happen tomorrow. What is your life? You are a mist that appears for a little while and then vanishes.*

But Larry, probably my favorite of all the scripture verses I found is Acts chapter 1 verse 7. It says

He said to them: 'It is not for you to know the times or dates the Father has set by his own authority.'

It's telling us, Larry, that we shouldn't be concerned with all that."

Brother Joe closed his Bible and allowed the Biblical barrage to settle in.

"You don't understand," said Larry, slowly and deliberately.

"Then explain it to me," said Brother Joe. "I want to understand. But you have to know that all I'm seeing now is a Brother turning away from the things that have made his life the entire time I've known him. He's obsessing - or something - about something, and it's driving a wedge between him, his daughters, and his friends."

Larry stood up, violently, causing his chair to flip over on its back. "You don't understand because you've still got your wife. Both of you do," he added and pointed his finger at Steven. "I lost mine and this might be the chance to get her back."

"Besides, who's to say that what I'm doing isn't what God intended? Who's to say that my changing time isn't part of His plan? If I can make it happen, what then? Will you change your tune and say it was God's will?" Larry was shouting now.

"Larry," started Steven, "settle down. We have no intention of making you mad. And you're right, the only thing we know of God's will comes straight from His word."

"That's right," added Brother Joe, "He gave us the Bible for us to use. It has all the answers to anything, any problem that comes our way. He very clearly tells us that He has an appointed time and place for everything. Everything. It was Gracie's appointed time."

"Tell me why, then," shouted Larry, reaching back and opening the door, "did he take her? What part of His plan did that fulfill? Huh? Tell me that?"

Steven and Brother Joe sat silent. The two men saw the horror on the face of Larry's daughters standing just outside the door. How long they'd been there, neither man knew. The both knew, however, that they'd fully heard everything Larry shouted at them from the moment he opcncd the door.

"Don't have anything to say now, do you?" said Larry. "Get out, just get out!"

He stepped away from the door, giving the men space to walk by him. They slowly stood. It was then that Larry noticed his daughters standing in the doorway, both on the verge of tears.

"Now look what you've done," said Larry.

"Larry," started Steven, standing beside his friend, "this is exactly the thing we're talking about. Look at your daughters. The Larry I know never would have had such an outburst. You're not yourself."

Larry leaned close to Steven. "Who am I then? Huh?" He pinched the skin on his arm pulling it up in front of Steven's face.

"Look!" Larry continued, "This is my skin, my arm. I'm me! Deal with it."

Cindy burst into tears and Larry stormed down the hallway. Reaching his bedroom, he slammed the door shut.

"Why didn't you tell us you were coming," asked Becky, tears in her eyes, but not yet crying. "We could have tried to help."

"Girls," started Steven as he took Cindy in his arms, "we thought that maybe if just the two of us were able to talk to him, man to man, he'd open up to us."

"We had no idea he'd react this way," said Brother Joe.

"What is it?" asked Cindy through tears, "What's wrong with him?"

"We don't know," said Steven.

"What can we do?" asked Becky.

"Pray," answered Brother Joe.

"We've been doing that," answered Becky.

"Pray, and continue to love him," said Steven. "Try not to do anything to set him off. Continue to be the devoted, loving daughters that I know you to be. Maybe seeing the two of you remain stable at a time like this will help bring him out of it."

Steven knew that really what the girls needed was a stable father, not the other way around.

"We're going to go now," said Brother Joe, squeezing once and then releasing Becky. "But don't hesitate to call on us if you need anything at all, okay?"

The girls nodded they would.

"And keep an eye on him" added Steven. "Pay special attention to the things he does different. Maybe you'll spot something that will help us deal with him. Brother Joe gave him a lot of good verses to think about today. Maybe they'll cause him to wake up and return to reality. We'll pray that it will."

The two men walked away. Steven turned to briefly glance back at Larry's home. Both girls stood half-in half-out of the garage door, watching him and Brother Joe walk away. They were scared and he knew it.

"Hey girls," he said, turning to them. "Would you like to come stay at my house?"

They looked at each other.

"Are you sure that's a good idea?" whispered Brother Joe.

"No," he whispered back, "but they're scared. I don't think they'll come, but I want them to know they're welcome."

"No thanks, Dr. Dale," answered Becky. "But thank you anyway."

"If you change your mind," he continued, "you don't even have to call, just come on over."

The two men returned to Steven's car and Steven made his way back to the Church.

"This is going to be touchy," he said as they pulled into the parking lot.

"Yeah," answered Brother Joe. "I've gotta admit, this isn't something they prepare you for in seminary!"

"I'll see you this evening" said Brother Joe, closing the door. "Call me if anything happens." Steven nodded he would, and drove away.

Although he hadn't been to seminary, Steven felt as unprepared about this whole situation. So many things he was just unsure of-what to do, what to say. The one thing he was sure of was that he would be spending this afternoon in prayer for his good friend. He was going to pray like he'd never prayed before.

* * *

The last time he had used crutches was during his junior year in high school. He'd been chopped blocked during a football game and it had torn the ligaments in his knee. He used the crutches for six weeks and never played football again.

Even though he was in pain now, Mike had to see him. He'd made his way home after being released from the hospital just a few hours ago. He changed his clothes and looked up the address. It wasn't hard to find.

He struggled into the truck, one that he normally used only for work purposes, had his company name and logo on both doors. Ignoring the pain in his left leg, he drove to the address he'd written down.

Now, as he hobbled up to the front door, he bowed in what he thought might be a prayer to give him courage and strength. The whole praying thing was new to him, but he'd seen it in action, so he knew it worked.

He knocked on the door, a loud, solid rap. Three times. If anyone was home, they'd hear him.

He turned to look back out into the street. If anyone peeked out the curtained window, he didn't want to be caught appearing to peek inside. It also gave him the opportunity to take a deep breath and not be seen by anyone inside.

While he wasn't sure of the time, it was early evening now, around 6 p.m. He hoped that he wasn't interrupting dinner.

The wooden door slowly opened.

"Yes," said the voice. Mike hadn't looked up at the face yet, but when he did, he immediately recognized Larry Pace as the man who'd been praying for his recovery for so long. The look on Larry's face was a confused one.

"Mr. Larry Pace?" asked Mike.

"I'm Larry Pace," he said.

"Mr. Pace," began Mike with a sigh, "I'm not sure if you recognize me or not, but my name is Mike Thompson. I've been in the hospi-"

"That's how I know you," said Larry, realization coming across his face. Larry opened the screen door to let Mike come in. "Come in," he said.

"No thank you," said Mike. "Really, I've just come to say a few things and then I really need to get home to rest."

Larry stepped outside to join Mike, letting the screen

187

door close behind him.

"I didn't realize you were out of the hospital," said Larry, "when did you get out?"

"Just a little while ago," answered Mike. "I went home to change into clothes and then came straight over here."

Larry looked out at Mike's truck, wondering if someone had driven him here.

"Did you come alone?" Larry asked.

"Yes," answered Mike, "I didn't want anything or anybody to disturb or take away from what I have to say."

"Well," said Larry, "you've obviously got something on your mind, so go ahead."

"Okay," said Mike, taking a deep breath and looking down at his feet. "Mr. Pace, I would like to offer my very sincerest apologies for being directly responsible for the death of your wife. I hope you will believe what I say when I assure you that it was an accident."

Larry crossed his arms and leaned back on the doorframe. A very small smile crossed his lips, but it was closer to a smirk than a smile. Mike noticed this and it made him even more uncomfortable. He imagined that Larry would scream and shout at him.

"I would gladly give up my life if I thought I could bring her back," Mike continued.

"You can't, though," Larry suddenly said.

"Mike," Larry began, "I appreciate your apology and I know it was an accident. At first I was very angry at you. And then, I started thinking what would my wife do-it's a shame you didn't know her, she was a great lady. And so I started praying for both your recovery and for your salvation. That's what she would have done and so I tried to do that.

"And so during the course of all that praying," Larry said, "God worked on my heart and I don't hold you responsible at all."

"Thank you," said Mike, "and thank you for all the time you spent praying for me. It worked. But there's something else I have to say, too."

"Okay," said Larry with a smile, "shoot."

"I know about the time travel you've been doing," said Mike. Larry visibly stiffened. His face turned red.

"That's really none of your business," Larry said, forcing

a nice tone on his voice.

"I know, I know," said Mike. "But you've done so much for me by continually praying for me, I feel so obligated to do what I can to help you."

"There is nothing you can do now," said Larry, his voice void of emotion. "So just drop it."

"It's wrong what you're doing, though," continued Mike.

"What would you know about right and wrong?" Larry unfolded his arms and leaned ever so slightly at Mike. "How do you know about what I'm doing anyway? And who says it's wrong?"

"You're right," said Mike, taking a short hop back on his crutches, "I don't know much about right and wrong, but I'm learning. Tom told me about the time travel."

"Tom Morgan?" asked Larry.

"Yes."

"Why would he tell you?"

"Tom and I are good friends," offered Mike. "I don't know that we share our deepest darkest secrets, but we know a lot about each other."

"Well," said Larry, "I'll tell you again. It's none of your business."

"Mr. Pace," said Mike, hobbling forward a couple of inches again, "I know it's not my business, but you can't imagine the guilt I feel about your wife. I want to do what I can to make-"

"You can't!" yelled Larry. "There is nothing you can do to make it up. Period." Angry, Larry opened the screen door, nearly shoving Mike back off the small porch.

"I mean, listen to yourself. You. You killed my wife. What you were doing was wrong. Every idiot knows you shouldn't get behind the wheel of a car after you've touched alcohol. But you did it anyway. And now you're trying to tell *me* what's right and wrong?"

"You should have stopped at the apology. Now just get out." With that, Larry slammed the door shut.

The reaction was what Mike had expected about the apology. He certainly hadn't expected it regarding the time travel. Though Mike was still leery about whether he even believed it or not, he'd heard the preacher saying that it couldn't be right. Even though he wasn't sure why, he believed the preacher and thought by communicating that to Larry, he could help out some.

He didn't expect Larry to slam the door in his face about it.

* * *

Larry was fuming. He watched Mike hobble back to his truck and drive away. Larry was so angry that he picked up his keys and stormed out the back door. His daughters had left for evening services at church so even though he had the house to himself, he had to get out.

Though he told himself he didn't know where he was going, he headed north, straight to the home of Big Ben.

Parking his truck, he stomped up to the front door and knocked. The dog didn't bark at him, instead he wagged his tail, saying hi to a friend. Larry glanced at the dog and looked away. He didn't have the patience for a dog right now.

The door opened and Big Ben stood holding a cigar in his right hand and a glass of something-Larry guessed alcohol-in his left.

"Larry," said Big Ben, sounding surprised, "what brings you here? It's Sunday night, shouldn't you be in the house of God?"

"Normally that's where I would be," answered Larry, "but not today."

"Listen," Larry continued, "how secret are we supposed to keep this time travel stuff?"

"Secret?" asked Big Ben.

"Yeah," said Larry, "are we supposed to tell people?"

"Well," Big Ben shrugged, "generally...would you like to come in Larry?"

"No thanks."

"Suit yourself. Generally, I leave it up to the individual. Most people are too afraid to tell all but their closest friends. After all, it all sounds like something a crazy person would make up, wouldn't you agree?"

"That's what I thought the first time I heard it," said Larry.

"Same here," agreed Big Ben.

"So, really," Big Ben continued, "it's all up to you and

how much you want to be labeled a nut."

"What about Tom Morgan?" asked Larry.

"Ahh," said Big Ben, taking a big puff on his cigar, "Tom Morgan is a different story. He's a newspaper man. But why do you ask, Larry?"

"No reason except that he told one of his friends who came to me about it."

"One of his friends came to you?" asked Big Ben.

"Yeah," answered Larry, "It's a long story. I just wasn't sure what the rules were."

"Well," said Big Ben, "again, it's not really something I worry too much about. And I'd suggest the same strategy to you: don't worry too much about it."

"I guess you're right," said Larry.

"Besides," said Big Ben behind him, "don't you believe that worrying is a sin?"

Larry looked Big Ben in the eyes.

"I want to go again," said Larry.

"You want another trip already?" asked Big Ben.

"Yes."

"Larry," Big Ben began, "you know that I would love to...but are you sure?"

"We changed it," said Larry.

"Changed it?"

"Changed time. Changed events. Whatever you want to call it," said Larry, "Tom and I changed it."

Big Ben was obviously very interested in hearing what Larry had to say.

"How?" he asked.

"I'm not sure," said Larry, "to be brutally honest. We met each other before the accident and-"

"You mean, in the past, you directed yourselves to meet each other even though you didn't really meet until after the accident?"

"That's right," answered Larry.

"So," began Big Ben, the wheels in his brain turning, "your wife is alive?"

"No."

"I don't understand," said Big Ben.

"The odd thing is that the accident still happened, but it happened differently. Mike's vehicle still hit Gracie's car, but Tom wasn't in it. Tom was in the truck with me."

"So, your wife still died-forgive me for sounding so uncaring-and Mike still went to the hospital?"

"That's right."

"So nothing really changed then," observed Big Ben.

"Tom wasn't in the car with Mike and he never went to the hospital. Tom was untouched."

"What did that do to the Tom of today?"

"I don't know," said Larry, "I haven't talked to him since we came back. But I want to go again. I know what I have to do."

"I'll go get the papers," said Big Ben. He almost sounded excited about the whole prospect himself, and Larry still guessed there was something he would like to undo even if he wasn't telling anyone.

He walked away from the door, leaving it open. Larry put his hands in his pockets and looked around. He imagined what his life would be like with Gracie back in it. It was a comforting thought.

Big Ben arrived much quicker than Larry had expected and he offered Larry a pen with a contract to sign.

"Larry," he said, "I want you to call me when this is over. I want to know what happens."

"You mean you want to know if it works?" asked Larry with a smile.

"Quite frankly," said Big Ben, "yes. You must understand, everything I know about this says it is impossible. If you make it happen, then there's no telling what is possible. It changes everything."

Larry signed the paper, another contract, and handed it back to Big Ben.

"Are you sure you don't want to come in for a while?" offered Big Ben.

"I'm sure," Larry declined, "but thanks anyway."

Larry stepped off the porch and in the direction of his truck. The dog, seeing Larry leaving, arose and walked to the edge of the porch, tail wagging, saying goodbye.

"If you hear from Tom," called Big Ben from behind him, "have him call me, too."

"Sure," said Larry. But his thoughts were on sleep and not on Tom. He appreciated Tom's help in the matter earlier. But now he knew what must be done and he could do it alone.

* * *

Mike knew Tom would not be expecting him now. He'd seen Tom only a few hours ago when he was released from the hospital. Tom had come up to see if anything was different, he'd said and was surprised to find out he was being released.

Tom had asked Mike questions about the accident, feigning a loss of memory or something. But Mike remembered the conversation Tom had with him when he thought he was out, and broached the subject with him. Tom spilled his guts-everything, including Larry Pace's traveling.

Just as he was finishing the story, Dr. Steven Dale, the first man Mike saw as he regained consciousness, happened up. The preacher was right behind him. They both caught the end of the story, but Tom wouldn't say anything more and abruptly left.

Mike wasn't so disinclined and told the men everything Tom had told him. They were truly shocked and close to disbelief. However, they'd warned Mike that it was dangerous and that he should stay away from it.

It was at that moment that Mike decided to go see Larry Pace and try to make up for some of the pain he'd caused by helping him.

Now, Mike was headed to his friend's home to share Jesus with him. Mike didn't know everything there was to know about Jesus, but he knew enough to know that He could change lives-He'd changed his, and was still working on him.

Continuing to ignore the pain, Mike hobbled to Tom's door and knocked. It swung open slightly at his touch.

"Tom?" he called out.

"Door's open," came Tom's voice from inside. "C'mon in."

Using one of his crutches, Mike pushed the door wide enough to allow him entrance. He hopped through the door and was immediately assaulted at the stench filling the place. What was it? If he didn't know better, he'd think that Tom was hiding a dead body underneath all the trash strewn about his apartment.

Mike had been to Tom's before, and while he remembered it being messy, he didn't remember it stinking like it did.

It was also dark. Every third bulb had burned out but still filled up socket space, Tom failing to replace them.

"Where are you, buddy," he said, "it's so dark in here I can't see you."

"Right in front of you on the couch," Tom said.

Mike's eyes adjusted to the much darker room and spotted Tom on the couch with a remote control in his hands. He glanced over to the television and saw the picture scrambling in reverse.

Mike carefully placed his crutches strategically in the mess, trying to find solid ground so he wouldn't slip. He stood next to Tom and searched for a place to sit. Noticing his friend standing above him, Tom realized he had no place to sit.

"Sorry," he said, quickly grabbing the pile of junk off the chair next to him and shoving it out into the floor, another inch or two higher now in that place.

"Here," he said, "sit here."

"Thanks," answered Mike. He grabbed both his crutches in his left hand and hopped on his right leg, using his right hand for support on the arm of the chair.

"I like what you've done with the place," Mike said, plopping down in the seat. He laughed. Tom did not.

"I haven't had time lately to do any cleaning," Tom said. His finger released the button on the remote and he suddenly brightened up.

"We've talked about this movie before, haven't we?" he asked.

"What movie is this?"

"*It's a Wonderful Life.*"

"Uhmm," answered Mike, "I'm not sure. What about it?"

"You've seen it, right?"

"Sure, hasn't everybody?"

"Well, I don't know about that. Tell me, though, what do you think about this segment here," said Tom, pointing to the television screen.

Mike looked at the screen and recognized the actor but couldn't think of his name.

"I recognize the guy," Mike said, "who is he?"

194

"James Stewart."

"That's right! James Stewart. Who's the old guy he's talking to?"

"That's Lionel Barrymore, he plays Mr. Potter," answered Tom.

"Mr. Potter. He's the guy who wants to buy him out, right?"

"Right. Now listen here..."

"No securities, no stocks, no bonds. Nothin' but a miserable little $500 equity in a life insurance policy. You're worth more dead than alive."

Tom hit the pause button.

"What do you think about that?" asked Tom.

"Pretty low of the guy, ain't it?"

"Yeah," answered Tom, "but that's not what I mean. Do you reckon that there are people who really are worth more dead than alive?"

Mike didn't like where the questioning was going, but realized it might just be the chance he needed.

"Oh, I don't think so," he answered, sounding as chipper as he possibly could. "Wasn't the whole point of this movie that Stewart had been a positive influence and that if he hadn't lived things would be much worse?"

"Yeah, commercially that was the point," answered Tom.

"Commercially?"

"Well, they had to sell it didn't they?" came Tom's response.

"But what about someone like me," Tom began, "now hear me out on this. I know you've heard me talk about death and all before, but hear me out."

"I'm listening."

"Let's say I have no insurance, and I die. Who picks up the tab?"

"Family usually does, don't they?" answered Mike, not really sure where Tom was headed with that particular question.

"What if I don't have any family?" continued Tom.

"No family?" asked Mike. "Who doesn't have family?"

Mike regretted saying that the minute it escaped his lips. He knew Tom's situation. For all practical purposes, he had no family.

"Just pretend for a minute," said Tom, "okay?"

"I can do that," said Mike. "I don't know, I guess the government. Who is responsible?" Mike finally asked.

"That's just it," Tom said, "I don't know."

"Tom," said Mike, hesitant to begin, "what do you know about Jesus?"

"Jesus?" came Tom's surprised answer.

"Yeah."

"He's supposed to be the son of God, right? Like Hercules is the son of Zeus."

"Well, Hercules and Zeus are just mythology, though," said Mike.

"Who says Jesus and God aren't?" asked Tom.

"I do," he answered.

"*You* do?" said Tom in surprise. "Cripes, did you go and get religion?"

"Yeah, you could say that," answered Mike, "and I really want to tell you about it. Tom, it's changed my life."

"No," said Tom, "you almost died. That *changed* your life. My life is still the same as it ever was."

"But it doesn't have to be," said Mike. "Jesus is willing to take anyone. Doesn't matter who you are or what you've done."

"Mike," started Tom, "I think that accident must have affected you more than you realize. Didn't you have a head injury?"

"You're right, Tom, it did. What would you say if I told you I saw angels?"

"Angels?" Tom laughed. "I'd say the drugs they had you on made you delusional. Angels?" Tom continued to laugh.

"Y'know, Tom," Mike continued, a little louder to be heard over Tom's laughter, "I saw people pray for me. Me! I'd just killed someone they loved, accidentally, but just as dead, and they were praying for me. Look me in the eye and tell me they don't have something that you and I don't have - didn't have. Can you do that?"

Tom's laughter died down.

"You've met the Pace family, huh?" he said.

"I have," said Mike, "and I could see over the course of the days I was in the hospital that they had something different, something special. And I wanted it."

"Oh, I still don't understand it all," Mike continued, "but

I know I'm changed, I feel it here." He touched his chest, his heart.

Tom shook his head slowly back and forth. He couldn't believe what his longtime friend was saying. But he didn't want to hear it anymore.

"Mike," he said, standing, "I appreciate what you're saying and all. But I'm fine. You're doing all this because you almost died. If I'd almost died, who knows, I might be doing the same thing. I might even get religion, too."

He stepped over Mike's crutches as he walked the path to the hallway.

"But I didn't almost die. I don't need that religion stuff. I wish you luck with it, but I don't need it."

"Tom," Mike began.

"Look," Tom interrupted, "I'm tired now. My days are all mixed up because of all the time travel nonsense. I just want to go to sleep. I'm glad you're out of the hospital. Close the door on your way out."

Tom disappeared into the darkness of the hallway and Mike heard his bedroom door shut. Noticing the glow from the television, he leaned forward and grabbed the remote Tom had left in his spot.

He pressed the rewind button and rewound the tape.

"No securities, no stocks, no bonds. Nothin' but a miserable little $500 equity in a life insurance policy. You're worth more dead than alive."

He'd seen the movie before, but that scene had never really stood out to him. He mostly remembered the stopping and starting of the snow when the angel changed time.

He'd never realized just how hopeless that line sounded. It nearly drove Stewart to suicide in the movie he remembered. Mike wondered if Tom really thought that about himself.

He shut and locked the door behind him on his way out. He'd come to Tom's hopeful; hopeful that he could help spur some realization, some change in Tom, the way he felt the change in himself.

Well, they'd told him about prayer, so he decided he would get his own tired and aching body home and try it out. He wasn't sure exactly how it was all done, but he wasn't going to let that stop him.

* * *

When Larry arrived home, the house was empty. While he wasn't exactly sure where his daughters were, it wasn't unusual that the Church's youth group did something on a Sunday night. He assumed they were there and likely to come in around 9:30, 10 p.m. being their curfew time on Sunday night.

He wasn't hungry even though he hadn't eaten since lunch. He opened the refrigerator and stared inside. The plate dinner that the girls had made for him the other night sat wrapped and on a shelf. He picked it up, sniffed it, and then set it back on the shelf.

He opened the freezer door, contemplated the hot pockets, and opted for the chocolate fudge bar instead.

He tossed the wrapper in the trash and headed for the bedroom. With the bar crammed mostly in his mouth, he dug a sheet of paper out of the nightstand by his bed. He was going to go to sleep and he wanted to ensure that he wasn't going to be disturbed. He still didn't know what would happen if he woke up before the travel time was over.

He wrote a note to his daughters;

Becky and Cindy,

 I've gone to bed early again. Please do not disturb me. It is very important that I get this sleep. I expect everything to be back to normal and I can fill you both in on it tomorrow. Maybe your mother will even tell you!

  Dad

Licking the bottom of the fudge bar to stop a drip from hitting the bed, he fumbled with a roll of tape in his one hand. Unsuccessful at tearing it, he crammed the fudge bar fully in his mouth, unable to barely move his tongue. The fudge bar hit a spot on his teeth and sent a sharp pain through his jaw. He loosened his mouth around the bar and breathed in and out quickly, trying to warm up his tooth.

Quickly, now with both hands free, he tore a piece of tape off the roll and raced to his bedroom door. Taping it dead center in the door and about eye level for his daughters, he was satisfied it would do the trick.

He removed the fudge bar from his mouth, and ran his tongue around the inside trying to warm his teeth. That task completed, he stuck the remaining part of the fudge bar in his mouth and pulled the stick out, leaving the ice cream inside.

He tossed the stick in the garbage can by his bed and crawled under the covers. The ice cream bar had caused him to get cold, even though the temperature in the house was set on 75.

He turned the light off and quickly put his hands back under the covers, pulling them up tight around his neck. He rubbed his palms together and shoved them between his knees. If Gracie had been in bed with him, he would have been tempted to try to sneak a pinky finger onto her back just to get a reaction out of her.

Leaving his hands tucked between his legs, he turned over on his stomach. His arms were under his body nearly their full length.

Uncomfortable on his pillow-he couldn't breathe-he pulled his hands up and stuffed them under the pillow, fluffing the pillow up just right for his face.

He always enjoyed putting his face on the cool surface of a pillow. He would often flip his head to the other side before he'd generated so much heat as to make the pillow hot so that both sides of his face could enjoy the coolness.

He thought about Tom for a moment. Maybe he should have checked on him today. How had not being in the accident affected him? That event had happened in the travel time, so did it affect the real time?

What was real time and what was fake time, or travel time now? It was still very confusing to Larry. The one thing he knew was that Tom wasn't in the accident with Mike when they traveled back last. So what did that do to real time?

Larry actually sat up and considered calling Tom to find out. It might make a difference in what he was going to try to do this time. Nothing had changed for Gracie or Mike, but it had changed for Tom.

He lay back down on the bed a little frustrated. Why hadn't he thought about that before now? Why hadn't he even thought about it while at Big Ben's? Why didn't it click for him?

No matter. He didn't want to get up. He didn't want to make any phone calls now. He was committed to this trip and he was bound and determined that it was going to work. He knew it would work.

While he felt somewhat guilty about running folks off, they'd just have to deal with it. He couldn't tell them what he was doing or they'd surely have him committed and sent off to the funny farm. Heck, if he'd traded places with any of them, he knew that's what he'd do.

Time travel. What a ridiculous idea. It was only something in books of fantasy.

Maybe he'd even write about it in his next novel. He'd been working on one that mirrored the American Revolution except instead of countries, it was planets and their colonies. Not exactly an original idea, he knew, but Larry's involved a heavy use of religion, much like the American Revolution did, even though schools were now trying to make the religious part of the war an insignificant item.

Larry could go on about stuff like this for hours at a time with Gracie. Her comments were usually just "uh-huh," and "I can't believe that." Just enough to spur him on. She wasn't as caught up in all that as Larry was. But on some issues, she could get wound tight and Larry would be the one grunting responses.

Warming up, Larry stretched his arms out to his side.

"Your hands are cold," came Gracie's voice.

Larry sat straight up in bed. Had he really fallen asleep? Why was it he could never remember falling asleep?

"Oww," said Gracie as the covers pulled away from her, quickly whipping from around her neck and arms so that it burned her.

"Sorry sweetheart," said Larry, plopping back down in bed and snuggling up to Gracie's back as she turned over.

"You're cold," she said.

"I was only out of the covers for a second," Larry responded.

He sniffed her hair, enjoying the scent of her shampoo. He mentally kicked himself for not knowing what kind she used. He waited for her to ask him what he wanted for breakfast. Bacon and eggs was his favorite, and he knew she'd ask him this morning...knew she had asked him that, and had done so every time.

"What's today?" he asked.

"It's time for you to wake up," Gracie said, unmoved.

"I didn't hear the alarm go off," he said, turning his head to look at the clock. The numbers were blurry and he couldn't read them. He tried rubbing the sleep from his eyes, but it didn't help.

No matter. He knew about what time it was anyway. But it really didn't matter. The time of day was not going to matter at all today. Because this trip he was going to change it all.

Realizing she hadn't answered the question he'd asked, he asked again.

"What's today?"

"Today is tomorrow yesterday," said Gracie.

"What?" Larry said. He had no idea what she was talking about. Why hadn't she asked him about bacon and eggs?

"Aren't you going to ask me what I want for breakfast this morning?" he asked, snuggling up close again and nuzzling his nose in the back of her neck.

"No," she said.

"No déjà vu on this trip," Larry mumbled to himself.

It was Gracie who sat straight up in bed this time. As she did, she turned to look him straight in the eyes.

"That's right," she began, "no déjà vu, because there is no déjà vu. Larry, what are you doing?"

Larry had trouble catching his breath. What did she mean? What had happened? What was causing this reaction?

"I don't know what you mean, Gracie," he said defensively. He sat up next to her and put his arms on her shoulders.

"Yes, you do," she said. "What? You think you can hide the truth from me now? When have you ever been able to hide the truth?"

"Gracie?"

She put her own arms around his waist.

"Larry, why are you doing this? It's not right."

"What do you mean, Grace?" he asked, unsure.

"You know what I mean," she answered. The tone of her voice had changed. It was now very soft, very comforting, full of all the love Larry knew she had for him. "Why do you keep coming back? What do you hope to accomplish?"

"Coming back?" asked Larry. The room began to spin. What was happening? Was Gracie talking to him? Actually talking to the Larry of today and not the Larry of yesterday?

Did she know he had time traveled back? How could she know?

"Yes, dear," she answered, "coming back."

Larry decided she knew. He didn't know how she knew but she knew. He pulled his hands from her shoulders and cupped his face in them. He had to stop the room from spinning.

"Larry?" she said. "Why are you doing this?" She put one hand on his shoulder, the other on his hands, gently rubbing them as she spoke.

"Because you're dead," he finally said, bursting into tears.

"I'm not dead, Larry," she answered. "Don't you remember what Vance Haviner used to say about his own wife when people said they were sorry he'd lost her? Don't you? You used to laugh about it often because you thought it was funny. He always told them he hadn't lost her; he knew exactly where she was. She was in heaven."

"Larry," she continued, "don't you know where I am?"

"I do, Gracie, I do," Larry said, tears still streaming down his cheeks. "But I miss you so much."

"I understand that, dear," she said, "but what you're doing is trying to play God. You're trying to tell God He was wrong with His timing. We had this discussion so many times when I was alive. God knows the perfect time and the perfect place for everything. We don't necessarily understand it, but it was my perfect time to go home. Let Him get the glory in it."

Larry's head was bowed, still crying. Gracie put her hand under his chin, gently pulling his face up to look her in the eyes.

"Larry," she continued, "it was my perfect time to go. I'm home now. Home. Your time will come, but you've still got God's work to do. Remember, we're just passing through in this life. Our journey is home, home to heaven."

"Larry," she leaned forward and kissed him gently on his lips, "Please stop this time traveling business. It's very dangerous what you're doing."

Larry embraced Gracie as he cried even harder. Gracie simply held him in her arms. The minutes ticked by.

"Larry," she said, after a few minutes, "I know you love me. We lived that life. I rest assured knowing that you know

I love you. It's not something I ever doubted, you knowing my love or me knowing you love me. I know. And you know, too. Stop doubting."

Gracie slowly pushed Larry back down onto the bed. She lay down with him, resting her head on his chest. Larry's right hand placed firmly around her waist, he stroked the top of her head and hair with his left.

"I'm sorry, Gracie," he said.

"Don't be. Be ever thankful that we had our time together. And be thankful that God gave you two beautiful daughters who still need their father."

"I am," he said.

"And be thankful that we have a God who loves us, no matter how many idiotic things we do."

"Gracie?"

"Yes, dear?"

"I love you."

"I know," she answered. "Larry?"

"Yes?"

"I love you, too."

"I know."

Monday, July 31

When Larry awoke, he was still crying. The pillow was soaking wet. The sheets around him were wet. He'd been crying for a long time. He was exhausted.

And he felt like an idiot. When he bought the time from Big Ben initially, he'd predicted he'd be a fool, and he was right. Only the time travel proved true...he was just a fool for buying it.

His first thought was to apologize to his daughters. How could he have treated them the way he had the past few days? They'd done nothing to deserve that sort of treatment or abandonment during their time of need.

Throwing on his robe, he opened his bedroom door.

There sat both his daughters, praying.

They jumped when the door opened. He saw a concerned fear in their eyes. It broke his heart. They slowly began to get to their knees. Larry didn't give them the opportunity. He fell to his knees and embraced them both, pulling them close to him.

"I'm so sorry, girls," he said. "I've been acting like such an idiot and I'm so sorry." Tears welled in his eyes once again.

The girls pulled back from his tight hug so they could see his face as they talked to him.

"We love you, Daddy," said Becky, and then kissed him on the cheek.

"We want to help you not hurt, Daddy," added Cindy. Larry's tears began to run freely and he hugged his daughters tight again.

"I know," he said. "I've known it all along but I was just too hardheaded to listen."

"But it's not like you to be that way," said Becky. "What did we do?"

Larry pushed them back and looked them both in the

eyes, from one to the other.

"No, no, no," he said. "Don't ever think that. It wasn't anything either of you did. It's what I did. I let Satan get a hold on me."

"Girls," he continued, "Satan knows where and how to attack you. You've heard me say that for years. He knew where I was weak, and he attacked me there."

"But what was it, Daddy?" asked Cindy.

"Let's just say I put your mom on a pedestal and I didn't realize it. I tried to play God."

"Look," he said standing and pulling his daughters up with him. He stopped and grabbed them again. "Were y'all here praying for me all night?"

They looked at each other, uneasy. They both nodded their heads. Larry hugged them again.

"I'm so proud of you," he said, "and I know for a fact your Mom is, too!"

Larry quickly made his way down the hallway and into the kitchen. He grabbed the phone off the wall and began to dial.

"I know that you both want to hear the whole story," he said, "and I promise to tell you. But I have a lot of apologizing to do, don't you think?"

His daughters smiled and nodded. This was the Dad they knew. This was the Dad they loved. This was the Dad they were thankful to have back.

"Steven?" Larry said into the phone. "Hey, it's Larry... Yeah, I'm at home... Yes, the girls are here with me...Yes, they're okay...Wait! Listen. I've got something to say. Buddy, I'm sorry about the way I've been acting. Can you forgive me? ... No, God is sovereign... Yes, it's really me again. Can you come over? ... Yes, right now. There's some stuff we've got to finish... Great, I'll see you in a few minutes."

He looked over at his daughters and winked at them.

"One down," he said, "next!" and he began to dial the phone again.

"Do you want us to make some breakfast?" asked Becky.

"That's a great idea," he answered, "plan for..." he ticked the numbers off in his head, counting, "four others."

"Four?" asked Cindy.

"Yeah," he answered. "You'll see-Brother Joe? Hi, it's

Larry...Yes, Larry Pace...it's good to hear your voice, too... Listen, I need to apologize for the way I've been acting... Yes...that was fast...no lectures?" he laughed.

"I have another favor to ask," Larry continued. "Can you come over right now? ... Yeah, it's pretty important... don't worry about that, the girls are whipping something up here... Great! I'll see you in a few minutes."

"Two down," Larry said as he hung up the phone.

"Dad," started Cindy, opening a package of sausage, "why are you inviting them over? It seems to me to be more appropriate to go see them yourself. After all, *you're* the one who messed up."

Becky shot her sister a sharp glance. Larry looked at her in surprise. Cindy's face turned red as she realized what she said.

"I mean..." she mumbled.

"No," said Larry, "It's okay. You're right. However, wait until you hear the last two folks I invite before you say anything more. Deal?"

"Okay," she answered.

Larry flipped through a phone book searching for the number he wanted. Putting his finger on a number, he began to dial.

"Mike?" Larry said, "Hi. This is Larry Pace. We spoke yesterday... Yes, I'm sorry about the way I spoke to you. Listen, would you mind coming to my house again? My daughters are fixing breakfast and I'd like to talk to you about Tom."

Larry cut his eyes over to his daughters when he mentioned Tom's name. They were busy preparing breakfast, but they exchanged whispers when he mentioned Tom's name. He smiled. He liked to create suspense for them.

"Great," he said, "can you come now? ... Fine, I'll see you in a few."

Larry hung up the phone and stretched.

"That's three," he said. "Girls, if you'll excuse me, I'm going to make my last call in my office. If anyone gets here before I return, which I doubt will happen, let them in."

He stole a glance behind him as he walked away. Both were standing wide-eyed as he left. They'd been a part of the first calls, now the last one would remain a mystery to them. He turned around quickly so they couldn't see him smile. It was amazing the relief he now felt.

Larry made his last phone call and returned to the kitchen to find Steven whispering to his daughters at the sink.

"Steven," he proclaimed loudly, "glad to see you made it."

Steven turned. His face had the expression of a kid caught with his hand in the cookie jar. He stuck his hand out to Larry.

Larry slapped it away. Steven and his daughters stood stunned for a moment. Then Larry smiled and embraced his friend.

"I had you worried," Larry said, "didn't I?"

"Yes," Steven said, "yes you did." He patted Larry on the back and then pushed him away. "What in the world got into you?"

"Patience," he answered, "wait till the others arrive."

"Others?"

"Yeah," said Becky from the stove, "Dad's already planned a big welcome back party for himself!" They laughed.

Brother Joe walked in momentarily and Larry did the same thing to him. The group shared another laugh at Brother Joe's expense and then sat down at the table.

"Mike," began Larry, "the guy who drove the vehicle that hit Gracie. He's on his way over here, too."

"Are you aware of what's gone on with him?" asked Brother Joe.

"Vaguely," answered Larry. "I know he's changed."

"He gave his life to Christ," answered Brother Joe, "I prayed the sinner's prayer with him."

"And he's anxious to learn and grow, Larry," added Steven.

"Well," continued Larry, "that's one of the reasons I invited him. He may be the only way we can get through to Tom."

"Tom?"

"Yeah," answered Larry. "Tom was the passenger in the car with Mike. He thinks it's all his fault. The accident, I mean."

"Also," Larry went on, "Tom thinks his life is worthless. Told me so himself. I tried to talk with him some the other day, but quite frankly, my mind was focused on other things and I was not myself."

"You can say that again," said Becky putting plates of food down in front of each man. Steven and Brother Joe laughed.

"Laugh all you want," said Larry, "but y'all don't know how terrible I feel."

"We don't mean to laugh at you Larry," said Brother Joe.

"Yes we do," said Steven. "And you know that you'd do the same if the situation were reversed. Now, you want to bless this food...I'm starving."

"Let's wait for Mike," said Larry.

"He's pulling in now, Dad," said Cindy, looking out the kitchen window. "You might want to go help him, he's on crutches."

All three men arose from the table and went to the back door. Offering hands, Mike ignored them all but thanked them for moving items out of the way.

After they were back in and seated, Larry gave thanks for the food.

"Okay," Larry began, after swallowing a bite of sausage, "here's the deal. Before you ask any questions, just hear me out.

"This time travel thing is very real. Now, I believe as you do preacher: that it is something I should stay away from. But it is very real.

"I traveled back in time three times. It's not like you think, there's no way possible I could see myself because I simply am myself.

"There's no time machine to hop, you simply sign a contract with the salesman-which, by the way, I now believe is a literal contract with the devil-and then you go to sleep."

Larry noticed his girls were listening intently. They saw him notice them and he gave them a quick nod assuring them it was very much okay for them to hear.

"When you wake up, you're in your own body back where you wanted to be. For the most part, it's kinda like watching a video tape-home movies or something. Except that you can feel everything, smell everything."

"Did you take a pill or something?" interjected Steven.

"No, no pills. That's just it. Here's the other thing. Tom and

I traveled back and were actually able to change something. So I think changing the past may very well be possible, but I couldn't even begin to imagine the ramifications.

"Also, it's very addictive, the salesman even warned me about that. Simply, I liked going back. That's why I kept shutting you girls out-I wanted to get in bed and get to sleep. When I slept, I would travel.

"Where did I travel? It should come as no surprise that I went back to see Gracie."

"You saw Mom," asked Becky, now sitting at the table listening intently.

"I did," answered Larry. "Each time I went back, I went back to the day she died. I felt so bad that she had gone, initially I just wanted to be sure she knew I loved her on her last day on earth. Then, I got to thinking I could change it and still have her around."

"What snapped you out of it all?" asked Steven.

"Gracie did."

"I don't understand," said Brother Joe, "how did she do it?"

"Y'all," Larry began. His bottom lip began to quiver slightly and he stared down at his hands now resting in his lap. "Last night, when I traveled, she talked to me. Me! I don't mean she simply repeated what we'd done that day. She stopped and asked me why I kept traveling back in time. She knew. And she told me to stop playing God."

Larry studied the faces of all those seated around him. They sat in stunned silence.

"Wow," said Steven finally. "God is good."

"No," said Larry, "God is sovereign."

"So how does Tom figure in to all of this?" asked Mike.

"As I said earlier, Tom is miserable and feels he is worthless. One of the things about time traveling is that it takes days off the end of your life. Tom is so miserable here that he keeps traveling to the past. Not only has he gone back to a time trying to change what happened with Gracie, but he's gone back other times that he won't talk about. It's a very destructive cycle that will kill him quickly if he doesn't stop. That's something else the salesman warned us about. Repeated travel will bring on death much more quickly."

"So," said Brother Joe, "what do you suggest? I'm betting

you have a plan."

"I do," answered Larry. "Don't know how good a plan it is, but I want us to all go see him. Basically gang up on him and just pour out God's love on him."

"I tried that already," said Mike. "He turned me away."

"It's all in God's hands anyway," said Brother Joe to Mike. "We just do what we feel God has led us to do."

"Like praying every day for you," said Cindy.

Mike smiled and turned slightly red.

"I've got a lot to learn," he said.

"And we're here to help you," said Brother Joe. He held up his Bible. "But this is the key to your relationship with Christ."

"I talked to Tom just after I called each of you," Larry continued. "He's at his apartment. He traveled last night also and said he was planning to stay inside today. I suggested that I'd come see him and talk about our next plan. So, I say we all go over there right now. Are you game?"

Everyone agreed and the four men piled into Brother Joe's van, leaving the girls behind.

In only a few minutes time, they were walking up to Tom's apartment.

Larry knocked on the door and called out to Tom, identifying himself.

"It's open," said Tom from inside. Larry pushed the door open and the other three men followed him inside.

It was dark, the only light came from the glow of the television screen. As Larry half expected, Tom was watching *It's a Wonderful Life* again.

"I come with friends this time," said Larry. The place reeked and Larry turned to look at his friend, more to turn away from Tom than anything, and wrinkled up his nose. It was obvious by their expressions that they smelled it, too.

Tom turned slightly to look at who was coming through his door.

"Great," he said, "we'll have a party." But Tom didn't budge an inch. The men filed in and tried to get as close to Tom as possible, a feat difficult to do because of the clutter. Larry stepped over Tom's legs to the other side of the sofa.

"Sit there, Mike," he said, and pointed to the chair next to Tom that was still clear of clutter. It was the same chair Mike had occupied yesterday.

210

Brother Joe helped Mike into the chair and then propped up on the arm of the chair. Steven stood in place.

Larry picked up a pillow and tossed it on the table in front of him. It was then that he noticed the pistol in Tom's right hand.

"Whoa! Tom," he exclaimed, "what's with the pistol?"

Tom held it up looking at it as if it was the first time he'd seen it.

"Never know when you might need one," he said.

"I see you're watching *It's a Wonderful Life* again," said Brother Joe. "I told you that I'd love to talk to you about that movie. What's your favorite scene?"

"Do I know you?" Tom asked, staring over at Brother Joe. It was hard to tell in the dark, but it appeared that Tom had been crying and crying hard. Maybe even drinking. The smell of stale alcohol permeated the room.

"Yeah, I came to see you a few days ago. You said I was welcome to come again. I hope that still holds."

"Sure," Tom answered. "What do I care?"

"You want to know my favorite scene?" Tom asked. "S'funny, I happen to be on it right now." Tom turned the volume up some so all could hear.

"No securities, no stocks, no bonds. Nothin' but a miserable little $500 equity in a life insurance policy. You're worth more dead than alive."

Tom hit the pause button, but before he could say anything, Brother Joe spoke up.

"Oh, I like that one, too!" he said. Tom's brows furrowed. He was confused.

"Aren't you the preacher?" he asked.

"Yes," answered Brother Joe, "yes, I am. Does that matter?"

"Well, no. But why do you like that scene?"

"Man," started Brother Joe, "that scene is just loaded with a wealth of truths. You know what I mean?"

"Yeah," answered Tom, "maybe it's better off if I die."

"No," said Brother Joe, "It's not that at all. Tom, we're just pilgrims passing through this life. We're here and then we're gone."

"You can't take any of this stuff with you when you die," he said, and motioned at all the 'stuff' around Tom's apartment.

"So, monetarily, it doesn't matter. It's the eternal value that we have," Brother Joe finished, his voice excited.

Tom stared at Brother Joe. If Steven hadn't known the situation to be as serious as it was, he might have laughed at Tom's expression.

"Isn't that great?" Brother Joe finally asked Tom.

"Great ain't the way I was thinking about it. If you've got nothing, you're a failure and ought to be dead."

"But," Brother Joe continued, "technically speaking we are dead. Of course, I mean that after this physical body dies, we'll live an eternity somewhere. *That's* when we start living."

"I just get all excited about that," Brother Joe said, "makes me want to sit down and watch this movie all over again."

"May I see the remote?" said Brother Joe, "I want to show you some of my favorite parts."

Tom numbly handed the remote to Brother Joe.

"I don't see that at all," said Tom. "Mr. Potter is trying to tell George that he's worthless. That he's a failure."

"Yeah," said Brother Joe, "but that's Mr. Potter speaking. You gonna believe that guy?"

Brother Joe pressed the buttons on the remote and fast-forwarded for several minutes.

"Watch this," he said.

Clarence, the angel, was speaking to George Bailey. "You see George, you've really had a wonderful life. Don't you see what a mistake it would be just to throw it away?"

"Yeah," said Tom defiantly, "but he's an angel, that's what he's supposed to do: make George feel like it's a mistake to commit suicide. That doesn't change the fact that George is worthless."

"Worthless?" asked Brother Joe, his voice raising an octave or two in his excitement. "What makes a man worthless?" Brother Joe's hand was already on the fast-forward button again.

"He had no money," said Tom, "and nothing else in his life to show for it. Sure, he'd saved the life of his brother and all. But what did that get him? What did his good works get him? Nothing."

"Faith without works..." said Steven, barely audible.

"Huh?" said Tom.

212

"Nevermind," said Brother Joe, "just watch this part now?" Clarence again was speaking to George, 'Remember, George: no man is a failure who has friends.'

"Friends?" asked Tom. "I've got no friends."

"What am I?" asked Mike.

"You're just here because these guys asked you to come."

"No, I'm not," Mike said, "I'm here because I want to be. I came alone yesterday, didn't I? Sat in this very chair."

"And we're here, too," said Brother Joe.

"You're just a preacher," Tom said.

"What? Don't you think I have friends?" Brother Joe asked. "Sure I'm a preacher, but I'm no different from you. I'm just a man. I make mistakes just like you. Just like Mike."

"And I've made the biggest mistake of all," said Mike, "my mistake killed Dr. Pace's wife."

"Yeah," said Tom, standing and waving the gun around. It wasn't a threatening motion, more like he forgot it was there. "And what's that all about? This joker kills your wife. Why are you hanging around him?"

"It's not through any power of my own," answered Larry, "if it was me and me only, I would have sought revenge— maybe even tried to find a way to take Mike's life. But I do my best to let God control my life and when He takes over, forgiveness reigns."

"So that's why you did all the time traveling, huh?" asked Tom.

"No," said Larry, bowing his head. While he was indeed sorry he'd done it, he exaggerated the motion for Tom to see. He knew that Tom was nearly blinded by emotions now. "I made a mistake doing that, Tom. I put myself back in control instead of leaving God in control. I'm sorry for doing that and I won't do it again, at least I'll try not to. I'm sorry I got you involved in my idiot plans, too."

"See," said Brother Joe, "just like *It's a Wonderful Life-*"

"Shut up!" Tom yelled, waving the gun around. It still wasn't exactly a threatening motion, but none of the men felt safe. "It's just a stupid movie. If you put so much stock in the movie, where's my Clarence? Huh? Where's my angel?"

"Tom," began Brother Joe.

"Shut up!" Tom yelled. "There is no angel and life isn't

213

so wonderful!"

"Tom," Brother Joe started again. He spread his arms in a symbol of peace, and pointing to the other men in the room, "have you ever considered that maybe that's what's going on now? No, we're not angels, but certainly you must admit that we care about you. Or else we wouldn't be here."

"But you don't know my life," Tom said as he began to cry.

"No," said Brother Joe, "nor do you know mine."

"Or mine," said Steven.

"Or mine," said Larry, "beyond the fact that my wife died and that it was hard on me."

"But you do know mine," said Mike, "we've been friends for a long time and you know a lot about me that other people don't. If God can forgive me, don't you think He can forgive you, too? Don't you think you're worth something to Him?"

Tom tossed the gun down onto the floor and dropped to his knees. Putting his face in his hands he began to sob uncontrollably. Brother Joe, Mike, Larry and Steven all gathered around him placing their hands on him.

Thursday, August 3

*L*arry kicked back with his feet propped up on his desk. It was hard to get back in the swing of classes again, but he was beginning to do it. His good friend Steven Dale sat in the chair near his door.

It had been three days since they'd gone to Tom's house. Tom had prayed to receive Christ in the middle of his living room.

"What an incredible past few days, huh?" he said to his friend.

"You're telling me," Steven answered.

"You know," Larry continued, "we talk about this a lot, but don't often get to see it in action, or rather, we may not realize it when it's happening. But everything works out for the glory of God, doesn't it?"

"Yes," answered Steven, "it does. Gracie's death-didn't I hear one of your girls call it a homecoming?"

"Cindy did."

"Gracie's homecoming, that should be home*going*, was directly responsible for bringing two men to Christ. And if you were only asking me," Steven continued, "I would say it was a very unfair trade. I mean, Gracie for what some might call worthless."

"Yep," said Larry.

"But," said Steven, "we're all equal in God's eyes. He brought one home to Him and in doing so, two more were added to His family."

"But you know, Steven, I know that Gracie would have volunteered to die if she thought it would bring two people to Christ. Heck, she would have if she thought it would bring one person to Christ. She was just that way."

"She was a good woman, Larry. You were very fortunate to have had her for a wife. God really blessed you."

"Yeah," Larry answered, "that's what I've been saying in

my prayers. Basically, I thank God for letting her be part of my life while she was here. I'm thankful it was me and not someone else, you know?"

"I know what you mean."

"Can I ask you something, Larry?"

"Sure, shoot! Anything."

"This whole time travel stuff still has me a bit confounded."

"Well," said Larry, "I'm not sure that I understand it all, if you're seeking to completely understand it."

"If it's all true," said Steven, "and I believe you when you say it, why does God allow it?"

"I dunno. I think it must be like alcohol, or smoking, or drugs, or gluttony, or really any other sin. God allows us to make our own decisions, trusting us to rely on Him for the answers to right or wrong. Not us, but Him."

"And time?"

"Well," Larry began, "it's like money. God gives it to us to spend, it's up to us how we spend it. But time, like money, can only be spent once. You can't use the same money over and over in the same way you can't use the same time over and over."

"Make the most of it while we can, huh?"

"Yeah, and you know," said Larry, "that really brings to light some of the urgency we hear in the New Testament writers. They knew this stuff way back then. You've got one chance to get it right, you'd better do it right the first time."

"That's deep, Larry."

"It is, isn't it?"

"God is good," said Steven.

"Yes He is, my friend," Larry replied. "And," he continued, "God is sovereign."

End

Discussion Questions

1) Has someone close to you ever died suddenly and unexpectedly? Did you feel their death was in error, meaning that it wasn't what God had planned? If so, explain.

2) Have you ever lost someone and wished you had another chance at a last conversation with them? Who is it and what would you say?

3) Setting often plays an integral role in works of fiction. What role does setting play in *Buying Time* and is it important to the story? Could this story work without the elements of faith?

4) If time travel worked as Big Ben describes it (meaning that we only observe and can't change the events), would you be willing to relive a part of your life just for the experience of living it again? Why? Or what experience in your past calls to you so strongly?

5) Assuming time travel as described in Buying Time were real and Larry was your personal friend, what advice would you give him and what scripture would you use to support your advice?

6) What themes in *Buying Time* are important for believers?

7) Do you believe that God has a time and place picked out for your death? Why? What scriptures support your belief?

8) If time travel were a reality and you could change an event in the past, do you feel it would be ethically or morally right to do so? How does this line up with what scripture tells us?

9) If Tom was your friend and you knew that he felt worthless and that his life had little meaning, what would you do or say to convince him otherwise? What scripture would you use to support your opinion?

10) *It's A Wonderful Life* is an important movie to Tom. Why do you think it means so much to him? How does his repeatedly watching the one scene reflect the way he feels?

ABOUT THE AUTHOR

Roland Mann was born in Memphis, Tennessee and spent his growing years in Mississippi. He earned a Bachelor of Science degree in Creative Writing from the University of Southern Mississippi in 1988. Immediately upon graduation, Roland found himself in comic small press as partner/editor in the packaging company Silverline. Roland wrote many comic titles during this time; *Cat and Mouse* was the first. It ran for nearly two years, won critical acclaim and led Roland to other work. Among the titles he wrote were *Rocket Ranger, Miss Fury, Planet of the Apes: Blood of the Apes, Krey* and *Demon's Tails*.

In 1992, Roland moved to California and became an editor with Malibu Comics where he eventually became Managing Editor of the company when it was purchased by comic giant Marvel Comics. He edited such titles as *The Night Man* (which became a television show), *Prototype, Ex-Mutants, Protectors* and *Dinosaurs For Hire*. In 1996, Roland returned to the life of freelancer and ran the small press publishing company Silverline where he published such titles as *Switchblade, SilverStorm, Cybertrash and the Dog, Marauder* and *The Scary Book*.

In 2000, Roland earned a Master's degree in English and taught at the university level for nearly five years. Roland also spent time as editor for a weekly newspaper in Northeast Arkansas where he thoroughly enjoyed writing columns. He now lives in Oxford, MS with his wife BJ, daughter Brittany and son Brett. Roland is enrolled in the MFA program at Spalding University. *Buying Time* is Roland's first novel. He has completed a second and is working on his third. He blogs regularly at www.rolandmann.wordpress.com

Coming Soon from Roland Mann

In a day when Christianity has been outlawed, what's a Christian superhero to do?

THE
GIFTED

The day is tomorrow. The Bible is considered hate propaganda and religious gathers are banned. Afraid, most Christians have remained silent at this destruction of religious freedom.

Most.

The hero known as "The Cross" will not remain silent. In fact, he has created The Refuge, a place for Christians to seek asylum and escape persecution by the government controlled corporations. 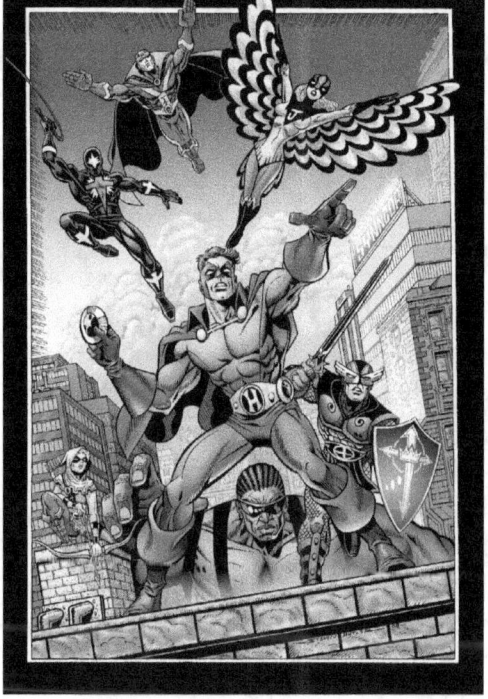 But The Cross is especially interested in those who have been "gifted," given extraordinary gifts. His goal: to build a team of these gifted Christians...but can he do it before they are rounded up and imprisoned?

The Gifted is the first book in a series of novels for Young Adult readers.

Chapter 1: The Incineration Program

"My accusers did not find me arguing with anyone at the temple, or stirring up a crowd in the synagogues or anywhere else in the city."
    Acts 24:12

The thick double doors of the church exploded inward with a loud crash. Shards of the once big oak doors hit dozens of people sitting in the back rows. Pieces as big and sharp as small spears impaled several startled onlookers nearby causing them to cry out in pain as well as surprise. Smaller fragments scratched and cut several others.

"This is an illegal gathering," rang out the metallic voices of the PolBots, or Police Robots, as they stormed inside. Their unified voice filled the room with electronic fear. The clanking of their metal feet reverberated in the foyer as they aimed their weapons, primed and ready to discharge a sharp bolt of electricity at anyone who threatened them; a bolt powerful enough to render the person unconscious.

"This is an illegal gathering," the metallic voices rang out again. "Hate speech is not allowed." Only the gears moving their legs could be heard once they stepped onto the carpeted floor of the sanctuary.

Nearly twenty of the PolBots took up positions intermittently along the center aisle. The people on every row from front to back began to inch away from the center and towards the outer walls.

"This is a peaceful community meeting," said the man at the opposite end of the room standing behind a podium. He had been addressing the crowd of approximately one hundred when the PolBots entered. "Don't citizens still have the right to meet?"

"You will come down and join the other lawbreakers." The PolBot nearest the man stepped closer and motioned for him to move from behind the podium. The man's hands moved discreetly behind the podium as he slowly stepped away.

The PolBot lifted its mechanical arm and fired a blast of energy. The blast screeched a short distance through the air hitting the podium, which erupted in a ball of flame.

"No!" said the man as he jumped back toward the podium, grabbing for something in the flames. He franticly beat at the fire engulfing a book.

The PolBot clanked onto the stage and yanked the burning book from the man's hands. A loud hiss of moist air sprayed the book extinguishing the flames. The PolBot held the burnt book high for all to see.

"This man has been found in public possession of a document containing hate propaganda and potentially riotous inducing text."

"It's the Bible!" shouted a man from near the back. "It's not riotous! It contains a message of forgiveness."

"It contains a message of love," said another voice, this one belonging to a female.

"Only your government is authorized to forgive transgressions. Possessing this hate propaganda with the intention of spreading its unpatriotic message is a crime against the State that carries the punishment of death.

"You have been found guilty and punishment will now be executed surely and immediately."

The Bible in the PolBot's hand burst into flames and was immediately incinerated. At the same time, the PolBot pointed its other arm at the man and fired another blast of energy. A flash of bright light enveloped the man and then he simply faded from existence as the light faded.

A child screamed and several PolBots near the entrance suddenly toppled over like bowling pins.

"Run!" came a man's muffled voice from outside the door. Still stunned, everyone in the building turned to look at the source of this bold new voice.

The owner of the voice barreled through the door knocking down another two PolBots. The bright yellow image of a cross could be clearly seen on his chest, despite the darkness of his costume. A full mask, hiding his identity, covered his face. And even though most of the people in the room had never seen one before, they each knew this man was a living breathing superhero.

The superhero ripped the arms off the PolBot he'd tackled, sending sparks everywhere.

"Run!" he shouted again. "Now!"

Panic set in and the people began to run for the exit.

"Do not flee," hummed the PolBots in unison. "Running must be interpreted as attempting to avoid due punishment. Immediate action must be taken. Do not run!"

The fleeing people ignored the PolBots and scurried toward the door like cockroaches escaping light. Several grappled with PolBots in the aisles as everyone tried to usher the children out.

"Hurry!" said the superhero, swinging the torn PolBot arms above his head trying to clear a path to the door for those fleeing. He released the robotic arms and they wrapped around the head of the closest PolBot. The superhero grabbed the arms again and yanked, snapping the head off the PolBot. Sparks danced from the neck as the PolBot collapsed.

"Do not flee," repeated the PolBots. "You have ten seconds to comply or face appropriate punishment."

221

"If you don't get out of here now," said the superhero above the screams, "they'll start shooting! They mean business. Now move!"

"10" the PolBots began to count down in unison. One standing near the back aisle grabbed a little girl and held her in its arms. The mother of the child cried out as she pulled desperately on the robotic arm, trying to release her little one. The superhero spun and kicked the back of the PolBot's legs, causing it to fall and release the child.

"9"

"Here," said the superhero, taking the child and handing her to the mother. "You've got to get out of here as fast as you can. Go!"

"8"

He watched as the mother exited the door safely with her child tucked away in her arms. Other people followed her out.

"7"

The superhero turned to help someone else and instead met the metal fist of a PolBot. The force of the Polbot's punch slammed him face first to the floor.

"You are guilty of obstruction of justice," said the PolBot, the numbers 2,5 and 9 stenciled down the right side of its chest.

"6. Punishment is now executed surely and immediately."

The superhero shook his head to clear his blurry vision. He looked up in time to see PolBot 259 aiming the weapon directly at his head.

"5"

The superhero pushed up with all fours like a cat and flipped over in a backhand somersault. He paused next to another PolBot currently entangled with a man, woman and young boy.

"4"

The first PolBot spun to take aim at the agile superhero again. The superhero, finding himself in a spot he liked, turned to the family and told them to duck!

"3"

The PolBot fired again. The family broke free and the superhero ducked at the same time. PolBot 259's blast hit the second, immediately turning it to cinders.

"2"

"You'd better get outta here," said the superhero to the family. "It's about to get very ugly."

The family dashed for the door. The superhero quickly surveyed the room. Almost everyone had escaped in the confusion he caused. Almost. In the middle of the room seven or eight people were completely surrounded by PolBots.

"1"

He could do nothing more. He'd simply run out of time. It wasn't the first time he'd interrupted a raid on an illegal Church gathering. He knew what was about to happen, and the thought of it made him angrier. He reacted to the rage that welled up in him.

"Hey PolBots! Over here," he yelled at the top of his lungs. The PolBots all turned to face him. When they did, one of the remaining people shoved the backmost PolBot causing it to fall into another beside it. The once surrounded group of people all dashed through the small opening in the circle of PolBots. Somehow they sensed this was their last chance at freedom.

"Commence punishment," the PolBots said. Almost at the exact same moment those few PolBots with a clear shot, took it. Three people ceased to be.

The superhero tried to take a step forward and found the air forced out of his lungs. PolBot 259 had grabbed him from behind in a fresh attempt to detain him. The superhero struggled to break free, but the PolBot was too strong.

Out of the corner of his eye, he saw another escapee blasted out of existence by a PolBot. Each person killed tore at his own heart. He often wished he was both stronger and faster, like some of those Gifted he'd recently seen. He wasn't, though, and he'd long ago accepted the Gift that God had given him.

The PolBots near the front of the building had already begun their incineration subroutine. Liquid fire blazed out of their arms in all directions, engulfing the building in flames.

The superhero felt a small shove forward and the PolBot suddenly turned him loose. He spun at the same time the PolBot did and both of them saw a teenaged boy with a baseball bat. The superhero realized he'd just used it on the PolBot to set him free.

With no hesitation, the PolBot raised its arm and aimed it point blank at the boy. The incineration subroutine already started, liquid fire shot out. The superhero tackled the PolBot at the same time. The boy screamed and tried to get away but the fire partially caught him as he turned to run.

"I can't see!" yelled the boy, the lower half of his body completely engulfed in flames. The superhero forced the PolBot over until it fell to the ground.

He jumped up and grabbed the burning boy by the arm and led him outside. Across the street, many of the former occupants stood watching, ready to run away again at a moment's notice.

A man carrying a blanket met the superhero, and he quickly wrapped it around the boy, smothering the flames. Seeing the boy, a middle-aged woman ran up next to him, called him by name and hugged him.

"He's going to need extra care from you now," said the superhero. He quietly wondered if the boy would ever walk again. Then, he pointed to the burning Church and spoke louder, addressing all those nearby.

"Don't ever forget what has been done here. But don't let them change you. They might be able to legislate what we can say and what we can do...but they can't legislate what...or who, is in our heart!"